Foremost

Books by Jody Hedlund

Young Adult: The Lost Princesses Series
Always: Prequel Novella
Evermore
Foremost
Hereafter

Young Adult: Noble Knights Series
The Vow: Prequel Novella
An Uncertain Choice
A Daring Sacrifice
For Love & Honor
A Loyal Heart
A Worthy Rebel

The Bride Ships Series
A Reluctant Bride

The Orphan Train Series
An Awakened Heart: A Novella
With You Always
Together Forever
Searching for You

The Beacons of Hope Series
Out of the Storm: A Novella
Love Unexpected
Hearts Made Whole
Undaunted Hope
Forever Safe
Never Forget

The Hearts of Faith Collection
The Preacher's Bride
The Doctor's Lady
Rebellious Heart

The Michigan Brides Collection
Unending Devotion
A Noble Groom
Captured by Love

Historical
Luther and Katharina
Newton & Polly

Foremost

JODY HEDLUND

NORTHERN LIGHTS PRESS

Foremost
Northern Lights Press
© 2019 Copyright
Jody Hedlund Print Edition

ISBN 978-1-7337534-2-5

www.jodyhedlund.com

Scripture quotations are taken from the King James Version of the Bible.

This is a work of historical reconstruction; the appearances of certain historical figures are accordingly inevitable. All other characters are products of the author's imagination. Any resemblance to actual events or locales or persons, living or dead, is entirely coincidental.

Cover Design by Emilie Hendryx of E. A. Hendryx Creative

Chapter 1

Maribel

I crouched next to Edmund behind the boulder. The harpy eagle circled overhead, her gray-and-white markings blending with the frosty winter sky.

"She is beautiful today," I whispered reverently, my breath rising in a puff and freezing on my already-chilled cheeks.

Focused on Sheba, Edmund was lost in silent communication with the mighty bird of prey. As a Fera Agmen—an animal trainer—Edmund had raised Sheba from the moment she'd hatched five years past, and the two had a special bond I'd always admired.

The Highlands stretched out below us as far as the eye could see. The desolate, mountainous terrain was covered in a thin blanket of snow and ice, broken by sharp, rocky crags and the rare deciduous, now leafless and gray. A few evergreens—hemlock and spruce—stood in remote clusters like sentinels guarding the convent.

"Has she found the valerian yet?" I rubbed my

mittened hands together for warmth.

"Patience, Maribel," Edmund whispered, his eyes still trained on the enormous eagle. He had every right to be exasperated with me, but his voice remained level and calm.

Patience wasn't one of my strengths, although I'd tried hard to cultivate it. I pressed my hand against the outline of my rosary and crucifix beneath my heavy woolen cloak, reminding me to pray. I had only six months until I turned eighteen and became eligible to take my vows and become a nun, but I had much growing to do before I'd be ready for the honor.

I lifted a silent petition that God would help me curb my faults, for I wanted nothing more than to take my vows and spend my life serving Him in the convent.

Edmund rose and whistled through his teeth. The call was lilting and commanding at the same time, a wordless language belonging to the eagles, one he'd learned and perfected during his years of apprenticeship as a Fera Agmen.

I followed Sheba's wide circle above a copse of spruce until she swept down and disappeared among the branches. I was ashamed to admit that, if not for Edmund, I likely would have gone down the mountain to pluck the valerian myself, heedless of the strict boundaries set by the abbess.

I'd done so a time or two or even three when my medicinal supplies had run low and I'd needed one of the rare herbs that grew in the Highlands—one I didn't cultivate in the convent's boxed gardens. I only went beyond the boundaries on those days when the nuns' rules felt especially suffocating. Most often, like today,

I obeyed and enlisted Edmund's assistance.

Stretching to my full height, I waited beside Edmund, my shoulder almost brushing his. He was taller than I was by a thumb's length. Thin and wiry, he didn't appear brawny. But all his years of sword drills with Wade had made him stronger than he looked. He hadn't developed into the serious soldier Wade had desired. But he was proficient with weapons, which was why the sisters allowed me to go out with him.

Of course, Edmund's friendship with a number of animals in the Highlands made him even more of a protector, especially when so many wild and dangerous creatures roamed this part of Mercia.

Besides, Edmund was one of my dearest friends, along with Colette. The three of us were all orphans, having arrived at the convent after King Ethelwulf's invasion of Mercia. We'd lost our parents during the bloodbath that followed when the king had slain entire noble families in order to ensure loyalty to himself. Someone had brought me to Sister Agnes when she'd lived at St Cuthbert's in the eastern Iron Hills. From there, Sister Agnes had carried me to refuge at St. Anne's.

We hadn't stayed at St. Anne's long before we'd moved again—several more times—before finally joining a handful of other sisters fleeing the king's persecution. We'd formed a new convent among the natural caves in the Highlands in a spot so remote no one had discovered our presence there during the past seventeen years.

Wade was the only one who ever went down from the high country, and he only left twice a year to purchase provisions we couldn't make or grow for ourselves. I couldn't deny that in recent years I'd watched his tall, strong figure hiking down the rocky path with more than a little longing to go with him. I'd tried to dampen that sinful desire to see beyond the Highlands, to walk in the Iron Cities, take a boat down the Cress River, and eventually reach the royal city of Delsworth on the East Sea.

However, no matter how hard I attempted to squelch my wish to see more of the world, much to my dismay, the desire had only grown. I needed to be content with the solitary existence we had in our lonely caves. I needed to appreciate the simplicity of life here and even the hardships—of which there were plenty. I needed to be grateful for the small group of people I could call my family. Even if Sister Agnes had passed away two years ago, I still had the other dear nuns who had become loving mothers to me.

I was blessed. I couldn't forget it.

Even now, I was blessed because Edmund was so willing to endure my many whims and faults. I hadn't required the valerian today. Yes, I was running low in my supply. But more than that, I'd longed to get outside for a while, to feel the cold sting of air against my nose and cheeks, to drag in deep lungsful of the thin mountain air, and to see the openness of the wild, but beautiful land.

As a postulant preparing to become a nun, I was required to adhere to the strict rules and prayer schedule of the convent. I had less freedom now than as a child, and rightly so. Nevertheless, I was thankful Edmund gave in to my herb-hunting requests as often as he could.

Edmund shifted his gaze to me, his bay-leaf-green

eyes dark with understanding. "Sheba will have it soon."

"She knows she must get the root of the plant, does she not?"

"She's done it before, Maribel."

"Yes, of course."

He focused his attention on the spruce grove concealing Sheba. At twenty-one his profile had long since lost its boyishness and was now sharply defined with an aristocratic nose and chin. His hair, which had once been as light and fair as mine, had ripened into a warm brown. Concealed beneath the hood of his heavy cloak, it was still as straight and fine as it had always been, long and tied back with a leather strip. The winter wind had teased strands loose, and they blew across his cheek.

Even though we both came from noble families, over the years he'd adopted the role of a lay worker, joining Wade in taking care of the livestock, creating and repairing our iron tools, cookware, and utensils, and hunting and fishing for game. Perhaps this wasn't the life either of us had been born to lead, but we knew no other. And we were happy.

Weren't we?

I wrapped my cloak tighter around my formless gray habit and let my gaze linger on the rocky horizon. "Have you ever thought of what life would be like out there?"

He followed my gaze. "You know I haven't."

In spite of having the conversation on previous occasions, I was sure one of these times his answer might be different. "Not even a little?"

"I'm content here." He slanted a sideways look at me.

"Then you still have never considered leaving?"

"Why would I? You're here." He shifted as if his admission embarrassed him.

"Surely you would be glad to leave behind all my escapades."

"Who would get you out of trouble, if not me?"

I laughed lightly. "Truly. I would be lost if not for you."

"Then you see, I can never leave you."

"But after I take my vows, I shall not need so much rescuing." I wouldn't need *any* rescuing. I'd finally have to settle down and become serious, devoting myself to a life of quiet and solitude expected of nuns.

"You don't have to take the vows." The earnestness of his tone surprised me.

I turned to face him, wanting to read his expression and his eyes. But he stared straight ahead, providing only his strong profile to study. "I have always believed I would become a nun when I come of age. You know that."

The muscles in his jaw flexed. "Maybe you'd be happier doing something else."

I'd never considered anything but being a nun. After watching Sister Agnes work as a physician and learning everything from her, I'd assumed I'd follow in her footsteps and become the convent physician. Already the nuns looked to me for medical treatment and sought out my remedies for their ailments.

"I cannot think of anything else I would be happier doing," I responded. "Besides, I have nowhere to go— no family, no friends who would take me in. This place is all I have."

He pivoted to face me, the angular lines in his

expression drawn taut, his eyes more intense than usual. "I'd take care of you."

For a moment, I sensed something deeper, something different in his declaration that went beyond the bounds of our friendship. But before I could question him, his attention shifted beyond me, and he stiffened, his dagger out of its sheath and wielded before I could blink.

"Move behind me very slowly." His voice was low and urgent.

I couldn't stop myself from glancing over my shoulder, and I sucked in a sharp breath at what I saw. There, less than two dozen paces away, a cougar crouched low, its bright-gold eyes riveted on me. It was thin and mangy, every rib evident beneath its lusterless winter coat.

"Now, Maribel." Edmund grabbed my arm and shoved me behind him.

The cougar snarled, revealing its sharp incisors, which it clearly intended to sink into one of us for a long-overdue meal.

Edmund snarled back and then released a low growl with a guttural call. The cougar's hungry eyes shifted to Edmund. It responded with a rumble in the same guttural language. I wanted to ask Edmund to interpret the communication. But his fingers only tightened and positioned me more securely behind him, which told me the conversation with the cougar wasn't going well.

The beast was likely too hungry for Edmund to reason with. Although summer and autumn had provided a bountiful crop and had brought an end to the drought that had plagued Mercia, the population of game in the Highlands was still low. And after a winter of having so little to scavenge, this cougar was desperate.

Edmund released a sharp, piercing whistle and then thrust his knife at the cougar. He hated to injure or kill the wild beasts that roamed the Highlands, even the most dangerous. He preferred to reason with them first. But sometimes he failed and had to resort to violence.

"Sheba is coming for you." He moved again, keeping himself between the cougar and me.

I glanced to the low clouds, watching for the eagle's appearance. "What about you?"

He crouched lower into a fighting position as Wade had trained him. "I'll be fine."

"I do not want to leave you behind."

"I'll defeat him easier without you here."

Before I could formulate a retort, Sheba's cry warned me of her approach, and I braced myself for her impact. Her wingspan was over six and a half feet in length, longer than Edmund's height. Her talons were larger than bear claws. And now that she was full-grown, her body weight equaled that of a boy.

The brush of wings and wind was rapidly followed by the pinch of her talons around my upper arms. In an instant, my feet lifted from the ground and I was airborne. I gritted against the pain of her claws, thankful for my heavy cloak and habit that provided some padding, but knew I'd suffer welts from her hold.

I could feel her strain to lift me. At five feet six inches, I was slight and slender, but even so, Sheba was accustomed to carrying the lighter weight of hares, raccoons, and sometimes foxes. She had borne me before during the few times I'd given in to Edmund's requests to provide the eagle the practice. But she'd never carried me far and never for long.

As Sheba ascended above Edmund, the cold January wind swirled my cloak and habit, crawling underneath and sending chills up my legs. At the same moment Sheba spirited me upward, the cougar pounced upon Edmund.

My heart leaped up and lodged in my throat, rendering my scream silent. Thankfully, Edmund's reflexes were honed, and he dodged the advance, running his blade across the cougar's flank. Even from several dozen feet above, I could see the line of crimson forming across the cat's body. It released a pained screech. And Edmund responded with another guttural call.

Sheba's wings flapped furiously until my feet bumped against an outcropping of rock, and I realized she was depositing me upon the flat surface of a tall boulder too high for the cougar to scale. As the leather soles of my boots came into contact with the stone, she released her grip. I'd not yet perfected a graceful landing, and the momentum sent me to my knees in a painful crash.

Sheba shrieked and flapped away. I wished I knew her language so I could ask her to assist Edmund. Instead, she surged into the air and circled above us, looking down as Edmund spread his feet and held out his knife, readying himself for another attack.

For several long minutes, Edmund and the cougar faced off, but it didn't lunge again, apparently too weak and hungry to use its agility and strength to its advantage. Edmund held himself steady until the cougar slunk away, sensing defeat.

Only after the cat disappeared down the mountain, did Edmund turn and look at me, his eyes wide with anxiety. "Are you all right?"

"I fare well." I rolled my arms to ease the ache from Sheba's talons. "And you?"

"Not a scratch. But I can't say as much for the poor creature. If only it would have listened to reason."

"Will it die?"

"Probably." Edmund's pained expression revealed his abhorrence at the prospect of the cougar's death, whether from wounds or from starvation. But Fera Agmen, as skilled as they were, had limits as to how much they could influence an animal's behavior.

Edmund whistled, and within seconds Sheba ceased her circling and began to swoop toward me. I rose and straightened my shoulders. At that moment, I felt as though I stood on the highest point of the Highlands. I could see, for a league in all directions, the barrenness of the mountainous table. Its desolateness spread out before me, icy, jagged, and lonely.

So lonely . . .

A movement by a distant crag at the eastern ravine snagged my attention. My breath caught as a figure in a hooded black cloak stepped out from behind the rock. The person was too far away to distinguish. But from the pointed way he stared in my direction, I knew he'd clearly seen me.

I considered dropping to my belly and attempting to hide, but Sheba's talons clamped around my upper arms again. In one easy motion, she propelled me down until my feet touched the ground in front of Edmund. His hands reached for my waist, steadying me and keeping me upright.

As Sheba flapped her large wings upward and away, all I could picture was the black-cloaked figure. The very thought that we'd been discovered after years of secrecy turned my blood to ice.

"We have to return to the caves." I broke from Edmund and began to scramble up the hill.

"The cougar won't come back today."

My heartbeat drummed at double speed. "Someone is here and saw me upon the rock."

The rapid crunch of gravel behind me told me Edmund sensed the urgency of our situation. "What direction?"

"To the southeast. Down near the ravine."

"How many did you see?"

"Just one. But there could be others in hiding."

"Was it a soldier?"

"He was wearing a black cloak." I grasped a rock ahead for leverage, and my fingers trembled within my mittens. Everyone knew King Ethelwulf's elite guard wore black. And if the figure belonged to the king's specially trained soldiers, then we weren't safe. Not in the least.

Chapter 2

EDMUND

"WE NEED TO GET THE WOMEN INTO HIDING," I CALLED TO WADE as I entered the enclosed forge.

In front of his anvil, Wade's hammer froze in midair. The light from the blazing charcoal stove broke the darkness of the windowless cave and made the sweat on his face and bald head shine. The room was warm even in the depths of winter and caused my frozen fingers and toes to tingle with the thawing they needed.

As a former elite guard during the days of King Francis's reign, Wade had been one of the fittest, strongest, and fiercest warriors in all of Mercia. His bulky frame hadn't changed much over the years. He was still nearly as strong and well-built as the day he'd pulled me out from behind the barrel where my father had shoved me on the way to our execution.

"We have no time to waste." I grabbed my sword from the ladder-like hooks on the wall where we kept the weapons we'd forged.

If my order regarding hiding the women was shocking,

my willing retrieval of my sword must have been even more so, for Wade took a step back from the anvil. "Why don't you tell me what's going on, lad?"

Although I had to disclose the truth sooner rather than later, I hesitated. I never liked disappointing Wade. But what was done couldn't be undone, no matter how I might wish it. "During our excursion, Maribel spotted a man in a black cloak."

Wade's glistening muscles visibly tensed. "Please assure me you didn't let him see the two of you."

I wanted to drop my head in disgrace, but I refrained. I wasn't a little boy anymore, even if I had broken all the rules today. The truth was it was getting harder for me to say no to anything Maribel asked of me. And this wasn't the first time I'd gone along with her schemes and taken risks in being seen.

Sensing my unspoken answer, Wade tossed his hammer down with a clatter and strode to the sword rack. "I hope you at least covered your tracks."

I twisted my sword aimlessly. "I was in a hurry to get Maribel back."

He stopped short, and his dark, bushy brows came together in a glare—a glare I'd oft earned over the years. He couldn't fault himself that I hadn't become the warrior he'd expected. He'd tried hard to train me as he'd once been trained. But I hadn't been able to physically accomplish the feats or endure the rigors required of an elite guard.

While I was grateful for the many skills Wade had given me, I'd long since realized my strengths were different from his. I felt no shame in the man I'd become. And I think Wade mostly accepted me for who I was now too.

But there were times, like now, when I knew he wished I was more like him.

With a shake of his head, he quickly donned his chain mail and then his belt, all the while muttering under his breath. "Well, don't just stand there," he barked at me finally. "Arm yourself."

I did as he said and within minutes was prepared to fight. The two of us together would be able to hold off any invaders for a short while, at least until the women had sufficient time to hide.

Our weapons clanked against our chain mail as we ducked into the main tunnel that connected the various areas of the convent. Torchlight down the corridor revealed Maribel already going from room to room and whispering instructions for the nuns to follow her.

"Oh, Edmund." Colette glided away from the others and approached me, her sweet face puckered with worry. "Maribel said we may have an unwanted visitor and that we need to take precautions and hide."

"Until we know we're safe." My gaze strayed to Maribel. She'd tossed back her hood, revealing the silky blond hair she always wore in a single plait down her back. I dreaded the day she would cut it all off, not just because she would shear her beautiful hair as was required of nuns but because she would be cut off to me forever.

The day she took her vows was the day I would lose her. Never again would I be able to spend time alone with her or talk to her or go on outings like we had today. Never again would I get to make her laugh or make her happy.

Maribel slipped her arm around the stooped back of the oldest nun, Sister Margaret, and gently led her. As she turned to hand the torch to the nun following them, I glimpsed her heart-shaped face, her cheeks pink from the cold mountain air, her blue eyes so bright, and her perfect lips uttering whispered words of encouragement.

There were times when I couldn't seem to get enough of her, when her loveliness seized my heart into a tight grip and wouldn't let go.

Colette wrapped her arm through mine, gaining my attention once more. "I want to stay with you, Edmund." She peered up at me with a trust and devotion I wasn't sure I deserved. "Please, I would feel much safer with you."

Wade snorted and strode ahead, leaving me behind with Colette. I loved Colette like a sister, but sometimes— especially in recent months—I'd found myself irritated by her growing clinginess. Like now.

I pried her arm out of mine. For a young woman as short and petite as her, she had surprising strength and didn't release me easily. "If Wade and I have to fight off any intruders, you'll be safer in the hidden caverns."

Her eyes widened. "Do you think we shall have fighting?"

I bit back a groan. I shouldn't have mentioned the possibility. Now Colette would be even more frightened. "Go on." I maneuvered her toward the sisters. "You must stay with the women."

She reluctantly joined the others but cast a furtive glance over her shoulder at me. I nodded at her in encouragement, and thankfully she continued on her way. Her appearance and bearing couldn't have been more different than Maribel's. The two were as dissimilar as an eagle and a mouse. Nevertheless, their friendship had always been strong, mostly because Maribel was easy to be with.

I gave myself one last look at Maribel before sprinting the opposite way. When I caught up with Wade, he was already at the cave entrance.

He raised a brow at me. "You should just ask that poor girl to marry you and put her out of her misery."

The comment, though slung in jest, threw me off guard. "Marry her?"

"Aye, you're old enough to get married now."

I couldn't think of a response. As one of the king's elite warriors, Wade had never considered marrying, having pledged celibacy. I'd assumed he'd expected the same of me.

"You can't tell me you haven't thought about it." He hefted the stone doorway and rolled it slightly open.

Had I considered it? I suppose in some part of my mind I'd harbored hope she'd decide not to take her vows, that we could stay as we were, that I wouldn't lose her. I'd even contemplated the possibility that I'd take care of her and protect her. But marry her? I shook my head. She'd never agree to it.

Would she?

My heart gave an extra thump at the thought. "Do you think she'd want to marry me?"

Wade snorted again. "Of course she would. She can never do anything without coming to you first."

Now it was my turn to snort. "Maribel? Hardly. She's got a mind of her own."

Wade paused in his effort to open the door and studied my face. "I wasn't referring to Maribel. I was talking about Colette."

"Oh." Under Wade's scrutiny, I felt myself grow warm. To hide my embarrassment, I dropped my shoulder against the stone door and added my muscles to his effort. Within seconds, the door slid open, and frigid mountain air engulfed us.

Thankfully, Wade's attention shifted to the landscape. He was too alert to the danger in our situation to say anything more about my marriage prospects. He scrutinized every detail of the crags surrounding the entrance. The large boulders rose out of the ground all around, making the area difficult to traverse. Wade motioned to me. "You scout the east side, and I'll scout the west."

I nodded and then followed Wade's lead, crouching low and darting behind the nearest boulder. We split ways, and I scurried behind outcroppings, attempting to assess whether King Ethelwulf's men had pursued our trail up the mountain. I earnestly prayed they hadn't, but I also realized the king had Fera Agmen working for him training wolves and dogs to sniff just about any scent. If he'd sent such animals, they'd soon discover our whereabouts.

As I moved along the ridge, I considered calling Sheba. I'd sent her away once Maribel and I had reached the convent. I could use her as my eyes to scout from the sky. And as a loyal and true friend, she'd willingly do just about anything I asked of her. But I hesitated, not sure I wanted to put her in harm's way.

From the opposite rim of our mountain home, Wade motioned in the warrior sign language he'd taught me. His message was clear: he'd spotted someone. But only one person.

We both sat silently in the cold, waiting, attempting to gauge if our visitor was truly alone or only the forefront of a much larger contingent.

Finally, Wade signed again, this time conveying that

the person had given the secret hand signal for St. Anne's.

St. Anne's?

Of course Wade would know the signal. King Francis's elite guards had been trained in more than just fighting. They'd memorized maps, routes, secret hideaways, tunnels, and anything that could be useful in the defense of king and country. In addition to the elite guards, the only other people who knew the secret hand signal for St. Anne's Convent were nuns who'd once lived there before moving to the Highland caves and calling it the Highland Convent.

It could be a trick, I signed back to Wade.

He nodded, knowing better than I did the deceits involved in warfare. King Ethelwulf could have learned the secret gesture from one of the nuns he'd captured and tortured in his efforts to track down all his enemies— namely the lost princesses of the former king.

When King Ethelwulf of Warwick had attacked Mercia, he'd enlisted the aid of the fierce, seafaring Danes and the stealthy, lethal Saracens. With his army of mercenaries, he'd been unbeatable. He'd surrounded the royal coastal fortress at Delsworth, and within weeks he'd penetrated the walls.

During the battle, Queen Dierdal had died after giving birth to twin babies, and King Francis had succumbed to mortal wounds. Without the king to lead, the fortress had fallen within hours.

Tales abounded regarding what had become of not only the twin babies but also the crown princess, who'd been two or three years of age at the time. Some said King Ethelwulf had already found the heirs and had put them to death to eliminate any competition for Mercia's throne. Others speculated the princesses had been smuggled to safety in lands far away. And still some believed the princesses were hidden here in Mercia.

Six months ago, when Wade had returned from his most recent trip into town, he'd brought back news of the oldest princess—how she was alive and safe in Norland, the kingdom to the north of Mercia. Apparently, rumors were circulating regarding the possibility she was forming an army of rebels over the border and was planning an attack on King Ethelwulf in the spring or summer.

I'd expected Wade to scoff at or dismiss the rumors. He was always so rational. But to my surprise, he'd exuded an excitement I'd seldom seen him display. I'd even begun to wonder if he might leave and attempt to find the so-called rebel army. Although he'd never admitted his desire for ousting King Ethelwulf, I knew it was one of his greatest wishes. So when he'd lingered at Highland Convent with no mention of departing, I'd been surprised again.

Wade cautiously peeked over the top of his hiding spot before ducking and signing. *Watch my back.* Then he slipped around the boulder and began the descent toward the lone figure.

I unsheathed my dagger. While I wasn't nearly as skilled as Wade, I could still hit a target several dozen paces away. Wade had made sure of that. He'd drilled me until I could do it without thinking.

Surveying the barren land once again, I searched for anything unusual, any sign of movement, any spot of color out of place. From all appearances, the cloaked figure was alone.

With a sixth sense I'd honed over the years, I attempted to gauge the presence of any animals in the area other than Sheba, any I'd trained that I could call upon for help. In the cold depths of winter, most creatures still hibernated, although it wouldn't be long before hunger drove them out of their warm dens.

If in a bind, I could call Barnabas. The young gray wolf was loyal to me since I'd trained him from birth, even more so since I'd rescued one of his pups from a ravine last autumn.

I remained tense and alert, my weapons at the ready. Wade approached the intruder cautiously, his sword in one hand and his mace in the other. When he was only six paces away, the person tossed off the hood of his cloak.

I shuffled back a step at the sight that met us. It wasn't a man. Rather it was an old woman with a hunched back and deformed face. Her hair—at least what was left of it—was pure white and grew in strange patches on her scalp. The curves of her face were splotched with pink skin that stretched taut.

Wade didn't lower his weapons but instead sniffed the air and seemed to test for the presence of other invaders.

The old woman spoke to him, but I couldn't hear what she said. After a moment of conversation, Wade nodded and started back toward the convent, the woman following behind with slow, awkward steps as though walking presented the greatest of challenges.

Wade signed for me to stay on guard outside.

I nodded my reply, but couldn't keep from wondering who the old woman was and why Wade was allowing her into our convent. After seventeen years without seeing anyone except the people here who'd become my family, I was unsettled by the prospect of a visitor, even if she was only an old woman.

When they disappeared into the tall stones leading to

the caves, I released a puff of breath.

I didn't want things to change. I preferred to go on living with Maribel the way we always had in the simplicity of our lives, without interference from the outside world. But I had the premonition our small corner of Mercia was about to be shaken and things would never be the same again.

Chapter 3

Maribel

I crushed the white willow bark and cat's claw with the pestle and mortar. The tangy scent filled the apothecary around me.

"Maribel," came Colette's short-winded voice from the doorway. "I should have realized you'd be here."

I didn't have to see her face to know she was excited. She'd been fairly humming with anticipation from the moment word had reached us in the hidden caves that we could come out, that our visitor was Sister Katherine, a nun who had once served with Sister Agnes at St. Cuthbert's in the Iron Hills.

Dear Sister Agnes had always spoken fondly of the nun but had indicated Sister Katherine died after being captured by King Ethelwulf. The king had imprisoned and tortured many sisters during those early days of his reign, as he'd heard rumors the nuns had helped the lost princesses escape from Mercia.

Apparently, Sister Katherine had indeed been within the king's clutches and subjected to his brutal torture. Though I had yet to meet her, a few of the nuns who had already seen her were whispering about her battered condition.

Wade hadn't wanted to allow Sister Katherine into the convent until he was certain she hadn't been followed. But the abbess had taken one look at Sister Katherine, had broken down weeping, and had insisted her old friend be brought into the refuge of our cave home.

The abbess and Sister Katherine had been closeted away in the abbess's room for the past hour, and no one else had been allowed in.

"All of the hustle and hiding has exacerbated Sister Margaret's back pain." I ground the two herbs into small particles that I could brew into tea for the older nun.

"You will have to finish later," Colette responded. "The Reverend Mother has asked for you specifically to come to her room."

My hands stilled, and my attention snapped to Colette. The light from the wall sconces reflected off her delicate features, outlining her luminous eyes and her anticipation. "Did she say why?"

"No. I was hoping *you* might have a clue why you've been summoned."

"Perhaps to assess Sister Katherine's physical well-being and administer any treatments that might help her?"

Colette's shoulders fell just slightly. Clearly, my practical answer disappointed her. I suspected my summoning had more to do with being the first to spot Sister Katherine. Even though my recklessness hadn't caused disaster, I was sure to be chastised, if not punished, for giving away the location of our convent.

I pushed aside the pestle and mortar on my worktable and straightened, careful to avoid bumping the bunches of herbs strung on twine similar to a laundry line. The combination of sage, mint, anise, and chamomile gave the room a homey, comforting appeal.

The apothecary was the closest space to a home I'd ever known since it was where I spent most of my time. Wade had built shelves, which lined one wall of the cave. They were filled with meticulously labeled clay canisters and vials of remedies Sister Agnes had created as well as some of my own medicinal experiments.

On the opposite wall, Wade had fashioned a stove for heating and distilling various concoctions, syrups, and tinctures. The rear of the room contained a raised pallet and a small shelf lined with surgical tools, bowls for bleeding, leeches in a jar, and an assortment of other equipment I used when performing surgeries or medical procedures.

I stepped to the stove and with a towel moved the boiling water off the heat. "Will you finish making Sister Margaret a cup of tea? I promised I would deliver it—"

"Maribel," Colette said sharply. "There are more important things to do right now than make tea for Sister Margaret."

Our daily routine of prayer interspersed with work rarely varied. To have potential intruders and be sent into hiding would have been excitement enough. But now, with Sister Katherine as a visitor, we didn't know what to expect or do next. Why had she come? What news did she bear? Were we in danger? The questions had rolled through my mind as I mulled over her appearance.

"Stop stalling, Maribel," Colette said. "And go at once, or you will get us both in trouble."

As trouble was something I seemed to have a knack for even though I didn't like it, I hastened across the room and followed Colette into the main tunnel. Quiet had descended once again upon the convent, and we walked with slow, muted steps as we'd been taught to do.

We passed the refectory with its trestle tables and benches, which Wade had hewn many years ago when we'd first arrived. The scent of boiled hare came from the kitchen, Sheba's recent gift to us. Though the meat would likely be tough, Sister Ingrid was an excellent cook and would use the onion, parsnip, and carrots that remained from our autumn harvest to give the meal some flavor. Even if it was simple fare, we'd eat it gratefully, for there were many times in recent years when our low rations had left our stomachs grumbling from want.

The chapel, too, was vacant, although our afternoon prayer hour of None approached, and we would all soon file into our places.

Beyond the chapel, we turned the corner into a dark passageway that led to several workshops, including the forge, the laundry, and the looms where Colette worked with two other nuns weaving the cloth used to make all our garments, towels, and bedding.

After another bend in the tunnel, we stopped outside the closed door of the abbess's office, and Colette knocked lightly. Without a word, the door opened. The sconces on the walls and a candle on the abbess's writing table illuminated the abbess as she stood at the door. She had clearly been waiting for my arrival.

The abbess was a kindly but plain woman. Like all the other nuns at Highland Convent, she wore the traditional gray habit, tied around the waist with a leather belt. Over the tunic she'd donned a scapula and a chain with a rugged wooden cross upon it. Her head was covered with a tight-fitting veil and a wimple that surrounded all but the circle of her face.

I bowed and moved to kiss her hand as was our custom, but before I could do so, she instead bowed to me.

Colette's startled intake of breath from the passageway echoed my own surprise at the strange reception.

The abbess finally lifted her head and studied my face as if seeing me for the first time. Behind her, Sister Katherine sat upon a bench, her hunched back to us. "The Princess Maribel?" she murmured.

I took a quick step backward and bumped into Colette. *Princess Maribel?* What was she talking about?

"Yes," replied the abbess, still looking at me with a strange awe that unsettled me. "This is she."

Sister Katherine didn't move. "Please forgive me for not standing, Your Highness. I fear my legs have given out for the day."

Your Highness? I exchanged a glance with Colette, one that silently pleaded with her to explain what was going on. She shook her head, her wide eyes revealing a confusion that matched my own.

"You must forgive me as well, Sister Katherine," I said. "But I am not a princess. I am a simple physician's assistant."

"If you are the infant Sister Agnes cared for and raised, then you are indeed a princess of Mercia, the daughter of King Francis and Queen Dierdal." Sister Katherine's voice was soft and somewhat raspy, but her words came across all too clear.

"Sister Agnes never made mention of any such identity. You must have me confused with another child."

"It will be easy enough to prove," Sister Katherine said, still unmoved from where she sat on the bench. "Reverend Mother, send for Sister Agnes's personal possessions and have them brought to me."

The abbess gave orders for Colette to go to the chapel and to retrieve a small locked chest there. After Colette was gone, Sister Katherine spoke again. "May I see you, Your Highness?"

I looked to the abbess for permission. She nodded and motioned me toward the old nun.

As I stepped around Sister Katherine and stood in front of her, she lifted her head and removed the hood of her cloak. At the sight that met me, compassion surged within my chest. The whispered rumors were true. The nun had been sorely abused. Her scalp and face were torn and burned. She was missing one eye and many teeth. She'd lost fingers, and the few remaining stubs were uneven. I didn't need to see beneath her robes to know the rest of her body was probably in the same condition, if not worse.

This woman had indeed endured much, had likely been pushed to the brink of death many times, but never killed. Why? What had she done to suffer this way?

As she stared at me with her one eye, it filled with

tears that spilled over and began to streak her cheek. "It is you," she whispered through trembling lips. "God be praised."

How could Sister Katherine know who I was simply by looking at me?

"The resemblance to your mother and sister is very strong," she said, answering my unspoken question. "You have their pale hair and blue eyes and beautiful features."

"My sister?" I could hardly get the words past the constriction in my throat. But now that Sister Katherine had spoken, I had to know everything.

"Queen Constance," she replied. "She's also taken the name Adelaide, given to her by the Langley family who took her in and raised her. Thus, most are calling her Queen Adelaide Constance. She's in Norland with her new husband. She's made an alliance with King Draybane of Norland, and they are amassing an army and preparing to invade Mercia."

My heart gave a tiny shiver of anticipation. So the rumors Wade had brought back from the outside world were true. The rightful queen of Mercia had come forward and was making plans to take the throne away from King Ethelwulf.

"However, the queen won't be able to defeat the forces of evil without the help of an ancient treasure."

I'd heard of the treasure during history lessons. Sister Agnes hadn't just taught me everything she knew about being a physician and surgeon. She'd also made sure I was educated in many other subjects, including history, geography, languages, physical science, and mathematics. Although I'd never harbored a fondness for those other areas of study, she'd been adamant I be as learned as possible.

Now I knew why.

"Sister Agnes told me tales about an ancient treasure, King Solomon's treasure, that it is buried somewhere on the Great Isle. She said it was brought here during ancient times for safekeeping against the invading barbarians."

"Yes, the treasure is greater than we can fathom."

Sister Agnes's stories had always fascinated me and piqued my curiosity. Many times during our childhood, I'd convinced Edmund and Colette to join me on pretend treasure hunts, exploring the caves for the fabled wealth.

"And now the queen has need of the treasure," Sister Katherine continued in an earnest but raspy voice. "But she won't be able to find it and defeat evil without the help of you and your twin sister, Emmeline."

I had a twin sister? And her name was Emmeline? I reached behind me for the abbess's writing table and grasped it to keep from sinking to the ground.

Sister Katherine's words shouldn't have surprised me. If I truly was one of the lost princesses, then it stood to reason I had a twin. After all, everyone knew Queen Dierdal had given birth to twin babes the night Delsworth had fallen to King Ethelwulf. No one knew for certain what had become of the girls.

At least no one but Sister Katherine.

"Emmeline," I tested the name. "Were our names changed like the queen's?"

"We had considered it, but since we were hiding you both away from society in seclusion, we decided there was no need as your names were never formally announced and known."

My mind reeled from the revelations. Part of me couldn't believe I was a royal princess of the house of Mercia. But another part suspected Sister Katherine was not only telling me the truth, but that she'd risked her life over and over to keep my identity a secret.

I lowered myself to the bench next to the nun and reached for her deformed hand. At first, she attempted to pull away, but I grasped her stubby fingers within mine and squeezed them tenderly, hoping to convey that nothing about her body or appearance repelled me.

"Will you tell me everything, Sister Katherine? From the very beginning?"

For a long moment, she stared at my long, strong fingers against the jagged red stumps on her puckered hands. She stroked my fingers, and once again tears ran down her cheek. "I held you for the first time when you were less than a week old."

Sister Katherine invited the abbess to join us as she shared my story. A young noblewoman, Lady Felicia, with the help of one of the king's elite guards, had smuggled the newborn twins out of Delsworth castle. The guard, Lance, had led the way through a secret tunnel that ran deep under the moat. In the dead of night, they'd managed to outrun the Saracens who chased them. Eventually, they'd escaped by boat to the iron city of Everly, where they also rescued Princess Constance, who'd been evacuated to the royal residence there along with her nursemaid.

Only by the grace of God and Lance's superior training did they manage to stay one step ahead of King Ethelwulf. He sent vicious wolves, trained by

Fera Agmen, to track down the royal princesses. But Lance was a fierce warrior and managed to hold the wolves off, even after he was injured.

"They brought you to St. Cuthbert's for hiding," Sister Katherine said. "But once again King Ethelwulf discovered your whereabouts and sent soldiers to get you. We could see them coming from a far distance. So we made the difficult decision to split all of you up and take you to separate places for safekeeping until the time was right."

"So Sister Agnes took me to St. Anne's?" I asked.

Sister Katherine nodded. "Yes. That's where I looked for you first. But of course, it has lain deserted all these many years since King Ethelwulf went on his crusade to capture as many nuns as possible."

"I do not remember living there. I was yet a babe when Sister Agnes brought me to this convent."

"I did not know the sisters had found refuge here in the caves," she said, peering around the abbess's chamber at the thick stone walls and low ceiling. "They have done well all these years keeping themselves hidden from the world. I have been in the Highlands looking for you for months, and I would probably still be searching if I had not seen the eagle lift you onto the boulder."

"That was Sheba, a harpy eagle Edmund has trained from a hatchling."

"Edmund?"

"Another orphan the nuns took in and kept safe these many years."

"Then he's been trained as a Fera Agmen?"

I had the overwhelming desire to boast about my friend, about his skills with the animals, and about all our escapades growing up together. He and Colette had been like a brother and sister to me. Without them, I would have had a lonely childhood.

Before I could formulate my thoughts regarding Edmund, the abbess spoke up. "Edmund learned his skills as a Fera Agmen from one of the older nuns who has since passed on. But his main tasks at the convent have been hunting, working in the forge, and providing protection under the guidance of Wade."

Sister Katherine was silent for a moment as if taking in the information. "I would like to meet Edmund before I depart."

"Of course," said the abbess. "As soon as Colette returns with the chest, I shall send her for Edmund."

"You have just arrived," I said, settling my hand into Sister Katherine's more firmly. "Surely you do not intend to leave soon."

"I must be on my way at the break of day."

"But you are sore and tired," I protested. "Allow me to provide you with infusions and poultices to ease your aches and pains."

"You are kind, Your Highness, but I must find your twin sister and so complete my mission."

"I shall help you find her." I sat up straighter, suddenly eager to meet my twin. Until moments ago I hadn't known I had any family alive. Sister Agnes had only told me my parents had died during King Ethelwulf's invasion. She'd never mentioned I had sisters or a twin. And I didn't hold it against her. She'd known me well enough to realize such knowledge would have spurred me to try to find them, that I probably would have taken risks and caused danger to myself and the convent.

But now, the time was right. I could feel it deep inside.

"Emmeline is living in Inglewood Forest. And it will take many weeks of hiding and slow travel before I reach her."

The thought of riding out of the Highlands and seeing new parts of Mercia made my heart thud with the same longing I'd felt earlier when speaking with Edmund about what life would be like out there. What if this was my one and only chance to travel beyond the confines of the convent before I took my vows? What if another opportunity never presented itself?

"No, Your Highness," Sister Katherine continued. "You must withdraw from Mercia as soon as you are able and join the queen in Norland. You will not be safe here much longer."

I had no intention of leaving the convent permanently, but a short visit to Norland to meet my older sister wouldn't harm my plans to become a nun. Perhaps the trip would satisfy my desire to see more of the world before I returned and took my vows.

"Will the queen receive me?" I asked.

Sister Katherine smiled, revealing blank spaces where her teeth had been knocked from her mouth. Even with her missing teeth and other deformities, I could see the goodness and kindness of her spirit in her expression. "She is already searching for you, the same as I have been these past months. I have seen her men from time to time. She will rejoice to have finally found you."

"But how shall I prove to her that I am her sister?"

"She will recognize herself in your features."

At that moment, a knock sounded. The abbess rose,

slowly walked to the door, and opened it. She spoke in hushed tones to Colette before closing the door and returning to us holding a wooden chest in her hands. Made of solid oak, it was engraved with intricate carvings and encircled with decorative leather straps.

The abbess smoothed a hand over the box. "Before her death, Sister Agnes told me to lock away two of her possessions. I put them in here."

"The two possessions belong to Princess Maribel," Sister Katherine responded. "She is now ready to receive them."

The abbess unlocked the chest, lifted the flat lid, and gave me the first item—a large glossy ruby in the shape of a teardrop. I cradled it reverently in my palm, noting the dark-red tones mixed with faint hints of blue.

"It is a rare, flawless ruby," Sister Katherine explained. "There are only six of them in the entire world, and they were embedded on the royal crown that once belonged to Queen Dierdal of Mercia."

"Then this came from my mother's crown?"

"Yes, upon her death, she instructed her lady-in-waiting to take two of the jewels with her—one for you and one for your twin sister. Someday, if you need to prove your legitimacy as a daughter of Queen Dierdal and King Francis, this jewel will match with the other rare originals in the crown."

I turned the ruby over in my hand, marveling that it had once belonged to my mother and that she'd worn it in her crown. From the stories Sister Agnes had told me regarding the previous king and queen of Mercia, I'd known them to be just, merciful, and kind rulers. And for a moment, I was saddened I would never have the chance to meet them.

Nevertheless, I was too excited to dwell on the sadness, especially when the abbess removed the next item from the chest—a golden key the size of my hand, from my wrist to the length of my middle finger. It was elegant, with an oval bow and a long, thick shank. The bit on the end had a tiny symbol. I lifted it toward the light to study it. The engraving was an ancient one of healing and life: a circle containing a tree with its branches full and blossoming at the top and its roots deep and thick on the bottom.

Sister Katherine was watching my face and not the key. "It is one of three ancient keys that unlocks Solomon's treasure."

"If I have this," I said, "does that mean my sisters each have one too?"

"Correct," Sister Katherine replied. "The keeper of the keys was supposed to have the three in his or her possession at all times. However, when we separated you princesses, we split up the keys as well."

I examined the key again, marveling at its beauty and the fact that my father had once held it, along with the great rulers before him. "Where is Solomon's treasure? And is there any of it left? Surely the previous kings and queens have used it up by now?"

"Of course, stories and prophecies point to the treasure being brought here to the Great Isle. But due to the passing of time, no one knows exactly where it is or what's become of it."

"Surely there are clues leading to the treasure."

"Many believe the keys themselves are the clues."

The key was the clue to the treasure? I fingered the engraved symbol of the tree of life and healing. What could the picture mean? What was its secret?

"An old prophecy foretells of a young ruler filled with wisdom who will use the ancient treasure to help drive evil from the land and usher in a time of peace like never before seen or ever seen again. This is one of the reasons why you and your sisters need to be reunited. Together you will use the keys to unlock the treasure that can help restore the land."

The cool silence of the cavern room descended around us. I didn't understand all of what Sister Katherine had explained. In fact, more and more questions formulated within my mind, questions that demanded answers. But I had the feeling Sister Katherine had told me everything she knew, and now my curiosity would only be sated by seeking out the answers for myself.

Chapter 4

EDMUND

I'M TASKING YOU WITH THE JOB OF DELIVERING THE PRINCESS Maribel safely to her sister, Queen Adelaide Constance, in Norland.

From my pallet on the forge floor, I stared at the glowing embers inside the open stone oven. Sister Katherine's words hadn't stopped echoing in my head since she'd spoken them to me hours ago.

I'd been surprised when Colette had rushed into the forge earlier and told me the abbess and Sister Katherine wanted to speak to me. I couldn't remember ever being called to visit the abbess, and I assumed she planned to give me my due punishment for endangering the convent and Maribel on our escapade down the mountain.

As I'd followed Colette to the abbess's chamber, I hadn't believed her whispered declarations—that Maribel was one of the lost princesses, that Sister Katherine had even addressed her as "Your Highness," and that the abbess had asked for Sister Agnes's personal items to be brought to her in order to prove to Maribel she was the princess.

I'd waited outside the abbess's chamber door for some time before Maribel finally emerged. Her odd expression as she'd passed by me should have been enough to confirm everything Colette had already spoken. But it wasn't until I was called inside and stood before the abbess and Sister Katherine that the truth hit me like an avalanche.

Maribel was a princess. I'd been able to sense it in Sister Katherine's demeanor and face even before she uttered a word. And I'd realized that's why the nun had come.

She wasted no time getting to the point of my summons. *I'm tasking you with the job of delivering the Princess Maribel safely to her sister, Queen Adelaide Constance, in Norland. You must be gone in two days and never come back.*

I flipped onto my back and expelled a sigh. Why had Sister Katherine given the job to me? Wade was the warrior. He was more capable of protecting Maribel and seeing her to safety than I was.

Wade's familiar, heavy breathing came from the opposite side of the room. He hadn't missed a beat of his hammer when I'd explained to him that Maribel was the princess. He'd accepted the news almost as if he'd already guessed the truth about her identity long ago. Maybe he'd always known. After all, he'd served King Francis and Queen Dierdal. Maybe he'd noticed the family resemblance in Maribel's features. Or perhaps Sister Agnes had confided in him about Maribel's identity.

I lifted to one elbow and watched the rise and fall of Wade's brawny torso under his coverlet, the wide chest that had protected me beneath his cloak when he'd carried me through the crowds, away from Delsworth, away from the lifeless bodies of my family swaying from the gallows.

Once he'd delivered me to the convent all those years ago, he'd had no reason to stay. He could have continued on to Norland where so many other elite guards had escaped. The nuns would have raised me regardless of his presence. Had he decided to remain because of Maribel? To be her protector?

I flopped back to my pallet. Sister Katherine should have asked the fierce elite guard to accompany Maribel to Norland. Not me.

Whatever the case, I hadn't been able to refuse the nun, not when she'd looked into my eyes as if she could see inside my soul. Her gleam had told me she'd guessed how much I cared about Maribel and would do anything for her, including laying down my life if need be.

Yes, I desperately wanted to go with her. Yes, I couldn't bear the thought of her departing without me. And yes, I'd do anything for her. But her safety mattered more than my desires.

Two soft scratches at the bottom of the forge door sent my pulse sputtering forward. The sound was part of the mouse communication I'd taught Maribel and Colette when we'd been younger. Back then, we'd used the secret language as a way to converse with each other when we were supposed to observe the rules of silence. In recent years, Maribel had taken to using the scratches when she wanted me to sneak out of my room and meet her in the chapel.

Wade was normally a light sleeper, trained to listen for every noise even in slumber. But the mouse scratches didn't rouse him. And most of the time my stealthy exits from the room didn't wake him either.

Within minutes, I was creeping through the dark passageway, my heart thudding with every step. I was more than ready to talk to Maribel and discover how she was feeling after learning about her identity. Knowing her as I did, I expected her to be excited but confused.

Had she heard that Sister Katherine had asked me to accompany her to Norland?

I rounded the bend, and faint light ahead guided my steps the last distance. We'd chosen the chapel as our rendezvous point because one of the candles on the altar was always lit. And Maribel said we could offer extra prayers in between our talking. She'd decided the sisters couldn't condemn us for that.

When I entered, Maribel was already kneeling on a prayer cushion at the front. Silently, I lowered myself next to her.

Her eyes were closed, and her lips moving in prayer. For a moment, I relished watching her without her realizing I was doing so. In the faint candle glow, her profile was almost angelic. Her veil had slipped off her shoulder, leaving more of her visible than usual. From her high cheekbones to her perfectly rounded chin, to her long neck, she was so graceful and beautiful she nearly stole the breath from my lungs.

She opened an eye and peeked sideways at me, as though she'd felt my attention upon her. "Are you as shocked as I am?"

"Quite."

"Then wait until you see what else I have." She lifted her hand out of the long, wide mouth of her sleeve and opened her palm to reveal a large, golden key. "Sister Agnes had it among her belongings."

I'd taken part in the education Sister Agnes had

insisted on giving us orphans. From our history lessons, I knew as well as Maribel what she was holding: one of the three keys belonging to royalty who'd been charged with their keeping. Keys that could supposedly unlock an ancient treasure.

While I'd assumed the lessons about the treasure and keys were more fable than truth, Sister Agnes had always insisted she had proof.

Now I knew why...

"I need your help in figuring out how this key is a clue to the treasure." She pressed the metal object into my hand. I wasn't sure I should touch it. But she released it to me, and I had no choice but to take it.

"You are the smartest person I know," she continued. "If anyone can decipher the meaning of the key, you can."

"I'm the smartest person you know only because you don't know many people."

She smiled and nudged me with her elbow. "Even if I knew everyone in the kingdom, you would still be one of the smartest."

I loved her confidence in me. She'd always believed in me and trusted me. I just hoped I wouldn't let her down.

I lifted the key and inspected it from the oval bow at the top to the bit at the end. I noted everything about it— its weight, length, and pattern. The engraving of a tree of life and healing certainly had great meaning. But I suspected there was something else about the key we needed to know first before we could understand the symbol.

"The weight of a solid, pure-gold key should be heavier." I examined the point where a thin band separated the shank from the collar. "Thus the key must be hollow."

Maribel bent her head closer to mine, and I caught the exotic scent of herbs that surrounded her all the time. I breathed her in and was tempted to lean even nearer. But I forced myself to focus on the key.

"Can you locate the hollow place?" she asked.

"My guess is that it's in the shank." I twisted at the thin band, but it didn't budge. It was likely tight from disuse. Or perhaps it had a secret catch somewhere inside that had to be pressed in order to open. Either way, I had to pry deeper.

After a minute of winding a piece of thread from my shirt into the band, it clicked and the shank loosened.

Maribel clapped softly. "You did it."

I guessed if anything remained in the shank, it would be wedged far inside to mask its presence—yet not so far it was unreachable. Whoever had designed the keys had made the hiding place difficult to find but not impossible. "We need a needle or a pin to poke up into the shank."

Maribel was on her feet and out the door before I could stop her. I guessed she was going a few doors down to the weaving room. She returned a few minutes later beaming and holding a needle.

It took me no time to pry loose a tiny piece of parchment. I unraveled it and squinted to see the faded print. "S.C. Abbey."

"S.C. Abbey," Maribel repeated.

We both sat in silence, staring at the scrap of paper. Until . . .

"St. Cuthbert's Abbey," we whispered in unison. A thrill shot through me. And when I met her gaze, I could see an excitement that matched mine. Our smiles broke free at the same moment.

"You did it." She gave a soft, jubilant laugh and then

threw her arms around me.

I was used to Maribel's occasional bursts of emotion, but it had been awhile since she'd hugged me. My head told me I needed to remain brotherly in return—keep her slightly at bay and end with a quick pat on the back.

However, my arms betrayed me and slipped around her entirely, pulling her tight so our bodies connected, and the side of her head brushed against the side of mine. I closed my eyes and basked in the pleasure of holding her near.

I realized I'd hugged her a moment too long when she wiggled to loosen herself. Reluctantly, I released her and tried to make my expression passive so she wouldn't see just how much her embrace had affected me.

I shouldn't have worried about her noticing my attraction. She never did. In fact, she reached for my hand and grasped it in hers, clearly not understanding how her merest touch sent fire into my limbs. "Let us go to St. Cuthbert's."

"Sister Katherine has charged me with escorting you to Norland."

"Then we shall go to St. Cuthbert's first." She accepted the news of my going with her as if it was a foregone conclusion.

"But it's the opposite direction."

"Not overly so."

"Anyway, don't you think Wade should be the one to accompany you?" She shook her head, but before she could say anything, I rushed forward. "He's the trained warrior. He'll be able to protect you and get you to Norland much better than I could."

"We shall be fine," she said with her usual confidence. "I would rather be with you than anyone else."

At her words, warmth seeped through my chest.

"Let us set out at once," she said. "If we depart without delay, we shall arrive at St. Cuthbert's tomorrow morning."

The abandoned abbey was a full day's ride in daylight and good weather. But in the dark of night in winter? "We ought to wait, Maribel. We'd be safer traveling by daylight. Besides, we should say farewell to everyone, should we not?"

"We shall return before going to Norland," she said. "And we shall say our good-byes then."

Past experience had taught me she'd do whatever she planned whether I supported her or not. If I decided against accompanying her, she'd go without me. And I couldn't let her do that.

She turned her face up, her blue eyes sparkling and wide with anticipation. "How can you wait? We have a clue that could lead us to the treasure. Sister Katherine will understand the urgency. After all, she is the one who said we must have the treasure before we can defeat King Ethelwulf's evil. If I am able to ride into Norland with my part of the treasure, then we shall bring something worthwhile to my sister."

"If she is as good and wise as people claim, then she will value you for who you are and not for what you bring."

Maribel made quick work of putting the key back together and tucking it into a pouch tied to her belt. "Can you not feel the adventure waiting for us, Eddie? We shall embark on a hunt for real treasure this time, not just for my herbs."

I hated when she called me Eddie. It was a childhood nickname I'd long outgrown. Thankfully, she didn't use it often, but when she did, I felt as though she saw me as a young boy and not the man I'd become.

She stood and straightened her veil. The gray fabric did nothing to mute or detract from her loveliness. In contrast, she only seemed all the more vibrant and alive. Certainly not the type of woman destined to become a nun. Perhaps now that she knew she was a princess, she would put the idea of being a nun out of her mind.

"Say you will come with me," she pleaded softly, looking down at where I still knelt on my prayer cushion. "Please."

I had the strangest longing to reach for her hand, bring it to my lips, and kiss her delicate fingers. Instead, I swallowed the unexpected desire and gave her the answer she wanted. "You know I will."

She smiled, and her eyes danced before she spun around and started to cross the chapel. "I shall meet you by the stables in ten minutes."

"Dress as warmly as you can," I whispered after her. She waved her answer and disappeared, leaving a mixture of longing and frustration swirling in my chest.

I wasted no time in returning to the forge, gathering my clothes and weapons. Wade's heavy breathing told me he still slept, and I prayed he would until we were well on our way to St. Cuthbert's. I doubted he'd approve of me giving in to Maribel's whim, especially to set off in the dark.

With all I needed in hand, I started to open the door, careful not to make a sound.

"Take Sheba." His whisper stopped me.

I spun to find his gaze upon me. I wanted to shake my head in denial but then thought better of it. After all, how could I explain why I had my weapons and every stitch of clothing I owned?

"Keep to the high paths until you reach the tunnels at the eastern end of the Iron Hills." His instructions told me he knew the details of our plans to go to St. Cuthbert's and search for the treasure. Had he pretended to be asleep only to follow me to the chapel? How many times had he done so in the past?

Embarrassed heat slid up my neck into my face.

"Do you remember the underground route that will take you into the ruins?" he asked.

I nodded. I'd traveled with Wade into the vicinity of St. Cuthbert's on several occasions, and he'd done his best to teach me all he knew about the various hiding places set into the Iron Hills and Highlands.

"Stay out of sight during the day and travel at night."

My shoulders dropped. "Maybe you should come with us."

Wade expelled a breath and closed his eyes. "No. She wants you."

If he'd listened to us in the chapel, then he would have heard Maribel's declaration that she desired me to accompany her and not Wade. How must he feel after sacrificing so many years of his life to stay near her and protect her only to have her choose me instead of him?

"I'm sorry, Wade."

"No, lad. It's as it should be. You're the one to go with her. Even Sister Katherine knows it."

"I'll take care of her."

"I know you will." Although not quite words of praise, it was the closest he'd come to acknowledging perhaps I wasn't a complete failure at all his training efforts.

"And we'll be back before dawn on the second day."

"It would be for the best if you can convince the

princess to leave directly for Norland. She won't be safe here anymore." The way he said "princess" left no doubt he'd guessed her identity long ago.

"Do you think King Ethelwulf's men will discover Sister Katherine's trail?"

"It's not a matter of *if,* but *when.*"

Danger awaited everyone who remained. Was that another reason Wade wasn't protesting my going with Maribel, so that he could stay and defend those left behind? "I'll do my best to keep Maribel away, but she is strong-willed and not easily persuaded."

Wade nodded his agreement, then rolled to his back and closed his eyes. It was his silent method of communicating that our conversation was over and I needed to be on my way.

I reached for the door.

"She doesn't see you the same way you see her."

Wade's comment twined around my gut and cinched tight. I didn't have to ask him what he meant. He was finishing the conversation we'd started much earlier in the day—the one about Colette and Maribel and marriage.

I wanted to be angry at him for pointing out something I'd already known about Maribel, something I hadn't wanted to acknowledge. That Maribel wasn't attracted to me as a man. In fact, half the time she considered me nothing more than a childhood playmate— even though we were both fully grown.

But instead of retorting, I swallowed my anger, which was really directed more at myself than at Wade.

"I just don't want to see you get hurt, lad," he said softly.

"I know."

"Colette loves you already and won't break your heart."

The problem was I didn't love Colette. How could I, not when I loved Maribel? I couldn't deny the truth any longer. I'd always loved Maribel and would forever. And if she never felt the same in return, I'd rather be by her side as her friend and companion than not at all.

"Go on, now, lad," Wade said, "and don't forget anything I taught you."

"I won't." As I exited, I had the awful premonition I might not see Wade again, that I wouldn't have the chance to thank him for everything he'd done for me—for rescuing me as a frightened boy alone on the street, for bringing me to safety, for taking the time and effort year after year to shape me into a warrior. For modeling hard work, sacrifice, and courage.

Maybe he hadn't loved me as my own father would have. But he'd loved me in his own way. And I would always be grateful to him.

Chapter 5

Maribel

The spiderwebs coating the tunnels were as thick as the snow that had fallen all night and covered our tracks. Well, maybe the sticky webs weren't quite as thick as the snow, but I shuddered with each dangling strand blocking our path. We'd been traversing the hidden passageways for the past two hours since riding down from the Highlands and entering the Iron Hills. Every time I asked, Edmund reassured me the tunnels would take us to St. Cuthbert's.

"Do you think this is the way Sister Agnes escaped from St. Cuthbert's when she took me away as a babe?"

"It could be." Edmund held the torch in one hand and his sword in the other. He slashed another spiderweb in half so we could make our way without tangling in the silk. The low ceiling forced us to crouch and at times had narrowed so much we'd had to crawl. Edmund had been wise to leave our mounts behind in the secluded alcove at the beginning of the old mine.

"It is difficult for me to imagine Sister Agnes

traversing these tunnels and rushing to get away from King Ethelwulf's soldiers." The old nun had always been big boned with broad shoulders and hips. As far back as I remembered, those joints had given her trouble, particularly when she walked for any length of time.

"Whatever route she took would have been hard for her," Edmund said, slashing at another web. "Especially carrying a newborn babe."

I stifled a yawn. My eyes were heavy from lack of sleep, and keeping up a steady stream of conversation kept my mind off how tired I was. Thankfully, Edmund was accustomed to my endless chatter and didn't seem to tire of it. "I wonder why she never told anyone, not even the abbess, about my identity."

"I suppose she decided the fewer people who knew, the safer you'd be."

"But she could have told me before she passed away." I'd spent hours at her bedside when she'd taken ill from an unexplained fever. Although I'd tried every remedy Sister Agnes had created and even new ones I'd devised, I hadn't been able to save her.

A familiar heaviness settled around my heart. I blamed myself for her death. I should have been able to cure a fever. A fever without any other symptoms. What kind of physician was I that I couldn't manage something so simple? Since that day, I'd vowed I would be an even better physician than Sister Agnes. I'd spend my life proving it if that's how long it took.

Edmund ducked under a low doorway. "Sister Agnes knew if she told you, you'd run off and do what you're doing now."

"Search for treasure?"

"Get into trouble."

I laughed.

Edmund smiled over his shoulder. "I'm serious."

"We shall not get into trouble. I promise."

"If I had a piece of silver for every time you've told me that, I'd be a rich man."

"I am not at fault for the decision to roll in poison oak."

"I suppose getting stuck up in the giant sequoia wasn't your fault either?"

My thoughts flashed back to those carefree days as children when we'd played together and roamed as much of the Highlands as Wade would allow. "I shall take responsibility for the bees' nest falling on Colette. I should have warned her to move out of the way before I cut it out of the tree."

Edmund chuckled. "The only reason you take responsibility for it is because she reminds you of her bee stings whenever she's upset at you."

Colette had been covered with welts. Thankfully, Sister Agnes had concocted a salve of honey and witch hazel and applied it all over Colette's little body. She'd been miserable for several days and had never forgotten it, much to my dismay.

Before I could defend myself further, Edmund stopped so abruptly I bumped into him. He reached a hand behind to steady me.

We'd come to a closed door in the tunnel.

"From here on, it's a steep uphill climb," he said.

"I can endure it." Once again, excitement coursed through my veins. I was on a hunt for the ancient King Solomon's treasure. What could be better?

We'd already discussed the best places to search.

That had been the main topic of conversation during the dark, cold hours we'd ridden across the Highlands. We'd decided we needed to locate keyholes and try the key into every one. How hard could that be? But of course, the always logical Edmund had cautioned me against getting my hopes too high.

"The keyhole won't be out in the open and easy to find," he'd said. "It's likely hidden in a special place having to do with the symbol on the key."

We'd speculated on the various items represented by the tree of life and healing. Perhaps the secret place was located in a well or former apothecary or even the garden beds. We had to search everywhere as quickly as possible. I'd promised Edmund we'd be on our way by nightfall since I didn't expect we'd need all day to find it.

When we reached the top of the steep incline leading to the former abbey, we had to climb several additional winding tunnels before we came into an abandoned mining drift. Continuing along, we eventually found ourselves in a wider room that contained a cold cistern of water fed by a spring cutting through the rocks. We refreshed ourselves there and let our breathing even out before moving onward and upward. I was grateful more than ever for Edmund guiding the way.

Even though he claimed to have been hunting in the eastern Iron Hills a time or two with Wade and was familiar with the area, I also knew Edmund had entire maps of Mercia committed to memory. Wade had required it of him during his training. At the time, I hadn't understood the importance of it, but now I realized Edmund was a huge asset, and I needed him more than I realized.

By the time we surfaced into the ruins of the abbey, the winter sun was peeking from behind clouds, indicating that most of our morning was already gone. The crumbling walls and the remains of small rooms brought a lump to my throat at the realization I'd once been here with my sisters. It was the last place we'd been together, the last place we'd been a family.

"Soon," I whispered into the cool air as I stepped into a tower room that overlooked Mercia's Eastern Plains. "We shall be together again soon."

Shrouded in the freshly fallen snow, the flat fields looked pristine and endlessly beautiful. To the west lay the Iron Cities of Everly, Middleton, and Stefford. The cities were set at the base of the Iron Hills, each upon a different branch of the Cress River. I could almost imagine I saw smoke rising into the air from the many smelters which took the raw iron from the mines and purified it into bars fit for making tools and weapons and household items.

If only I could walk among the cities one time, browse the busy markets, visit a smelter or forge, and step inside a cathedral.

I shook my head and rebuked myself for my wayward desires, certainly not the dreams of a young woman months away from taking her vows. In His Providence, God had chosen me—not my sisters—to go with Sister Agnes, to grow up in a convent, and to learn the physician's skills. It was my work, my life, my purpose. I might have a slight detour while I looked for the treasure and took it to Norland. But I wouldn't be swayed from my true calling to become a nun.

I turned away from the view and began scanning

every inch of the tower room for a keyhole.

"Have you found anything?" Edmund's voice broke into my inner chastisement.

"No, I have not found a single clue."

"Likewise." He crossed to the lookout window and gazed over the enormity of Mercia as I had just done.

"It is majestic, is it not?" I couldn't stop myself from moving next to him and peering out again, hungry for another view of the beauty so different from the barren wilderness of the Highlands.

"It is." His voice was wistful. Was he more eager to see the world beyond our convent than he'd admitted previously? Maybe accompanying me to Norland would give him a taste of adventure too.

"Thank you for coming with me." I shifted and studied his profile; his angular jaw, long nose, and finely sculpted cheeks. A wayward strand of hair lay across his forehead. Before I realized what I was doing, I smoothed the piece back.

His hand captured mine so swiftly I started. When he brought my fingers to his lips and placed a kiss upon them, I drew in a quick breath. Over the edge of our hands, his green eyes were wide as they met mine. And they were filled with the same something that had been there yesterday, something that made me realize Edmund was all man and no longer a boy.

For a moment, time stood still. My heartbeat and my breathing ceased to function. Somehow I'd missed the fact that he'd grown up. Did that mean we couldn't be friends in the same way anymore? What about when I became a nun? What about now that I was a princess?

I wouldn't allow anything to get in the way of our

friendship. Heaven forbid it.

Impetuously, I uncurled my fingers from his and cupped his cheek. "I want you to know that no matter what happens in the future, you will always be my friend."

I waited for a smile, for light to spark in his eyes. But instead, he nodded and took a step back, breaking our connection. I sensed my answer disappointed him, but I wasn't sure how.

"We need to keep looking." He strode toward the tower door without a backward glance.

"Yes. Of course."

Before I followed him, I turned to the view again, drinking it in one more time. Rather than marveling at the beauty, I could only feel the strange weight of Edmund's disappointment.

We continued searching, moving aside debris and leaving no corner or crevice of the abbey untouched. When the afternoon began to wane, a sense of urgency prodded me.

"It is not here." I released a long, loud yawn from where I perched on a lone stool—the only item left intact within what we guessed had once been the abbey's apothecary.

Edmund's face was lined with weariness. He sat on the floor and leaned against the wall, his head tilted back and his eyes closed. I wasn't ready to leave yet, but I'd promised him we'd go at dusk. Since he was clearly tired, I wouldn't push him to stay, even though I wanted to keep looking until I found the treasure. I didn't want to travel to Norland and meet my older sister without it. I'd be of no use to her. But neither would I break my word to Edmund.

"I guess we should go," I said, although I was unable to keep the reluctance from my tone.

Edmund didn't respond.

Forcing myself to rise, I walked over to him and stretched out a hand. "Come. Our horses are probably thinking we deserted them."

Edmund rested his head a moment longer before sitting forward with a start, his eyes opening and lighting with a characteristic glimmer that told me the gears in his mind were spinning and sparking. "We're looking in the wrong place."

"I thought for certain 'S.C. Abbey' stood for St. Cuthbert's."

"It does. But since the clue was likely penned more than a century ago, we must look for the original St. Cuthbert's, the one that would have been here when the clue was written, likely around the time of King Alfred the Peacemaker."

I'd assumed the parchment we'd found inside the key was written by the people who brought the treasure to the Great Isle hundreds of years ago. But as usual Edmund was one step ahead of me. St. Cuthbert's wouldn't have existed during ancient days. It made more sense the piece of parchment inside the key was placed there in more recent times, perhaps by King Alfred.

King Alfred had been one of the greatest kings to rule the united realm of Bryttania among a long line of strong kings. At his death, King Alfred had split the country into two separate realms, giving one to each of his twin daughters. He'd bestowed Mercia upon Leandra and Warwick upon Margery. They both ruled peacefully until Queen Leandra died. Margery fought

Leandra's heir for the right to Mercia's throne, claiming the whole kingdom of Bryttania belonged to her. Eventually, Margery lost the fight, only to have her grandson, King Ethelwulf, take up the conquest many years later.

Although I'd always listened to Sister Agnes's tales of the history of the kings and queens that had once ruled, I'd never truly given her words much thought. Until now. Now I understood all that had happened was the history of my family. My history.

King Ethelwulf had come into Mercia and had attacked Delsworth, taking the peaceful and prosperous kingdom away from King Francis and Queen Dierdal. But he'd done more than that. He'd taken my father and mother, my older sister, and my twin.

He'd also taken away Edmund's family. And Colette's. From the tales I'd heard, he'd hurt countless people in his desire to create a united kingdom. Instead of making a stronger and greater nation with Warwick and Mercia as one country again, his cruelty had created only more darkness and despair throughout the land, and his steep taxes had drained the already stretched resources.

Of course, since I'd lived a sheltered and isolated life in the Highlands, I knew only the information Wade gleaned during his trips to town. His news was never good. He complained bitterly of the lawlessness that prevailed throughout the land along with the fear and hardships the people endured under the king's policies.

If Queen Adelaide Constance took the throne, would the nuns finally feel safe again and come out of hiding? Perhaps people would seek out the convent for help and healing as they'd once done. Perhaps I would be able to bring wellness to many instead of to just a few.

Edmund reached for my hand and allowed me to help pull him to his feet. "We need to look down the hill. The original abbey was built closer to the mine."

We retraced our steps the way we'd entered. As we descended, Edmund veered off into another tunnel, this one slightly taller than the others. Finally, we reached a dead end.

He tapped against the stone with the hilt of his sword until the resulting thump gave a hollow echo. "We'll need to tear the wall down here."

I wasn't surprised when Edmund used his knife to dig through the mortar and pull the stones apart piece by piece. I attempted to aid him, but he worked with an efficiency and strength I couldn't match no matter how hard I tried.

When the opening was big enough to crawl through, he went first with the torch and I followed.

"Watch out for the spiderwebs," he cautioned as he ducked underneath one the size of a full-grown man.

Once inside, I sat back on my heels and looked around in amazement at the old convent that had been sealed off to the world. We'd apparently stumbled into the chapel, for against the far wall sat an altar fashioned from stone. The carvings on the front were covered by more cobwebs, but the detailed cross at the center was still visible.

On one side of the altar stood a tall stone holder that had probably held the Paschal candle. On the opposite side was a baptismal font made of stone, the basin cracked in half. Both were draped with spiderwebs so thick they could have been linen coverings.

Edmund stood and raised his dagger in a position of defense. "This place isn't safe." He sniffed the air and peered around the darkened room with narrowed eyes.

I got to my feet, ducking to avoid the webs hanging like drapes from the low ceiling. The air was damp and musty, and it contained a bitter odor I couldn't name. Even so, I approached the altar. "Surely we can spare a few minutes of searching."

Edmund stared intently at the passageway leading away from the chapel. "I think we should go."

I pushed the thick strands from the altar and smoothed my hand over the stone, noting the beautiful carved pattern of vines intertwined with grapes that decorated the outer rim. An altar represented sacrifice to God, laying down one's own plans and desires. Ultimately, it stood for death.

We needed to find something that symbolized life and healing. I turned first to the Paschal candle stand but stopped abruptly. If anything in this chapel embodied life, the baptismal font certainly did. What could signify new life and healing better than baptism?

Heedless of the webs snagging my veil, I crossed to the font. Like the altar, it was decorated with intricate engravings. I traced my fingers across the dusty but smooth pattern of ivy leaves. And flower blossoms.

The signs of life.

My heart thudded with an extra beat. I skimmed the font, searching for a keyhole or anything the key might fit into.

"We need to go." Edmund's voice was low and urgent.

I wrapped my fingers around the back of the font. Scraping aside the web coating, I probed the cool stone of the pedestal and then the base that held the cracked basin.

There was nothing. No keyhole. Not even a dent.

Unwilling to give up yet, I dropped to my knees and brushed my hands across the dusty floor, then returned to the pedestal itself.

"Now, Maribel!" Edmund was backing slowly away from the passageway toward the opening we'd created.

My fingers flew over the raised florets surrounding the base. One wiggled as I touched it. I tugged, digging into the crevices. It fell away, and a moment later I made contact with a keyhole.

"I found it!" I fumbled at my leather pouch for the key.

At a strange hiss and clacking behind me, the hairs on the back of my neck rose, but I made myself focus on getting the key out, reaching behind the pedestal, and inserting it into the hole.

"Hurry!" Edmund called.

My fingers shook, and I couldn't get the key in. "Calm down, Maribel," I admonished myself as I took a deep breath and willed my hands to still. Again, I attempted to fit the key, and this time it slid in perfectly. When I twisted it, a soft pop told me it had worked.

The hissing and clacking grew louder, but I didn't turn to the source. Instead, I fumbled at the back of the base. I couldn't see anything, but my fingers connected with the part of the structure that had come loose, like a drawer. I tugged at it and was surprised when it slid out.

"Maribel!" Edmund shouted. "We're out of time. We have to leave!"

I slipped my hand into the narrow space. It was lined in velvet, and a small rolled parchment lay inside. I'd expected to find a treasure, not another piece of paper. Nevertheless, I grabbed the scroll, patted around the bottom of the drawer to ensure I wasn't leaving something important behind, then scrambled backward.

Only then did I glance past Edmund toward the passageway. His torch illuminated a sight more frightening than anything from the worst of nightmares. A black-and-brown-striped spider was crawling across the ceiling toward us. A giant spider the size of a goat.

Chapter
6

EDMUND

NONE OF MY COMMUNICATION WOULD GET THROUGH TO THE giant arachnid. I'd only learned a little regarding the language of the lesser creatures, having focused mainly on the wild animals that roamed the Highlands.

Its eight black eyes were pinned on me, sensing my attempt to communicate. But still, it crept closer, the hairs on its legs raised, picking up our vibrations and our scent. In the passageway behind the spider came the clanking and hissing of more. The place was infested with the giant creatures.

I'd heard rumors of large, poisonous spiders once having lived in the Iron Hills in the days before the mines were fully developed. Their deadly bites had killed many miners until the spiders had been hunted to extinction.

How had these survived?

I thrust my sword, attempting to discern the best way to attack. Its hard exoskeleton would be difficult to penetrate. I'd likely have to start by slicing off its legs while dodging the dagger-like claws on each tip as well as the pedipalps next to its fangs.

With a last desperate effort at communicating, I issued a short hiss, telling it to withdraw. It hissed back, releasing an odor that told me it had every intention of killing us.

"Crawl through the opening, Maribel," I said as the creature neared, so close that it was almost overhead. Out of the corner of my eye, I glimpsed another one entering the room, as big as the first. Although I could possibly battle one, I wouldn't be able to defend Maribel from multiple spiders at once. Not from overhead and certainly not with so many claws and legs.

She moved to obey me but then stopped halfway through the space. "Give me your dagger, and I shall help you fight them."

"No! Make haste through the hole and leave space for me to dive out after you."

She did as I asked, no doubt hearing the strain in my voice. As a third spider crawled into the room, this one on the floor, I knew the only way we could escape was to attempt to outrun them.

As if sensing my plan, the spider above me lunged, releasing silk from its spinneret as it descended. I spun and tossed my torch and sword ahead.

"Start running!" I forced my head into the hole and scrambled to pull my body through. But I was too late. A jab into my calf was followed by piercing pain so intense I couldn't hold back a cry. The spider had punctured my tender flesh with one of its claws. Within seconds, it would riddle me with more cuts from its other legs before finally biting me with its poisonous fangs. There was nothing I could do to stop it except attempt to crawl away and get as much of my body out of its reach as possible.

"I have you!" Maribel shouted, clutching my arms and hauling me. I pushed with her, throwing myself forward. Another spider claw hit my thigh, grazing my flesh like a cat scratch.

With Maribel dragging me, I managed to wriggle both legs through. Once out, I jumped to my feet. Heedless of the pain in my limb, I shoved stones over the opening. Maribel joined my efforts. Working frantically, we tossed and stacked but managed to block only half of the opening when a spider leg shot out and almost pierced Maribel in the chest.

I shoved her away in the direction we'd hiked. "Time to go." Grabbing both the torch and my sword, I waved her ahead of me. "Run, Maribel!"

With the blood from my wound running down my calf and seeping into my hose and boot, I limped after her. The spider claw had penetrated deeply, but thankfully, from what I could tell, it hadn't damaged muscle or bone. I needed to stop and tend it, at least slow the flow of blood. But first we had to put distance between ourselves and the spiders.

"Would it help if I cover our trail with Mountain Essence?" Maribel called as she stumbled along the rocky path. The nuns had developed the herbal mixture long ago in an effort to keep tracking dogs and wolves from picking up their scent. It worked well in many instances and had been one of the ways Wade had been able to cover his scent during his forays up and down the mountains over the years.

"It won't suffice this time." My breath already was labored, and I was weakening from the loss of blood, but I pushed onward, praying I'd make it to the horses without passing out. "Even if you mask our scent, the hairs on the spiders' legs will pick up our slightest movements."

"Can we outrun them?"

"Yes, if we don't stop." It wasn't exactly a lie. But it wasn't the entire truth. Spiders could crawl exceptionally fast. Each of their eight legs contained six joints, making them versatile. Our only hope was that the stones in front of the opening would delay them enough to give us an advantage.

"Make haste," I urged Maribel even as I began to lag, the pressure and discomfort in my leg burning with every step. The pain rose up, making me nauseous, and I breathed deeply to stay conscious. Behind, I could hear faint hisses and scrapes, informing me the spiders had broken free of the stones and were on our trail.

After passing under a gate at the end of a low tunnel, I yanked on the rusty iron grill. Protesting and screeching, it gave way, sliding down far enough that it would impede the spiders—at least for a little while.

When we finally reached the mouth where we'd tied our horses, I fell to the ground, trembling and weak. Maribel paused in untying the lead rope of her horse and rushed to my side. She took one look at my leg, frowned, and then ripped a strip off the shift beneath her habit.

I needed to protest, tell her we didn't have the time to tend my wound, but I sensed myself beginning to fade. I felt her tie the linen above my wound to staunch the flow of blood. Then just as quickly, she pressed something into the puncture before covering it with another piece of cloth.

"Come now," she said gently, slipping her arms underneath mine and lifting me so I was sitting. "I shall help you onto your horse."

The clacking of the spiders was closer. We had only

minutes, if not seconds, before they surrounded us. As much as I wanted to push her away and tell her to go, I realized Maribel would never leave me alone to fend for myself. Her physician heart wouldn't allow her to abandon someone in need, and I'd only waste precious time arguing with her to do so.

With the last vestige of strength I could muster, I climbed onto my horse. Maribel scrambled onto hers, releasing a frightened scream as the spiders crawled one by one out of the tunnel into the cave, their multiple black eyes all focused on us. I leaned down into my mount, wrapped the reins around my arms to stay astride if I lost consciousness, and then whispered the words that would communicate to our horses the need to travel faster than they'd ever gone before.

We charged into the growing darkness, the coldness of the coming night slapping us with the reminder we were still in a wild and dangerous land, that anything could happen, and that I couldn't let my guard down for a second if I hoped to protect Maribel.

The movement of my horse jarred my calf wound, but whatever Maribel had put there began to numb the pain, making it more bearable. The scratch along my thigh stung as well, and the blood from it had seeped through my layers of clothing. It was apparently deeper than I had first suspected. I'd likely need stitches for both injuries.

As we rode, I could feel Sheba's presence nearby, which brought me a measure of relief. The harpy eagle had accompanied us through the Highlands. And now, if anything happened to me, I could count on her to take care of Maribel. The bird had picked up on how much the young woman meant to me and was as protective as if Maribel had been a hatchling.

After several hours of hard riding, we reached a small cave Wade and I used when hunting. In the moonlight, I'd noticed Maribel's growing struggle to stay awake and hold herself aright. It was no wonder, after being up all of last night and then again today. Since we were far enough from St. Cuthbert's and wouldn't need to worry about the spiders, I decided we'd rest a few hours before finishing our journey home.

Maribel started a fire with flint while I tended to the horses. She found the small iron pot and a few other necessities Wade and I kept in the cavern. As industrious as always, she melted snow and began to heat water. When I limped into the warmth of the cave a few minutes later, the pot was bubbling, and she'd set out the few remaining food rations we'd brought along—goat cheese, smoked venison, and dried apples. She also had her medicinal satchel untied and laid open and was threading a needle.

"Eat first," she said. "The nourishment will provide strength for my mending."

I lowered myself gingerly on the opposite side of the fire and cringed at the throbbing surge of heat in my calf. Whatever she'd given me to ease the pain was wearing thin.

As I ate, I sat back and watched her at work. Using a splash of boiling water, she mixed together several of the herbs she'd taken from her bag. She made two different kinds of paste and then finished with a tonic.

I never tired of seeing her mixing her medicines. Her long fingers were deft but careful, elegant and yet proficient. I followed her every movement, the way the firelight flickered upon her bent head, highlighting the blond and spinning it into gold, the way loose strands of hair brushed her neck, and the way her pretty lips pursed in concentration.

Finally, she turned to me, her blue eyes probing mine, gently questioning. "Are you ready?"

"Whenever you are."

She began arranging her supplies next to me. "I shall wash the wounds first with warm water then numb it with the paste." Her fingers shook a little. Was she nervous?

I reached for her arm and squeezed. "I'll be fine, Maribel."

She nodded but lacked her usual confidence.

"You removed two teeth from Sister Margaret's mouth a week ago," I said, wanting to see her lips curve into a smile. "Surely this will be easy in comparison."

Instead of smiling, she frowned. "This is different. What if I make a mistake? What if I make things worse instead of better, as I did with Sister Agnes?"

Her words confused me. How had Maribel made things worse for Sister Agnes? She'd stayed by the old nun's side day after day and night after night, administering every remedy she could concoct.

With a shake of her head, she gave a weak smile. "Listen to me. Letting my worry get the best of me." She reached for the closest poultice. "If we let worry control us, we shall never accomplish anything."

Was she worried about me? More than other patients she tended? The thought sent a warm trail through my heart.

She scanned my leg. "You must remove your hosen and breeches."

I shook my head adamantly at her brazen suggestion. "I'll roll up my breeches up."

"Nonsense." She reached for my boot and began to

unlace it. "I shall help you undress if it pains you to do so yourself."

Speechless, I watched her take off my boot and hose, first one foot then the other with her usual focused efficiency. Even so, I couldn't keep from experiencing a strange, low heat in my middle at her closeness and the fact that she was undressing me.

When she moved to my waist and tugged at the drawstring on my breeches, the heat swelled through my chest and up into my cheeks. I grabbed her hand and stopped her. "I can do it, Maribel."

"Are you sure?" Her expression held only tender concern. Nothing else.

"Of course," I replied as nonchalantly as I could manage. This experience clearly wasn't conjuring the same physical reaction in her as it was in me. She saw herself as the physician and me as her patient, while I couldn't keep from thinking I was a man alone with a beautiful and desirable woman.

Of the two views of our situation, hers was definitely the safest and most appropriate. And I should chastise myself for allowing my mind to go anyplace else. But my body seemed to have a will of its own, and I was attracted to her in spite of my best efforts to remain neutral.

I stood and made quick work of divesting my breeches. My braies underneath came to midthigh, but when I lay back down in front of her, I felt entirely bare even though I was modestly covered.

"Your braies are still in the way of the cut on your thigh." Her fingers brushed against my leg near my wound. The soft touch sent tingles across my flesh.

I sensed her request to take them off and interrupted before she could ask it. "Maribel, please. This is awkward enough." My voice came out more strangled than I'd intended.

As she lifted her eyes to mine, confusion and even a little hurt swam there. "Why is it awkward? I only want to help you."

How could I explain that even if she saw me as only another patient, as only her friend, I saw her as so much more? That I sometimes ached when I looked at her because of how beautiful she was. That sometimes I wanted to be in her presence more than I wanted to be with anyone else. That sometimes I needed to hear her voice and see her smile more than I needed nourishment.

I wasn't sure how or when my feelings for her had changed. Maybe I'd always been enamored with her. Maybe my childhood adoration had developed into an adult infatuation. Whatever the case, her feelings weren't catching up to mine.

Was that what I'd hoped? That eventually she'd feel for me the way I did for her? Of course, I hadn't told her how I felt. I suppose I'd hoped she'd just naturally experience the same. Or at the very least, I'd hoped she'd sense my affections went deeper.

"What is it?" she probed further, recognizing my need to say something.

The clock was ticking toward the eve of her eighteenth birthday when she'd take her vows and I'd lose her. Maybe I needed to make my affections clear. Maybe I needed to simply come out and tell her. But what if I disclosed my truest feelings and then learned she didn't reciprocate? I'd only make things worse.

"Eddie," she said, softly, almost pleadingly. "You can tell me anything. You know that."

"You shouldn't call me Eddie." My voice was thin with

my frustration. "I much prefer Edmund."

Her brows shot up, making the blue all the more vibrant and alluring.

"If you haven't noticed, I'm not a young lad anymore." There, I'd said it. Not my best explanation for what was going on inside of me. But it was a start.

She studied my face for a moment and then reached for the pot of hot water, but not before I saw the smile she was trying to hide.

I closed my eyes and bit back a groan. She was impossible.

"Very well," she said solemnly, although I could hear the mirth in her tone. "I shall call you Edmund from now on if that is what you prefer."

I didn't respond except to press my lips together to keep from blurting out something I would surely regret later.

Her fingers grazed my thigh again, sending another cascade of tingles over my skin. As she rolled up the hem of my braies, I gritted my teeth and attempted to think of anything besides her touch.

"I know this hurts," she said gently.

I didn't correct her mistake and instead allowed her to believe my grimace came from pain instead of pleasure. Inwardly, I counted myself a coward. And told myself I would have to speak the truth soon. Not today. But soon.

Chapter
7

Maribel

I brushed a strand of Edmund's hair off his forehead.
At my touch, he stirred as I'd intended.

With his head in my lap, my legs were numb from
the lack of movement. But I'd wanted to make him as
comfortable as possible. The perforation in his calf had
severed through layers of flesh—had almost gone in
one side of his leg and out the other. I'd needed to
clean deep inside, and the stitching had been more
complicated than I'd ever done before.

Throughout the entire procedure, he hadn't spoken
a word and had endured the pain bravely. But the
moment I'd finished, he'd fallen into a deep slumber
and hadn't awoken. I'd slept off and on, too, waking to
check his sutures, flushing the inflamed tissues with a
tonic, and reapplying poultices to the laceration.

Now that it was midafternoon, however, we needed
to be on our way. Edmund had insisted on leaving at
break of day, not wanting to linger too long in any one
place. I understood his caution. He was doing as Wade

had taught him.

But I was doing as Sister Agnes had taught me. The motion on the horse alone would jar Edmund's injuries again and interfere with the healing process.

He released a low moan and shifted his head. His normally smoothly shaven jaw and chin contained a dark layer of stubble.

If you haven't noticed, I'm not a young lad anymore. The remembrance of his petulant words made me smile. I wasn't sure what had brought about his statement. Pain often caused people to say the oddest things. But he was right. I'd already begun to recognize the changes in our relationship when we'd stood together in the tower ruins of St. Cuthbert's. It was past time for me to acknowledge we were growing up and no longer the same carefree children.

I ran my thumb across the stubble, the proof he was indeed a man. The bristly hair tickled my fingers, and I rounded his chin and trailed my thumb over his jaw, relishing the texture. Only as I traced a path toward his ear did I realize his eyes were open and he was looking up at me. His forest-green gaze was dark—darker than I'd ever seen it. And filled with an intensity that drew me into its lush thickness, pulling me, embracing me, and somehow caressing me.

The connection was unlike any I'd ever ex- perienced before, and it seemed to unlock something inside me and release a warm tumble of fluttering feathers. It was an unusual sensation but not unpleasant. Much to my chagrin, it made me want to run my thumb across his cheek and chin again.

I wasn't sure what was happening. I tried to find something to say to explain why I'd been touching his face. But I couldn't think of anything.

He broke eye contact, letting his focus drop to my lips.

The feathers fluttered again, this time faster. Why was he looking at my lips like that? Almost as if he wondered what it would be like to kiss me.

He wasn't thinking that, was he?

My gaze flickered to his lips, and the warmth and tenderness from when he'd kissed my knuckles came rushing back. Would a kiss on my lips be as warm and tender?

Just as soon as the question entered my mind, I stiffened, aghast at such a worldly thought. I was destined to take a vow of celibacy, to remain chaste, to dedicate myself to God for the rest of my life. Thoughts of kissing were completely inappropriate for someone about to become a nun.

"How are you feeling?" I asked, looking everywhere but at his face.

"Sore," he said quietly.

"I shall put on another paste to deaden the pain so you are able to ride more comfortably."

I wanted to put distance between us, but his head was still resting on my lap.

He glanced toward the cave opening. Upon seeing the light of day streaming inside, he sat up—so quickly he almost fell back.

I steadied him with a hand to his upper arm, feeling the contours of his muscles and much too conscious of them.

"How long have I been asleep?" he asked.

"It is past midday."

He dropped his forehead into his hands and gave

another moan. "Maribel, we should have left hours ago."

"I know." I crawled to my satchel and reached for the paste I'd made earlier. "But you needed to rest in order to heal."

"We're in danger staying in any place overlong." He pushed himself to his knees then stopped and sucked in a sharp breath. His face contorted with an effort to control his pain.

"Lie down and let me put the poultice on your wounds before you arise."

Bracing against the cave wall, he rose until he was hunched but standing.

"Please, Eddie—Edmund." I, too, stood and again placed my hand on his back, this time rubbing him gently. "Let me ease your suffering."

He lurched forward as if my touch caused him even more pain. "I'll be all right—in a few minutes." He moved to the mouth of the cavern and grabbed at the rocky rim to brace himself and take the pressure off his injured leg. He whistled and a short while later was rewarded by the flap of eagle wings. Sheba was carrying a hare in her talons. She dropped it to the ground at Edmund's feet before perching on the ledge nearby.

We'd eaten the remainder of our provisions last night, and now my empty stomach rumbled with the anticipation of a meal. Though I wanted to pick up the rabbit and begin dressing it in preparation for roasting, I stood back and waited.

Sheba's full white head was bordered by the gray in her breast and wings. As she settled her feathers, she shifted to look at me with her black eyes. Her stare seemed to assess me in a single glance before she swiveled her head and focused on Edmund. For a few moments, the two communicated in whistles and short birdcalls.

Finally, Sheba took flight, her heavy flap pushing a waft of cold air into the cave.

Edmund didn't turn but instead limped outside. He studied the rocky, barren landscape before spinning back to me, his expression grave. "Sheba has seen other humans in the area."

"Who?" We never had visitors in the Highlands. First Sister Katherine and now someone else?

"Men on horseback."

"Do we know if they are friend or foe?"

"Sheba cannot give me such specific details. Nevertheless, we should use caution. We don't want anyone seeing us."

A shiver ran up my spine. "Are they near?"

"I wasn't able to figure out exactly where they are, but we need to wait now, until nightfall, before venturing out."

I nodded. "Good. Then you will be able to rest longer."

He limped to his cloak and picked it up. "I'm going out to scout the area and see if I can discover anything more."

I sensed an undercurrent between us—one that had never been there previously, one I didn't understand. Normally, I would have protested his disregard for my instructions, and the physician within me wanted to rush to him and make him lie down again. Instead, I silently watched him don his cloak and gloves and then strap on his weapons.

While he was gone, I skinned and gutted the hare and started roasting it. During the solitude, I tried to make sense of Edmund's mood. He was clearly frustrated, and it went beyond my decision to allow him to oversleep. Did it have to do with his comment about not being a lad? Was I treating him like a child in more ways than using his childhood nickname?

Perhaps I needed to approach him with more respect, the way I did Wade. Our relationship obviously needed to mature into something different. I didn't know what. But I did know I didn't want to push him away, which was what I seemed to be doing.

When he returned later, his cheeks and nose were pink from the cold. I was glad for the color in his skin and also that his limp was less pronounced.

"I found hoofprints for maybe a dozen warhorses, likely Ethelwulf's men," he informed me. "They've headed away from the Highlands to the east."

"Then we are safe and undetected?"

"For the time being." He stood over the fire and rubbed his hands together. The seriousness of his expression and the manner in which he held himself reminded me again that my childhood friend had turned into a man and wanted to be treated as such.

I speared a piece of the roasted rabbit onto the end of my knife and handed it to him. He nodded his thanks, used his teeth to rip off a chunk, and began to eat. I stirred the fire, sparking the blaze so that it radiated more heat.

When I straightened, I decided now was as good a time as any to make amends. "Edmund, I sense I have displeased you—"

"We'll be fine," he said between greasy bites.

"From what I can tell, Ethelwulf's knights have picked up our scent and are tracking us to St. Cuthbert's. They'll search for us there and in the meantime, we'll say a hasty good-bye to everyone and be on our way to Norland."

"I am not speaking about our current predicament."

He stopped chewing and lowered the knife. His gaze snapped to mine, and his eyes were dark and brooding.

"I have not recognized the changes in our relationship as a result of growing up."

His Adam's apple rose and fell in a hard swallow, and his eyes widened in expectation. And . . . perhaps even hope?

I plunged forward, knowing I'd been correct in my assessment. "Now that you are a man, I have not respected you the way I should. And I am heartily sorry for it."

He waited.

"I shall endeavor to give you the esteem you are due and cease treating you like a child."

His shoulders deflated, and he glanced down at the meat remaining on the tip of the knife. "You have no need to apologize, Maribel. Whatever confusion in our relationship is my fault and not yours."

His answer wasn't what I'd expected and left me more confused than before.

"You are a good friend to me," he continued, twisting his knife around. "And I have no wish to push you away, although I fear I'm doing so already."

I smiled at his confession. "You could never push me away. Even if you do, I shall not go far. I am too stubborn for that."

"Quite true." He gave me a sideways glance, one that revealed the beginning of his smile.

If I'd been next to him, I would have nudged him back playfully. As it was, my smile widened, and the weight of worry lifted off my chest. All was right between us again. And I was glad for it.

"Since we have a couple of hours until dusk, shall we take a look at the parchment I discovered in the base of the baptismal font?"

"Since I nearly sacrificed my leg for the parchment, I'd say so." His voice contained forced cheer, and he focused on the bit of hare left on the knife and began eating again.

Perhaps not *all* was right, but whatever was bothering him, he would certainly work it out in his own time and way. At least I prayed so.

I untied the pouch at my side that contained the key, the ruby, and now the parchment, and I carefully pulled out the rolled-up sheet. It was no wider than my hand, but as I unraveled it, I realized that it was as long as my arm. I kneeled and spread it out on the stone floor, using two small rocks to hold it flat. Swirls of ink circled in various patterns, like an ancient piece of artwork.

"It's a maze." Edmund peered over my shoulder and took another bite of meat.

"A maze?" I examined the worn sheet again. Sure enough, the picture had neat lines running in connected rows, some coming to dead ends and others flowing together in a continuous path.

"But it's only part of the maze." He knelt next to me. "You can tell the parchment has been severed. Here." He wiped the grease from his finger and pointed to the top long edge. The remnant had darkened with age, especially along the sides. But the top length was more jagged and frayed.

"The maze's pattern must continue with another piece of parchment," Edmund said. "If I had to judge from the size, I'd guess there are two other pieces to this maze."

I attempted to digest the information that came so easily to Edmund. "Then do you think each of the three keys unlocks a part of the maze?"

"It's possible."

"But I thought the keys unlocked King Solomon's treasure."

"Perhaps they still do. If I had to speculate, I'd say the three map sections must be put back together to make a whole maze, which will then enable a person to discover the way through it. I wouldn't be surprised if the treasure is at the end and the keys are needed to unlock it."

I sat back on my heels and watched Edmund's keen eyes trace the maze. He'd always been much smarter than Colette and me in our studies. What he'd figured out in an instant would have taken me hours, if I'd been able to tie the clues together at all.

"You are brilliant," I said.

He smiled at my words of praise.

"Then all the parchments collectively form a treasure map?"

"It appears so."

The queen has need of the treasure, Sister Katherine had said. *But she won't be able to find it and defeat evil without the help of you and your twin sister, Emmeline.*

Now I understood why Queen Adelaide needed me.

She not only needed my key, but she needed my piece of the treasure map.

"But a maze?" I asked. "Yes, there are likely nobility who have erected mazes in their gardens. But this is one of great magnitude." The parchment contained hundreds of paths. "I cannot think of any place big enough, other than Inglewood Forest. Do you suppose the maze is there?"

"If it is, then it would be overgrown and nearly impossible to find." Edmund stared at the map, his brows knit.

I forced myself to concentrate likewise. "What if there was a maze long ago, one that has since been destroyed or covered much like St. Cuthbert's original structure?"

Edmund's eyes sparkled. "The Labyrinth of Death. What if the map is the solution to the Labyrinth of Death?"

"I have never heard of a labyrinth in Mercia—"

"It's in the western Highlands, deep underground."

"How do you know?"

"How do I know most of the geography of Mercia?" he asked.

"Wade." We said the warrior's name at the same time and then both smiled.

"The Labyrinth of Death has become the tale of legends and myths," Edmund continued, "but Wade taught me its location anyway, likely in the event we needed another hiding place."

"Then you could lead us there?" I asked, sitting forward.

The excitement upon his countenance dimmed. "No, Maribel. It would do no good to make the trip. If it does exist, we will only get lost inside without the other segments of the map to guide us. That's why it's called the Labyrinth of Death. Because so many people wandered within its depths and were never able to find their way out."

"But we have a partial map—"

"And there's rumored to be a creature living in the bowels of the labyrinth—a deadly creature who captures and kills anyone who crosses its path."

"If we could face all those spiders, we can survive one deadly creature in the labyrinth."

"I gave Sister Katherine my word I'd take you to Norland, and that is where we must go."

"No harm would come of passing by the labyrinth on our way. Surely 'twould not delay us overlong."

He started to shake his head.

"We would not have to go inside," I added. "We could simply take a look around and then hasten onward."

He sighed, but I could see the excitement in his eyes as he studied the pattern of the maze. He was just as interested as I was in having adventures. He simply needed a nudge to fly out of the nest.

I stood. "The matter is settled. We shall discover if a labyrinth still exists. If so, such information will be valuable to relate to my sister once we arrive in Norland."

When he didn't protest, I smiled to myself. Edmund might be more reserved and careful than I was. But most of the time, we were of one mind and soul. I didn't want to lose that connection—didn't want to lose him. Yet somehow I sensed him slipping through my fingers, and no matter how hard I tried to hang on, I had the feeling I was losing him anyway.

Chapter 8

EDMUND

I COULD SENSE SHEBA'S FEAR. HER MOTIONS HAD BECOME MORE forceful and erratic. The moonlight revealed her flying overhead in circles as I led Maribel along the hidden paths back to the convent. The eagle's fear had been palpable since the moment she'd come to me in the hunter's cave hours ago.

I'd hoped the further we traveled away from St. Cuthbert's and Ethelwulf's men, the calmer she'd grow. But her agitation had remained, making me more alert and on edge. Although the darkness of the winter night hid us well, I maintained a high level of awareness at every noise, scent, movement.

Sister Katherine had told us to leave within two days. I'd assumed we would be fairly safe until then and hadn't covered our scent as well as I could have. But apparently, Ethelwulf's men were closer than she'd anticipated.

Why hadn't Sister Katherine done a better job of masking her trail? Even as frustration coursed through my veins, I guessed the old nun had likely done the best she could, but her age and frailties had likely made the travel difficult and all too easy for Ethelwulf's men to follow no matter how well she attempted to evade them.

As usual, Maribel rode and chattered as though she hadn't a care in the world. She was oblivious to the danger closing in on us, which was just as well. There was no need to worry her. Not when I didn't have anything but Sheba's fear and the earlier sighting of horse prints to give credence to my anxiety.

"Wait until Colette sees the piece of the maze we found," Maribel was saying. "I wonder if she could recreate the other part of it for us?"

Colette was especially talented with artistry. After working at the loom most of the day, she spent her free time drawing and painting on the convent walls. She'd accomplished detailed murals of biblical scenes over the past few years. She'd even used my face for one of Noah's sons surrounded by animals. I thought I saw myself in several of her other murals, but not quite as distinctly as the portrait of Noah's son. At the time, I'd been flattered. But Wade's recent comments about Colette had been nagging me.

You should just ask that poor girl to marry you and put her out of her misery. That girl would do anything you asked of her. Colette loves you already and won't break your heart.

Had Colette's infatuation existed all along? Maybe I'd been too blind to see it, the same way Maribel was ignorant of my feelings. I couldn't fault Maribel for not knowing or reciprocating any more than Colette could blame me for the same.

I swallowed a sigh. My desire and feelings for Maribel were getting harder to contain, especially whenever she touched me. And now she knew something was wrong, had even apologized and said she would try to be a better friend.

I had to stop reacting to her, had to stay platonic, had to mask all that I felt. Obviously, if she didn't harbor affection for me, she couldn't summon it forth. I certainly couldn't for Colette.

"Is the map symmetrical?" Maribel asked. "If so, then the top would likely be a mirror image of the bottom. Surely Colette could draw it."

"I think it would be wise for us to keep the discovery of the map a secret," I replied. "Just between you and me. At least for now."

"But Colette will already be peeved at me for not inviting her to come along on our trip to St. Cuthbert's. I cannot bear to think of hurting her even further."

"She may be insulted, but she'll mend easily enough." Colette had a way of pouting at the smallest slights. It annoyed me more than I cared to admit.

Colette was still debating whether to take her vows and become a nun. She hadn't made up her mind yet the way Maribel had. Was it because she hoped I'd marry her?

I nearly coughed at the realization. Maybe I needed to speak frankly with her and let her know she shouldn't harbor any plans of a future with me. Then she could move on and decide what she really wanted to do with her life.

Maribel blew into her hands for warmth and rubbed her mittens together. The cold was taking its toll on her, but as usual, she never complained. Thankfully, we were almost home. "Do you think we should invite Colette to journey to Norland with us? She would enjoy the adventure, would she not?"

"The journey to Norland will be fraught with many dangers. Colette will be safer at the convent, and we'll be able to travel faster without her."

"What kind of dangers?" Maribel's tone seemed nonchalant, as though she was asking about the weather instead of life-threatening situations. How much should I share with her? I didn't want to upset her with the possibility that Ethelwulf would probably do everything within his power to capture and kill her. If his men were already in the area, from here on out, we would have to travel hard and cover our trail well to avoid them.

Before I could formulate a truthful but nonthreatening answer, I sensed increased tension in the air. At first, I thought Sheba was flying close and communicating with me, her agitation emanating with the flap of her wings. But then I realized the new sense of fear and turmoil was lower to the ground. At a nearby yip, I reined my horse.

"What is it?" Maribel halted several feet ahead.

"Barnabas is out." The wolf I'd raised made his home close enough that we still saw each other regularly and maintained a connection even after he'd found a mate last spring and had a litter of pups. Late in the summer, one of the pups had wandered off and had fallen into a tight ravine. Barnabas had come to me for help, and I'd been able to rescue the wayward wolf.

Ever since, I sensed Barnabas wanted to find a way to repay me for my good deed. And though I'd reassured him that I expected nothing from him, he'd watched over me more diligently lately, and tonight I felt his concern in its full force.

"How does Barnabas fare?" Maribel asked affectionately. "I pray all is well."

I glanced around the darkened crags eager for a

glimpse of the animal's glowing eyes or his outline in the moonlight. But I saw nothing and realized he was likely staying hidden so he wouldn't draw undue attention to himself or his family.

He yipped several high notes and then gave a low growl. He was warning me of impending danger, telling me to protect my family the same as he was doing.

I yipped back, hoping he would divulge more. But only silence and stillness greeted me, the sign Barnabas had done what he'd come to do and left.

Were we walking into a trap? Was the convent even now besieged by Ethelwulf's guards awaiting our return? Surely not. Sheba had seen the men riding away, and I'd clearly seen the tracks heading in the direction of St. Cuthbert's.

I slid from my mount and reached to help Maribel down. "We'll tie the horses over beyond Eagle's Ledge and approach the convent from the south."

Maribel allowed me to hoist her out of her saddle and set her on the rocky ground. "Is there a problem?"

"There may be," I whispered. "I want to take precautions just in case."

We secured our mounts in a safe place, and then I led the way around the convent, creeping low to the ground. As we finally neared the south path, the moonlight revealed horse and boot prints in the dusting of snow that remained. They were the same tracks I'd seen earlier in the day, which meant only one thing. The band of men had come here first—likely looking for Maribel.

Was it possible they hadn't picked up our trail but rather someone had told them where we'd gone?

I shook my head. No one but Wade knew our destination. And he'd likely informed the sisters we'd left for Norland.

When we reached a large rock a dozen paces from the entrance, I caught the movement of a shadow in the half-open doorway. I tugged Maribel down into a crouch next to me. In the stillness of the night, her breathing was too loud.

"Do you see—" she whispered before I clamped my gloved hand over her mouth.

In the darkness, I could sense more than see her eyes widening in surprise. I leaned into her ear and spoke as quietly as possible. "Be wary and silent."

She nodded.

Slowly, I released her. Something was definitely wrong. Wade would never open the door halfway, not even a crack. And if there was a hint of danger, he would have been outside keeping guard. He'd have seen us coming long before we'd seen him and would have met me by now.

My fingers circled the handle of my knife in an automatic reflex. Behind me to the north, I sensed Sheba's hovering tension even though she was silent.

We should have gone straight to Norland. I admonished myself as I scanned the surrounding boulders. It wasn't too late to circle the convent, return to our horses, and be on our way. I touched Maribel's arm and signaled that we were leaving.

Before she could protest, another motion in the doorway drew my attention. A cloaked figure slipped outside and hesitated, looking first one way and then the other. Although the darkness shrouded the person, the diminutive frame and movements gave her away.

"Colette?" Maribel whispered, surprise echoing like a thunderclap.

At the mention of her name, Colette swiveled in our direction.

What was Colette doing out at this hour of the night? I glanced around again, almost irritably. And where was Wade?

Next to me, Maribel started to rise.

I swung out my arm and stopped her, flattening her against the stone. "Stay here until I motion that you are safe to leave."

She didn't respond, except with increasing stiffness in her body, signaling her protest.

"Please, Maribel," I whispered even as I focused on Colette, who took a hesitant step nearer. "Let me find out what's going on before you come out of hiding."

Maribel released an exasperated sigh. "'Tis only Colette."

"I'll talk to her first and discover all that's transpired while we've been gone."

"Very well."

I crept out from behind the rock and sidled toward another large boulder. Once I was securely behind it, I leaned forward. "Colette. Here."

She spun and started toward me, her footsteps rushed, almost frantic. Something was most definitely wrong.

When she swerved and almost passed me in the darkness, I snaked out an arm, caught her, and pulled her behind the rock with me.

"Oh, Edmund," Colette whispered, her voice threaded with fear and desperation. She threw herself against me, her small body trembling. I drew her into an embrace, knowing I had to be more cautious about leading her to believe I cared beyond our friendship. But at the moment,

I sensed her distress and could do nothing less than offer my comfort.

"What is amiss?" I asked. "And where's Wade?"

She released a soft, strangled sob. "He's dead."

Chills skittered across my flesh.

"He tried to fight the king's men and held them off for hours," she said in a rushed whisper, "but his injuries made him weak."

In a flash, I pictured Wade standing at the mouth of the cave fending away man after man, his face set like flint, his body steel, his eyes burning like fire. He would have been fierce.

A rush of sorrow pierced my chest, but now was neither the time nor place to grieve for Wade. He'd given his life to protect the convent, the sisters, and Maribel. Now the least I could do was step in and do the same, which meant I needed to clear my mind of all emotions and focus on the present so I was aware of everything at all times.

I glanced around, noting for the first time the traces of blood that remained from the battle scene. "Where are the bodies of the slain?"

"The king's men took them away." Her arms tightened around me, and she burrowed her face into my chest.

"Everyone else in the convent? The sisters?"

Colette hesitated, and in that instant, I was wary again. I released her so I could assess her more fully. The moonlight didn't afford much light, but it was enough for me to see her features were taut with worry and something else. Was it guilt?

"The soldiers threatened some of the sisters," she whispered. "But no one is seriously hurt."

More chills raced over my skin, and my mind wanted

to travel back in time to that terrible day when my entire family had been marched out of the dungeons to the center of Delsworth. Images flashed through my conscience—the threats, the torture, the gruesome bloodshed. But I rapidly slammed the door in my mind, surprised it had opened even a crack when I'd so carefully kept the memories locked up all these years.

I hadn't wanted to remember the gentle, kind face of my mother, my two older sisters, or my two brothers. Seventeen years of shoving away every thought of them had erased their images from my mind. I could hardly picture what they looked like anymore. I only had the vague recollection that as the youngest, I'd been well loved by my siblings and parents alike. And I'd had a grandfather who'd been kind to me. But I didn't like remembering him either.

The people at the convent were my family now, the only family I needed or wanted.

"You're unharmed?" I forced myself to focus on Colette. "You weren't threatened, were you?"

"No." Her voice wavered just enough for me to know she wasn't sharing the entire truth.

"Colette," I whispered urgently, glancing around again. I had a sudden feeling of being caged. "You need to tell me everything."

When she followed my gaze, a terrible premonition tightened my chest. It constricted even more when guilt began to radiate from her eyes and tears brimmed over.

I grasped her arms and almost shook her. "Tell me what happened."

"I didn't know what else to do," she whispered, the tears coursing down her cheeks. "The captain was getting ready to sever Sister Ingrid's fingers. I had to tell him what

91

I knew. I couldn't just stand by and watch her suffer."

My heart dipped into my stomach. "What did you tell the captain?"

"That you and Maribel went to St. Cuthbert's."

"How did you know—"

"I overheard you talking in the chapel."

I tried to absorb what she was telling me, but Sheba released a low, urgent call—one that told me I was in trouble.

"Some of the king's men are still here, aren't they?" My words came out hard. She started to shake her head in denial, but then slowly nodded, letting her shoulders droop in a motion of defeat.

"You betrayed Maribel and me," I hissed.

"No, I am saving us all." She reached out to grab my arm. "The captain promised if I cooperated, we would all remain unharmed."

A short distance away, I heard Maribel gasp. She'd likely been listening to every word of our conversation. And now she knew we were trapped. I had no doubt the king's men were closing in on us even as we stood in the dark.

I released two soft whistles to Sheba, praying there were no Fera Agmen among the ranks of Ethelwulf's guard who'd be able to decipher what I'd just instructed the eagle to do.

Had the captain used Colette to bait us? Was that why she'd been waiting by the door? Waiting for our return, perhaps even for hours? At that moment, I wanted to thrust Colette away in anger. But perhaps she'd reacted again in fear. Under threats of torture, most people were helpless but to do whatever was asked of them. I couldn't blame Colette for going along with the captain to save herself, could I?

"You know they'll kill Maribel."

"She will be safe," Colette rushed, her tone growing more desperate. "The captain said the king has no plans to kill her, that he intends to marry her to his son and she will be the queen of the kingdom someday. What more could she want?"

"You know I'll never let them have Maribel."

Colette grasped my chest. "Why? She will never love you the way you love her. She is too caught up in her own life to think about anyone else."

"It doesn't matter," I lied. "It's my duty to protect her and see her safely to Norland."

The skin at the back of my neck prickled. One of the king's guards was drawing close. I whistled again, this time more urgently. Sheba answered.

"Please, Edmund." Colette threw herself against me. "I shall love you like Maribel never can. I promise to make you happy."

A sickening in my stomach swirled up into my throat. What if Colette had been jealous of Maribel and had willingly cooperated with the captain to turn her over? What if she hadn't been coerced at all?

The thought was there for only a moment before it was gone. I wouldn't think ill of Colette. Not now.

At the flap of wings, I turned to where Maribel was crouched. It was time to act. I had to do so decisively and without delay if I hoped to have any chance of survival.

"Maribel," I whispered. "The labyrinth. Wait for me there. If I don't come in two days, go on without me to Norland."

Before she could reply, Sheba swooped down and plucked Maribel from the ground, lifting her into the air.

In an instant, the shouts of angry warrior cries erupted around us. But Sheba flapped her powerful wings, taking Maribel higher until the blackness of night swallowed her. I didn't wait to see where they went. I had faith the eagle would take Maribel where I'd instructed her.

Instead, I thrust Colette back toward the convent door. In the next second, I struck down the closest soldier while vaulting onto a nearby stone. From there, I leaped from boulder to familiar boulder, jumped onto an overhanging precipice, and swung up until I was out of the reach of the swords of the king's guards.

I crouched low and assessed the situation below in one quick sweep, noting Colette was out of sight and that additional soldiers were now pouring from the convent, clearly having lain in wait for our return. In the torchlight, my gaze snagged on a face I hadn't seen since the day I'd been discovered by Wade and smuggled out of Delsworth.

Captain Theobald. My gut clinched at the sight of the long scar that started beneath his eye and ran the length of his face down to his beard. In his black chain mail and hood, he stood stiffly, staring up in the direction I'd disappeared. Even in the dark, I sensed the coldness emanating from his soul.

Although his expression was severe, it brought back a memory I'd thought was long buried—the sadistic smile he'd given my father before slitting his stomach and pulling out his entrails.

The echo of my father's screams of agony suddenly rang in my ears. I could hear his cries as he'd been forced to watch Theobald hang his wife and children, all while he'd been bleeding to death. Tears had streamed down his noble face as the jerking, swaying bodies had stilled into lifelessness.

Bile rose up in my throat as it had that day when I'd watched from behind the barrels. I wanted to bend over and vomit. At the same time, anger spread through my limbs like burning, melted iron.

At the moment, I didn't have the luxury of being sick, any more than I had the luxury of thinking about the past. I had to make my escape before Theobald could rally his men and hunt for me.

Nevertheless, I peered down one last time at the captain. I hated him and would take my revenge upon him for what he did to my family. I was tempted to throw my knife and kill him in that instant. But I held myself back. When I killed Theobald, I'd do so slowly and deliberately. And I'd make sure he knew exactly who was slaughtering him and why.

The snap and whiz of an arrow registered in my mind. It was coming from my left. But the darkness hid the bolt. I only had enough time to swerve before it pierced my shoulder.

Chapter
9

Maribel

I rubbed salve into the deep talon wounds in my arms.
Sheba hadn't meant to harm me. But after the hours of
carrying me, the eagle's grip had become so unbearable
I'd lost consciousness a time or two during the
journey.

I suspected the flight had been as equally taxing on
Sheba, because by the end of the night, she'd stopped
frequently for breaks. And she'd glided low, as if she
hadn't had the strength to lift me.

At dawn, she'd deposited me at the mouth of an
isolated cave deep in the Highlands and flown away.
I'd immediately fallen into a weakened and weary
slumber. Hours later, I'd awoken stiff and frozen,
hardly able to feel my fingers and toes.

I'd worked quickly to start a fire with the flint in
my medical bag and the few dry twigs I could find.
Once thawed, I'd tended my bleeding arms, grateful to
see abrasions and not punctures, and grateful I'd had
my satchel when Sheba had plucked me from danger.

My muscles were sore, and my arm sockets felt as though they'd been pulled out of joint. But after flexing and rotating them, I knew I'd survived without any major damage.

But what about Edmund? All throughout the long flight, I'd prayed he'd escaped the clutches of the soldiers. Even though I wanted to remain optimistic, the reality of his situation weighed upon me. He was one man against many. Yes, he was a skilled warrior, but how would he be able to fight them off? If the king's men had killed Wade with his brute strength and experience, how could Edmund survive?

My heart panged with the realization Edmund was in all likelihood dead. The ache moved into my throat and brought tears to my eyes. Everything was my fault. The soldiers had come for me because I was the princess. I was responsible for putting everyone in danger. I was to blame for Wade's death. And I was now the cause of Edmund's peril.

In spite of the threat, I had to cling to the hope that somehow, some way, he'd been able to evade King Ethelwulf's men and would reach me.

Leaning against the cold, smooth wall of the cave, I massaged the salve deeper into my bicep, my mind replaying the whispered conversation he'd had with Colette before Sheba had plucked me to safety.

You know I'll never let them have Maribel, he'd said.

Why? Colette had countered almost bitterly. *She will never love you the way you love her.*

Exactly how did Edmund love me? Of course, we all loved each other like siblings. We'd grown up as a family. But Colette's words seemed to indicate Edmund cared for me in a deeper way, a way that had more to do with the affection between a man and a woman.

Just thinking about that kind of love brought a rush of heat to my face. Surely Edmund wasn't attracted to me as a woman. Surely I'd misunderstood their conversation.

But even as I tried to deny what I overheard, I couldn't stop thinking about those strange, sizzling moments I'd recently had with him, those times when I'd caught him looking at me, especially when he'd focused on my lips as though he wanted to kiss me. Did he regard me differently now that we were older? Was that what he'd been trying to explain to me about the changing nature of our relationship?

He'd changed in how he viewed me, viewed us. But I hadn't noticed it.

She is too caught up in her own life to think about anyone else. The rest of Colette's whispered words resounded through my mind. How could she say such a thing? All I wanted to do with my life was to serve others by being a skilled physician. I wasn't selfish. I was merely determined. Wasn't I?

"No." My voice echoed against the low ceiling and close walls of the cave. "Edmund loves me as a friend. He knows how much I want to become a nun, and he respects that. I must not read more into Colette's words."

The disquiet of my thoughts and the rumbling in my stomach pushed me to my feet. I headed outside the mouth of the cave and found a smaller attached cavern. Rocky wasteland spread for miles all around me. If this was the location of the labyrinth, then perhaps many of the large stone formations were a result of excavations from long ago.

Covered with ice and snow, it was as silent as it was barren. Although I scouted the area for anything edible, all I found were a few dried yarrow plants. Without a pot for boiling, I gnawed the roots and ate snow.

With hunger still clawing my insides, I knew I needed to stay busy in order to keep my mind off my pain and empty stomach as well as Edmund's condition. So I created a torch and investigated the cave.

To my disappointment, I wasn't able to go far before coming to a dead end. Edmund would have been proud of me for using the hilt of my dagger to tap against the stone and listen for any hollowness that might indicate a false wall. But I couldn't hear any differences and finally gave up to search elsewhere.

By eventide, I'd hiked the hills and ravines surrounding the cave, exploring for other tunnels or caves that might lead to the maze, the Labyrinth of Death. Surely that was where Sheba had brought me. It's where Edmund expected to meet up with me—if he made it away from the soldiers.

Yet if the maze was nearby, I didn't see any signs.

Once I returned to my cave, I couldn't contain a smile as I stirred the fire and added the fuel I'd collected. If Edmund had been with me, he'd have already located the labyrinth entrance. He never overlooked a detail and would have noticed something I'd missed.

My smile faded and a sob rose in my chest. "Oh, Edmund," I whispered thickly.

A flap and the rush of cold air startled me. I tensed,

my knife at the ready. At the sight of Sheba perched at the mouth of the cave with a winter hare in her beak, I expelled a breath. "Sheba," I said. "I didn't have the chance to express my gratitude for your saving my life yesterday."

Her dark eyes surveyed me as though making sure I was still well. Then she dropped the hare to the cave floor before moving to take flight again.

"Wait!" I ran after her. "Do not go yet."

But she lifted her long, gray wings and soared away, leaving me standing in the fading daylight watching her. She circled ahead then looped back around as though to tell me she wouldn't be far away, that she was guarding me. Perhaps she was. Edmund had probably asked her to do so in his absence.

If only I knew at least a little bit of the language of animals, I'd be able to ask her how Edmund fared. And I'd order her to go back to him, wherever he was, and try to help him.

I stooped and retrieved the hare, grateful for the eagle's offering that would fill my belly this night. During my searching earlier, I'd dug up additional edible roots and accumulated a sufficient amount of snow to refill my leather drinking gourd. I'd fare well enough. I was warm, dry, and safe. And now, I had a hot meal to look forward to. I could only pray Edmund would arrive soon, within the two days he'd specified. I didn't want to go on without him.

Yes, I'd miss his companionship and help. But more than that, I couldn't imagine my life without him in it. That thought alone puzzled me the most.

By nightfall of the second day, dread crept out to taunt me. I'd been holding it at bay by staying hopeful and keeping occupied by further exploring the area. But as I sat in front of the fire, I shivered even though I was warmed all the way through.

I'd eaten the last of the hare for supper and hadn't seen Sheba all day. I'd attempted to gauge the passing of hours so I could pray at regular intervals the same way I did at the convent. And while I tried praying for Colette and the other sisters, my heart invariably kept returning to Edmund.

At last, I lay down next to the fire, wrapped in my cloak, my cheek resting on my arm. "I shall not go to Norland without him," I said. "I shall travel back the way I have come and search for him."

For a long moment, I waged an inner war, knowing Edmund would want me to travel on regardless. That's why he'd risked himself—so I'd have the chance to escape. He'd be angry if I returned to the convent and gave myself over to King Ethelwulf.

At the same time, Colette's whispered words haunted me. *She is too caught up in her own life to think about anyone else.*

All this time, I thought I'd been aspiring after noble and good deeds by helping those who were sick. But had I also been attempting to make myself look better?

Ever since childhood when I'd learned of King Ethelwulf's massacres, I'd longed to be an instrument to bring about healing. After Sister Agnes's passing, my desires had only escalated. I'd needed to devote my life to saving people even more and in doing so, perhaps one day, atone for her death.

However, was there a part of me—even a small part—that wanted the glory of helping save lives, the accolades, the praise, the prestige?

I groaned and buried my face in my hands. Colette had been right. How had I allowed myself to become so selfish?

A howl sounded outside the cave entrance, and I bolted up and unsheathed my knife. My heartbeat rammed against my ribcage, and all I could think about was the starving cougar that had nearly attacked me a few days ago. The wild creatures were hungrier than I was and wouldn't hesitate to claim me for a meal.

As a form slinked into view, I tossed a twig onto the fire, hoping the blaze would provide a barrier. Even so, I held out my knife and yelled in what I hoped was my fiercest voice. "Go away!"

The animal came closer into the mouth of the cave, low to the ground, its glowing eyes all I could see. It released another howl, this one louder . . . and almost sad. Certainly not the vicious call of a hungry beast.

My outstretched hand shook, the knife wobbling. I was a lifegiver, not a lifetaker. I wasn't sure I'd be able to harm the creature even in self-defense. Nevertheless, I hoped it would see the weapon and leave me alone.

The wild animal crept forward several more paces until the firelight illuminated its speckled gray fur, sharply pointed ears, and long, spindly legs. At the sight of the white patch on its chest that looked like a star, I let my hand drop.

"Barnabas." I pushed to my feet. "What news do you have for me? Where is Edmund?"

He gave another short howl and then turned and trotted back to the entrance.

"Will you not tarry a moment longer?"

His ears flickered, keenly in tune to every sound. But he didn't stop and instead disappeared into the darkness of the night.

"Barnabas! Wait!" I scrambled to gather my belongings and light a torch before hurrying after him. Outside, I lifted the flame over the rocky ground, hoping to find his tracks. I was surprised to see him only a dozen paces away, looking at me as though waiting.

"Come back." I held out a beckoning hand, but he bounded onward a few more feet before halting and peering at me again.

He was clearly attempting to communicate. Did he want me to follow?

I walked toward him, and he repeated the pattern of moving forward and then pausing. We traversed that way for some time before he began to trot faster, enough so I had difficulty keeping up.

On several occasions, I thought I lost him, but he always stopped just in time so I could spot him. I didn't know what he was doing and guessed that somehow Edmund had communicated with the wolf to lead me to another safe place.

I stumbled along the rocky terrain even when I grew cold and tired. Finally, Barnabas yipped and streaked off. I tried to run, but the uneven ground and sharp rocks made my movements difficult.

"Barnabas!" I called out, raising the torch high,

praying I would catch a glimpse of him. Thankfully, down a hundred feet, I saw his outline. Instead of looking back at me, this time he hovered over a motionless form.

I began descending the embankment. Had the wolf killed a stag for me?

When Barnabas nudged the shape with his muzzle and then gently licked it, my veins constricted, and my blood pulsed in choppy bursts.

"Edmund?" I called.

The figure lifted his head.

"Oh, angels and saints have mercy!" It *was* Edmund. And something was wrong. Terribly wrong.

I couldn't finish climbing to him fast enough. Upon reaching him, I knelt and held the torch above him, assessing him from his head to his toes. A broken arrow shaft stuck out of his shoulder. His cloak was saturated with blood around the wound—some dry and some fresh.

I probed him gently.

At the contact, he groaned. His lashes lifted, and glassy eyes met mine. "Maribel," he rasped.

I unplugged my drinking gourd and poured the liquid past his parched lips. He drank greedily before letting his head fall back.

Barnabas nuzzled Edmund, bumping his hand as though urging him to get up. I could feel the wolf's concern, for it matched mine. We needed to get him out of the elements where I could tend to his wound.

"Do you think you can walk?" I asked.

"No. Not far."

"The cave is close." Not entirely true, but I didn't have the heart to tell him. Instead, I slid an arm underneath him. "I shall help you to your feet."

I had to practically lift him. But somehow we managed to move forward. With his uninjured arm around my shoulder and my arm about his waist, we inched up the slope.

As we continued back the way I'd come, we had to stop every few minutes for Edmund to rest. By the time I glimpsed the light from the tiny fire I'd left burning in the cave, he was barely conscious. He used the remainder of his energy and strength to climb the last of the distance. And when we finally staggered into the cave, he passed out.

Exhausted myself, I slowly collapsed under his weight, bringing him with me as I went to my knees. Then I blinked away my weariness, breathed in a lungful of air, and laid Edmund out as carefully as I could in front of the fire.

I wasted no time cutting away his cloak, shirt, and linen shift so I had access to the spot where the arrowhead had penetrated his flesh. I shuddered to think that if the arrow had hit two inches lower, it would have punctured his heart and killed him. I probed the wound and felt the sharp corners of the tip. It wasn't embedded too deeply, and thankfully it was a thin head, the kind suited for attacking chain mail. I could make a few incisions with my scalpel and cut it out without damaging muscle.

However, he'd be fortunate if his wound didn't putrefy. From what I could tell, he'd been injured hours ago, if not the night we'd encountered King Ethelwulf's soldiers. I was surprised Edmund hadn't attempted to pull the head out for himself and guessed he'd been afraid he'd pass out or become too weak to travel.

With precise slices, I extricated the metal and flushed and cleaned the wound with a few drops of a wine tincture I'd concocted. Then I applied a poultice of dried yarrow, packing it directly into the incision.

One of his leg injuries from the spider attack was festering with pus. If I'd had my jar of leeches, I would have drained him of the bad humors. As it was, I could only clean the area and reapply the healing poultice.

Finally, I did my best to boil water in the tin cup I found in Edmund's satchel and made a tea of willow bark, which I made him drink in tiny sips to ease the pain that was sure to come when he regained full consciousness.

With Edmund settled, I toiled throughout the rest of the night to produce a stronger healing ointment. It was a project I'd been working on in the convent's apothecary over the past months—testing various herbs together. Even though I'd left my latest formula behind and was missing nettle, I did have sage, wormwood, vervain, and several other ingredients to recreate the remedy. Without a pestle and mortar for grinding, I made do with two stones. And by the time the sky began to turn pink with dawn, the ointment was ready.

Once again, I cleaned the wounds with the wine tincture, and then I applied the new ointment. Edmund's coloring was normal, his breathing even, and his heartbeat steady.

Leaving the injuries open to dry, I sat back and yawned. The anxiety that had been driving me all night began to ease. Maybe Edmund would survive. He was strong and healthy, unlike Sister Agnes, who'd been older and suffering from many maladies already.

Surely, my methods and medicines wouldn't fail this time.

Sheba brought more game. But I was too tired to prepare a meal. So, I added several pieces of wood to the fire and stretched out near Edmund.

I'd only just closed my eyes when he moaned and started thrashing. I crawled to his side and rested my hand against his cheek. He wasn't hot with fever. But I suspected he was feeling the pain even in his deep sleep. I smoothed his forehead, brushing back his hair, and then caressed his cheek again. At my touch, he quieted and grew motionless.

Another shuddering yawn racked my body, and my lids drooped with the heaviness of exhaustion. I needed to sleep if I wanted to remain useful to Edmund. With my hand still upon his cheek, I curled up next to him, closed my eyes, and let slumber claim me.

Chapter 10

EDMUND

THE PAIN IN MY SHOULDER WOKE ME. I WANTED TO CRY OUT AT the burning. But I bit back my agony. Instead, I slowly counted to ten, as Wade had taught me to do, and took a deep breath. If my mentor had discovered I'd passed out, he'd have scolded me severely. He'd drilled into me that a strong soldier always remained alert, no matter the injury, no matter the circumstances, no matter the personal torment.

At a soft brush against my cheek, my inner tirade and attempt to control my pain came to an abrupt halt.

My eyes flew open. The first thing I saw was the low, dark ceiling of a cave. For a moment, I was disoriented and couldn't make sense of where I was. Warmth enveloped me, stretched along my side, and softly tickled my chin.

I dropped my gaze to find fine silky strands of golden hair spread out in disarray and Maribel curled against me. Her arm lay across my waist, and her hand gently cupped my cheek. She'd rested her head on my uninjured shoulder, using it as a pillow. I couldn't see her face, but from the slow rise and fall of her chest, I knew she was still asleep.

Bits and pieces of the previous night came back to me. How I'd grown too weak to travel and had collapsed and been unable to get up. How Barnabas had nipped me and scratched at me to keep going. How I'd grown so cold and stiff.

But I couldn't remember how I'd made it to the cave. I was fairly certain I hadn't crawled there on my own. Had Maribel come after me?

I flexed my injured leg and my shoulder and sucked in a breath at the sharp pain. Even so, I could tell she'd removed the arrowhead and had put my body on the course toward healing. The scents of her many herbs hung heavy in the air, informing me I was slathered in one poultice or another.

Her fingers caressed my cheek in a soothing motion, a movement that was likely reflexive for her, one meant to bring comfort. But for me, the touch was so much more. I leaned my head into her hand, each stroke of her fingers striking something deep within me.

When she stilled, I suspected she'd allowed herself to sink back into oblivion, which was just as well. I wanted to enjoy her nearness for as long as possible without having to put on the mask and play the part of being only a friend.

She'd spread her cloak over the both of us, trapping our body heat. And suddenly, I realized why she was so close, why she was wrapped against me. It wasn't because she'd wanted to embrace or show her affection. No, she'd done it as she did most things, to help me and ease my discomfort. In tending my wounds, she'd removed my breeches and shirt so that I wore only my shift and braies. Then, in order to keep me warm, she'd lent me her body heat.

I started to sigh, but swallowed my disappointment. Now was neither the time nor the place to think about my desires for Maribel. We were in too much danger. Ethelwulf's elite guard was pursuing me.

I'd managed to evade them and cover my tracks and scent for at least the first day of traveling. But yesterday, in my weakness, I'd grown sloppy. It wouldn't be long before they picked up my trail again. And when they did, they'd follow it straight here.

Panic bubbled in my stomach. I wouldn't be strong enough to travel as fast as we needed. I'd only slow Maribel down. That meant I needed to ask Sheba to carry Maribel once more. This time all the way to Norland. It would be difficult for the mighty eagle to go the long distance. But she'd managed to bring Maribel here, so perhaps she could do it if she rested often.

I glanced at the cave opening to the brightness of the day. From the way the shadows fell, I guessed it was early afternoon. I didn't know how much time we had before Ethelwulf's men arrived, but we couldn't wait a moment longer.

Slowly, I shifted, attempting to move without waking Maribel. But the motion sent fiery agony through my shoulder—and caused Maribel to stir. She burrowed against me, nuzzling her nose into my neck and releasing a warm sigh that bathed my skin.

I shut my eyes and fought the urge to wrap her closer and bury my face into her hair. Instead, I waited a moment before again attempting to slip away from her. I managed to pull only halfway out from under her when she spoke.

"You need to lie still, Edmund, or you will tear your wound open."

I chanced a glance over to find her propped on one elbow, her long lashes drooping with the heaviness of sleep, her hair falling in tangled waves about her, and her lips quirked in a half smile.

I hadn't seen her with her hair down in years—not since she'd been a little girl. And now, with it freed from the usual plait and spilling over her shoulders, she was stunning. Her beauty took away every coherent thought and rendered me speechless.

When she got to her knees and gently pushed me back to the floor, I was unable to resist. I could only watch the way her hair surrounded her face and cascaded over her shoulders.

"I need to clean and add fresh ointment to your injuries." She bent in to examine my shoulder. As she did so, her hair brushed against my chest and fanned my face. It was finer than the most exotic silk.

When she started to back away and reach for her medical satchel, I snagged her arm. Before I could stop myself or question what I was doing, I tugged her so that she practically sprawled out on my chest, her face only inches from mine. Her palm lay flat against my abdomen, and the heat of the contact seared me.

At our proximity, her eyes widened with surprise, and as they did so, her gaze locked with mine. Questions flitted through the beautiful blue.

"Your hair is so pretty like this." The words escaped, the only explanation I could find for her confusion. My hand seemed to have a will of its own as my fingers found her hair and dove into the depths.

She held herself motionless, not even breathing. She

studied my face as if searching for clues to a puzzle. Then, her cheeks flushed, and she dropped her gaze. I could guess what she'd seen: the desire for her I'd been trying to hide. But at the moment, I didn't care if it was out in the open. I only cared about the thick silk tangling in my fingers. It was luxurious, decadent, and I wanted to lose myself there.

Her eyes dropped to my lips, which sent sparks of lightning through my midsection. Why was she looking at my mouth? She certainly wasn't thinking about kissing me, was she?

"Edmund?" Her whisper was strangled, and I could sense her mounting confusion and anxiety. Was my blatant affection scaring her? If I pushed her too quickly, I'd likely drive her away. And I didn't want to chance losing her. Her friendship was more important than anything else.

Using all the willpower I possessed, I loosened my grip in her hair. I made myself relax and smile. "Remember the time when we were younger and you decided to cut the end off one of your braids?"

Her eyes searched mine for a moment, and then, as if concluding we were back on solid, familiar friendship ground, she allowed her body to relax against me. "If I remember right," she countered with a smile of her own, "I wanted to see how long it would take to grow and catch back up to the other braid."

"You were quite the inquisitive child."

She laughed lightly and the sound of it rolled over me like music. "That is one way of politely saying I was a dunce."

"You weren't a dunce. Just too curious for your own good."

"Sister Agnes was a saint for raising me."

"Yes, she was."

Maribel nudged me with an elbow. "I was not always naughty, was I?"

"I choose to refrain from answering—"

At her laughter, I grinned. Inwardly, I released a heave of relief. I'd diverted her attention away from my attraction, and I'd kept things from becoming strained between us.

Sheba's call, though distant, broke into my conscience. She was sounding a warning that she'd sighted men. I sat up, all mirth falling away.

"What is it?" Maribel didn't try to stop me this time.

"Ethelwulf's men will soon be upon us."

Maribel scrambled toward her bag and the various items strewn over the cave floor and hurried to pack them.

I called to Sheba, giving her my instructions to carry Maribel to Norland. By the time I pushed myself unsteadily to my feet and began to don my garments, she'd arrived at the cave entrance.

I paused with my breeches halfway up, the pain from the movement causing me to break into a sweat. "Maribel, go with Sheba."

"No, I am not leaving you this time." She slung her medicine satchel over her shoulder and across her body.

"You are going. And you're leaving now." I spoke in my hardest voice, the one that told Maribel I'd reached my limits of patience with her.

She hesitated.

"Sheba will take you to Norland where you'll be safe."

Noticing I was struggling with my breeches, Maribel crossed to me. She helped me cinch the waist before assisting me with my shirt and cloak. Each movement of my shoulder brought a stab of fresh pain so severe I wavered with dizziness.

As I strapped on my belt with my weapons, Maribel's fingers circled mine and stopped me, drawing my gaze up to hers. Her expression was more earnest than I'd ever seen. "I know you only want me to be safe, Edmund. But I have already made up my mind that I shall not leave you to fend for yourself."

"You must go," I said. "You are far more important to Mercia than I am or ever could be."

"But you are important to me," she said softly, glancing down at my belt and straightening it. "I had not planned to go to Norland without you before, and I shall not go now."

What did she mean I was important to her?

When she lifted her eyes almost shyly, I saw something in their depths that hadn't been there before, something that sent warmth whispering through me.

Whatever the case might be, I couldn't let her stay with me. I'd most certainly be captured. And then I'd lose her forever.

"Listen to me, Maribel." I attempted to gentle my voice, to keep at bay my rising panic. "You ride ahead with Sheba. And I shall follow behind."

She shook her head. "If I stay with you, at least I can continue to treat your wounds and make your travel easier."

I groaned my frustration.

"Let us be on our way." She reached for my leather pack, replaced my tin cup, and added the game Sheba had hunted for us. Then she handed me the bag.

I didn't move to take it.

She stretched it out farther. This time her beautiful features implored me in that irresistible way she had, the one that molded me into doing whatever she wished.

"If you force me to go with Sheba," she said. "I shall only turn around the first moment she sets me down and run back to you."

I wanted to strangle Maribel and hug her at the same time. She was stubborn when she made up her mind to do something. "Very well, if you insist."

"I insist." She smiled, her eyes lighting as they usually did when I yielded to her. Most of the time, her delight gave me a moment of happiness. But not today. Not at this decision. Instead, doubt crept in to whisper I'd made a terrible mistake, that I was leading us both into captivity.

If we didn't die first.

Nevertheless, I shook off the doubts, took my bag, and attempted to lift the strap over my head. "If you will not leave me, then there is only one thing to be done."

"And what is that?" She gently raised my pack the rest of the way and settled the bag on my hip.

"We must go down into the labyrinth and hide there."

Chapter
11

Maribel

"I found no conclusive evidence of a labyrinth," I told Edmund as we explored the depths of the cavern. "I searched this cave as well as every rock and crevice in the surrounding vicinity. But I could find nothing."

Edmund ducked as the ceiling slanted lower. From his stilted movements, I could tell he was in terrible pain but was doing his best to mask it.

"The entrance is here somewhere," he said in a strained voice, skimming his fingers along the walls, assessing every detail.

"There are no hollow spots like we found at St. Cuthbert's." After lighting a torch, I doused the cooking fire with snow, putting out the flames and the warmth.

"Did you test the floor?"

"No. I did not think to do so."

He knelt and ran his hand over the roughened rock.

I stomped the wet wood and ashes, wishing we could hide the evidence we'd been there. But I suspected all my efforts would do no good. King Ethelwulf's guard likely had the use of specially trained dogs or wolves that would follow our scent from the previous night when I'd dragged Edmund to the cave. I hadn't taken the time to cover our tracks or sprinkle the Mountain Essence.

After several minutes of searching, Edmund paused, sat back on his heels, and peered around the cave with narrowed eyes.

"If I was the architect in charge of creating the maze," he mumbled to himself, "where would I put the entrance?"

"Apparently someplace impossible to find."

"No," he said, rising slowly and shuffling toward the now cold and wet remains of the fire. "I'd put the entrance in a place that would give my workers easy access for bringing up the tons of stones needing to be chiseled away."

He crouched beside the blackened wood and ashes and used a rock to sweep the residue away. Nothing unusual or different marked the spot except for the soot of many fires from long ago. Edmund brushed more remains away and then began to scrape. For a moment, I thought he was merely rubbing rock against rock. But as he dug deeper, I could see a groove forming in the floor.

With a burst of excitement, I knelt next to him, found a sharp stone, and began to scrape in what was clearly a crack that had been filled with mortar. The seal blended in with the stone, and over time had become nearly invisible.

"This is the entrance," I said as the groove deepened. "Is it not?"

"It must be," he replied. "Although I wouldn't be surprised if there is a false opening that leads to deadly traps."

I paused, my anticipation dimming at the prospect of the dangerous unknown. "Do you think this is one such trap?"

"We shall know soon enough."

His answer didn't soothe me. But I resumed my digging anyway.

His gaze flickered to me, giving me a glimpse of the seriousness in his eyes, along with something else. The same something I'd noticed there earlier when we'd awoken from our slumber.

I'd fallen asleep beside him to keep him warm and so that if he stirred, the motion would rouse me. What I hadn't expected was for him to awaken and bury his fingers in my hair.

When he'd told me my hair was pretty and looked at me as though I was the most beautiful woman he'd ever laid eyes upon, my body had warmed all the way through as it did when I drank hot spiced mead on a frigid winter day. I'd felt delicious and womanly in a way I'd never experienced before.

Now again, as he met my gaze, I could feel that same interest. Did he really think I was beautiful? I suppose his appreciation was no different than my acknowledging he'd grown into a fine-looking young man. With his well-defined features and lush green eyes, he could be considered handsome by those who emphasized such earthly attributes. Of course, as a postulant, I wasn't one to focus on that kind of thing.

But what about Colette? Had she thought Edmund was handsome? She'd certainly seemed enamored with him. Her whispered words returned to me: *I shall love you like Maribel never can. I promise to make you happy.*

Was she right? Could I never love Edmund and make him happy the way she could?

"I wouldn't fault you if you changed your mind and left with Sheba." He wiped his perspiring brow with the back of his arm.

"You will not be rid of me that easily."

He didn't respond, except to continue to pry away the seal. I knew he regretted his decision to allow me to stay with him. And doubts assailed me whether I'd been right to insist on remaining rather than escaping to Norland. What if King Ethelwulf's guard captured me? They'd take the ancient key and the piece of the map, making it impossible for Queen Adelaide Constance to find the hidden treasure.

I dug harder. We had to get into the labyrinth. We'd hide there for a few days. And then once the king's guards gave up the search and left, we'd make our way to Norland. It would be simple, I told myself.

When we removed all the mortar, we used our weapons to pry the opening upward. It was heavy, and with Edmund's injured shoulder, his strength was reduced by at least half. I tried to make up for it, but I was no replacement.

Even when Edmund formed a makeshift lever to pry the stone plate loose, it still took long minutes before it moved enough to wedge the lever farther under it. Finally, after more heaving, the stone scraped across the cave floor, revealing a dark sloping tunnel with the rusted remains of cart rails, likely once used in hauling rock pieces to the surface.

Edmund stuck his head inside and sniffed. "There

must be another entrance from the outside somewhere else."

I tested the scent, smelling nothing but mildew, soil, and perhaps the rancid odor of a dead rat. "How can you tell?"

"The air is still breathable, and I don't detect dangerous fumes."

We made preparations to descend, filling our water pouches and gathering roots and twigs, which we tied into a pack with Edmund's cloak. With the fresh provisions, along with Sheba's generous supply of meat, I was optimistic we'd survive the labyrinth just fine. If only we had a way to camouflage the opening so that the king's guard wouldn't discover it. But after struggling to close the stone to no avail, we knew we had no choice but to proceed even if the enemy decided to follow us.

As we descended, the rocky gravel made each foothold precarious, and I slid countless times. Torch in hand, Edmund led the way, going slowly and bracing me as best he could. When the passageway finally leveled, I was surprised to find that it branched into three identical tunnels. They were wide enough to allow a cart but too low for standing upright. Made of smooth gray walls, they were plain, with no markings to identify or set them apart.

I studied the entrance for each and shuddered at the prospect of winding through the tight confines. Even so, I squared my shoulders. "Which one?"

"Let's look at the map and pray it can help us."

I pulled out the parchment, unrolled it, and together we studied the maze. I searched for a place where three tunnels converged, but found nothing.

"Do you see anything?" I shifted to watch him. His noble features were taut with concentration, his eyes narrowed, his hair loose across his forehead. The sheen of perspiration on his upper lip and the flush in his cheeks told me how much pain he suffered. I should have insisted on repacking his wounds with fresh poultice and ointment before beginning our trek into the maze. But I'd been fortunate he'd allowed me to come at all, much less slow down our escape.

He circled his finger around and touched the western side of the map. "I think we are here."

"How can you tell?"

"From the rock deposits I passed on my way here, I believe we're at a western entrance of the labyrinth. Even if this piece of the map is for the eastern half, we should still be able to navigate as long as we remember to follow the mirror image of the trail."

I studied the area near his finger. "But here there is only one tunnel leading into the maze. Not three."

"Many labyrinths have multiple false paths at the opening. My feeling is that of the three, one is safe and the other two lead to traps that will likely kill us or anyone who takes them."

I walked forward to examine the entrances more carefully. "Perhaps the middle one?"

"Are you guessing, or do you have logic for your choice?" Despite the seriousness of the situation, his tone filled with mirth because he already knew the answer.

"Everybody knows the middle road is always the best to travel." I tossed a smirk over my shoulder, relieved again that even though we were having strange and intense new feelings between us, we could easily banter as we always had.

He paced from one entrance to the next. I guessed he was making use of all his senses to discover every detail he could—sights, smells, sounds, air movement, and more. After a moment, he stood in the far left entrance. "This one has the most airflow. The other two eventually lead to dead ends."

I started into the left tunnel, but he jerked me back. "Wait, Maribel. I want to test them first."

"How?"

"I'll walk into them and see if I come out alive."

I turned horrified eyes to him only to see him grinning. I swatted him, glad we could find humor even in the midst of the worst of circumstances.

Handing me the torch, he retrieved three medium rocks from the slope, kneeled, and pitched one down the far right tunnel. The steady clank of its movement down the slight hill picked up momentum and then stopped. Several seconds later a plop was followed by sizzling.

"What happened?" I asked.

"I suspect the path abruptly ends, that the rock fell off and landed into a pool of some kind of acid that has the power to eat anything it touches."

"A deadly brew awaiting unsuspecting travelers?"

"Exactly." Edmund tossed the second rock down the middle path. It rolled a few seconds longer, but then a whistling noise was followed by a sharp *thwack*.

"A rotating blade," Edmund explained. "It likely would have sliced the stone in half had it been softer."

I shuddered at the image of a human meeting such a fate.

He threw the third stone down the left path, and

this time it went unhindered until it hit a turn in the tunnel. Edmund examined the map. "Yes, I do believe we're on the western end."

"'Are you guessing, or do you have logic for your choice?'" I mimicked his earlier words.

"I'm guessing, of course," he said with all seriousness even though his eyes twinkled. "This area has a corner and a turn about the distance the rock traveled."

I was tempted to jest with him again, but he slanted a glance toward the opening far above, his expression losing all mirth.

"We need to be on our way." He stepped around me, holding the map in one hand and taking back the torch in the other. "I'll go first."

We ducked as we made our way through the passage. The air was cold and the stone walls equally chilly to the touch. The rugged, low ceiling presented dangerously sharp outcroppings in some places.

At every turn, Edmund stopped to study the map and gauge our position. He pointed to a circular area branching off one passageway near the middle of the map. "We might be able to hide there."

I nodded, trusting him to keep us safe. "Do you think the other opening is on the eastern side of our map? Perhaps in an identical spot to the one we entered?"

He peered carefully at the map. "It would appear the image is identical and so likely would have an entrance in the exact area. At least that's what I'm hoping for."

"Does this mean we shall attempt to make our way there?"

He traced his finger first along one route, then another, and another. He followed several more until sighing. "I'm not sure we can reach the eastern edge by sticking to the paths on our little piece of the outer rim of the map. I see only dead ends."

"So you think the route to the eastern entrance passes through a different segment of the map?"

"It's likely, and we cannot venture into the midsection without its map to guide us. It's too risky. We need to stay in this area and on the trails that are clearly marked, even if that means we have to wait to leave until Ethelwulf's forces are gone."

I deflated only a little. I wanted to remain hopeful that with our map and the knowledge there was another way out, we'd locate it. Perhaps in the process of exploring, we'd even discover more the hidden treasure.

We continued winding our way through one tunnel after another. Since each passage and doorway looked the same, I felt as though we were walking in circles and never going anywhere. I easily became disoriented and wasn't sure I'd be able to find my way, even with the map.

I prayed Edmund was more confident in his sense of direction than I was. From his slight limp and the echo of his strained breath, I'd have to encourage him to rest soon. He was taxing himself.

When he came to an abrupt halt, I almost bumped into him. I peered beyond him, but could see nothing but the curving tunnel. "What is it?"

He pressed a finger against his lips in a motion for silence and stood absolutely still as though concentrating. After a few seconds, he pursed his lips in displeasure and then spoke. "They've entered the labyrinth. We need to find that hiding spot."

By "they" I knew he was referring to King Ethelwulf's knights. I strained to listen, but the echo of our breathing against the stone drowned out any other sound. "Are they close?"

"No, they're at the beginning with the three tunnels. I heard the screams of those who chose wrongly."

A shiver raced up my spine at the realization of how careless I would have been had I explored the labyrinth on my own without Edmund. I wouldn't have thought to test each of the routes before starting.

I reached for Edmund's arm and squeezed. "I am grateful to have your wisdom and guidance, Edmund. Without you, I would have experienced their fate."

"I will remind you of your praise next time you object to something I request of you," he teased, starting forward faster.

I rushed to keep up with his stride, even with his limping. When finally the tunnel veered into a small cavern, we stumbled to a stop.

"Here we are," he said. "Our hiding place." He raised the torch high.

I gasped at the sight that met us.

Skeletons of all shapes and sizes littered the floor . . . including those belonging to humans.

Chapter 12

EDMUND

"WE CANNOT STAY HERE," MARIBEL SAID, HER WIDE EYES TAKING in the piles of bones—likely the remains of people and animals long lost in the maze. Or perhaps, this was a lair of the creature who lived in the underground tunnels, one of the places he ate his prey.

I had no doubt the beast was alive somewhere in the labyrinth. I'd caught faint echoes of the creature's language, a strange and ancient one. The beast was far enough away for now but was steadily moving closer, likely having heard us and picked up our scent.

"The bones won't hurt us," I teased, trying to ease her fear and mask my pain. The wound in my shoulder throbbed unrelentingly, making me want to drop to my knees and groan.

Maribel didn't return my smile. Instead, she trembled. "Did all these people get lost?"

I shoved aside a pile of the skeletons with my boot. "We're not lost, Maribel. We're exactly where I hoped we'd be. And now we need to get comfortable, extinguish our torch, and wait for Ethelwulf's men to leave." Without a map, the soldiers would have a difficult time navigating. But it was possible they could stumble across our hiding place. In that case, I'd have to be prepared to fight.

Maribel took a step back into the tunnel, her face pale, her eyes still wide. "Perhaps we made a mistake coming down here."

It was too late to rebuke her for being stubborn and remind her she could have gone with Sheba. But neither would it help to focus on how much danger we were in.

When Ethelwulf's men tired of looking for us or if the search became too hazardous, they'd wait at the top for us to emerge—like a fox waiting outside a hare's burrow, ready to pounce. I doubted they'd leave until they knew we were dead.

I hadn't wanted to tell Maribel we'd be trapped down here if I didn't find an alternate way out. Even without the other pieces of the map, eventually I'd need to explore further into the maze for another exit, testing scents, sound, light, and any other clues I could locate. But I'd do the searching without Maribel so that I didn't put her into any further danger. My first priority was to ensure her safety. And to do so, we had to make ourselves invisible until Ethelwulf's men grew discouraged looking for us.

I cleared aside more bones, enough that we'd have a spot to sit without Maribel fearing the skeletons.

"At least you will get to rest." She opened her medical bag.

I refrained from telling her I wouldn't rest much. I'd have to stay alert in order to defend her against any soldiers who happened upon us.

"Now sit." She retrieved a small clay pot and opened it. "I shall put more of the painkilling poultice on your wounds to ease your discomfort."

I didn't have the energy to resist. In fact, I relished the thought of the cool relief her medicinal supplies would bring. I leaned against the cave wall and slid down until I was sitting with my legs stretched out in front of me.

When she started to lift my cloak and shirt, I closed my eyes. I pretended to rest, but the truth was I didn't want her to see how much I liked her touch. I'd already made a fool of myself by reacting to her beautiful hair earlier. I had to stay in control and keep my feelings for her stashed away.

With my bare skin exposed and her fingers brushing my bicep, I tensed.

"It will only sting for a moment," she said softly. Her words were followed by burning pressure against my injury. The pain took my breath away and made me dizzy. Only then did I grasp the seriousness of my injury and the possibility it might not heal—that I could grow weaker and that I might not be able to lead Maribel to safety.

Mentally, I shook myself. I couldn't think that way. Wade had taught me the skills to survive any hardship. No matter what, I'd make sure Maribel was secure before succumbing to my injury.

Once she'd applied the poultice to my shoulder and the wounds on my leg, we refreshed ourselves with water, ate some of the roots we'd gathered, and then extinguished the torch. The darkness was so complete we couldn't see anything, not even the space directly in front of our faces.

"Do you think the soldiers have left yet?" she whispered.

"No, they wouldn't dare." Her leg brushed against mine, as did her arm, the sign she was sidling closer.

Although I wanted to draw her into the circle of my arm, I resisted the temptation.

"Perhaps the three entrance tunnels scared them away," she offered hopefully.

"Captain Theobald won't let anything scare him away." My voice came out more bitter than I intended.

"Who is Captain Theobald?"

"The twisted man who murdered my family." Once the words were out, I wished I hadn't uttered them. In all the years living at the convent, I'd never spoken of my family, of what I'd experienced that fateful day they'd died. As we'd grown up, Maribel and Colette had known I wouldn't talk about it, that their questions would be met with silence. So they'd never brought it up. Neither had Wade. I guessed he'd seen too much senseless violence and had wanted to forget about it every bit as much as I had.

Even now, Maribel didn't push me to explain, respecting my desire to forget after all these years. Through the dark, her fingers groped for mine. I gladly, willingly, let her find my hand and didn't resist when she laced our fingers together. I knew it was her unspoken way of offering me her support.

I clutched her hand, hoping she understood it was my unspoken way of saying thanks.

We sat in comfortable companionship. After a while, she rested her head against my uninjured shoulder. I wanted to tell her more, tried to think of what I could say to give voice to those awful days that had changed my life forever. Where did I even begin?

I opened my mouth, but couldn't formulate any words.

She squeezed my hand. "We had a good life at the

convent, did we not?" she whispered hesitantly.

"We did," I whispered in return. I would be forever grateful to Wade for the risks he took in smuggling me out of Delsworth, for bringing me to the convent, for the years he spent teaching me everything he knew. My throat tightened at the loss of such an honorable man. He'd been a strict instructor, but I wouldn't be half the man I was if not for him.

"Will we ever be able to go back?" Sadness tinged her voice.

I wanted to reassure her, give her hope, make everything right in her life. But she deserved my honesty. "No. At least not while Ethelwulf remains on the throne."

She sighed. "What will happen to the nuns? And to Colette?"

"We shall pray God keeps them safe." I hoped Theobald had no need of them now that Maribel was gone and would leave them in peace. But Theobald's methods were unpredictable and inhumane. There was no telling what he might do.

The soft clink of Maribel's rosary told me she was taking my request for prayers seriously. For long minutes, she touched the various beads, offering silent pleas. I added my own, although less formal, prayers to hers.

At the faint tap of bootsteps, I stiffened. Two pairs of boots.

"What is it—" she started, but I cut her off with a squeeze of her fingers and then leaned in to her ear.

"Don't move or speak."

She nodded.

I rose and crept along the perimeter of the wall until I stood next to the entrance, my dagger in one hand and my sword in the other. I would use the element of surprise to my advantage. I suspected the soldiers were working in pairs, which meant I'd have to act quickly to silence them both before they shouted an alarm that could give away our location to the others in the labyrinth.

Their torches illuminated the tunnel and brought enough light to our cavern that I could see Maribel's outline where I'd left her. She was trusting me, as usual, to get us out of a difficult predicament. I just prayed I'd have enough strength in my injured shoulder to lift the dagger.

As the sounds of the soldiers drew nearer, I could hear the fear in their hesitant steps. I doubted they'd known about the labyrinth before descending. Ethelwulf would have exploited it by now if he'd realized it was here. Even so, they'd likely heard tales regarding a Labyrinth of Death and the creatures that lived in its depths.

The glow from the flame grew steadily stronger, and my muscles tightened in readiness. As the first soldier held out the torch and ducked into the cavern, he made little more than a gurgle as I silenced him. At the same moment, I jumped in front of the opening and plunged my sword into the other soldier. He, too, had no time to make a sound or react. Instead, he crumpled to the ground next to his comrade.

I used one of their torches to examine them and to divest them of their weapons. Then I dragged them away from the opening, hiding their bodies behind the pile of bones. When I finally glanced at Maribel, she was watching me with a horrified expression.

"I'm sorry you had to witness that." I wasn't proud of myself for having to injure or kill other men. The only man I longed to kill was Theobald. However, I'd harm anyone who attempted to lay hands upon Maribel.

Was it possible Wade had taught me so diligently

because he'd known one day I'd have to take over protecting Maribel for him?

"Was it truly necessary to harm them?" Maribel's whisper was filled with condemnation.

"If I hadn't, they would have killed me and captured you." I wiped the blood from my weapons with the edge of the black cloak that had belonged to one of the soldiers.

She watched me a moment before biting down on her lip and looking away.

After confiscating any further valuable supplies from the dead men, I extinguished their torches, immersing us once more in utter darkness. I stood near the entrance again, waiting, expecting that additional guards would soon follow. Even if I'd been quiet, sound carried easily in the tunnels.

As minutes passed with no shouts or calls, the tension eased from my muscles, and I supported myself against the cave wall. Even though I hoped we'd have no more encounters, I suspected if one pair of soldiers had tracked us to the cavern, others would eventually as well.

After waiting at least another hour, I slid down and sat. My shoulder throbbed with returning pain. Maribel's ointment was wearing thin. I winced and leaned my head back. Perhaps it was time to move on and attempt to look for the other entrance. And yet, even as I considered standing up and searching, my body wouldn't cooperate. I was weary and wanted nothing more than to close my eyes and rest.

But as my lids drifted shut, a distant growl rumbled through the labyrinth, a sound that could only belong to one of the creatures living here in the bowels of the Highlands. It likely hadn't been disturbed by humans in a very long time.

As it released another drawn-out sound that was more of a hiss, I tried to analyze the cadence and intonations. It was a reptile of some kind. Not a snake, but perhaps a lizard. It moved heavily but slowly, with stilted steps, which told me it was large and old.

My mind worked to remember the old languages Sister Paula had taught me. At first, the old Fera Agmen hadn't paid me any attention. I followed her around every spare moment and started learning on my own just from watching her. After realizing how quickly I understood the difficult communication that had taken her years to master, she'd finally taken an interest in me.

Since I'd been Wade's apprentice, he'd insisted on my total devotion and commitment. In fact, I'd hidden my Fera Agmen training from him for many months, until Sister Paula had been the one to tell him. She wanted to have more structured time with me in order to tutor me properly and sought Wade out to ask him.

Initially, he opposed Sister Paula, not wanting anything to detract from my warrior drills. But eventually, he relented, likely realizing I'd never be the soldier he was. Or perhaps he decided my skill with animals could be another weapon to add to my cache. Whatever the case, he'd allowed me to have more time with Sister Paula.

Although my Fera Agmen apprenticeship had been cut short by Sister Paula's sudden death when I'd been but a lad of twelve, I'd already surpassed her by that point, having learned everything she knew. Since then, I'd sought to expand my abilities, listening and memorizing all I heard and testing the new communications.

In the darkness of the cavern, I fought against my pain and drowsiness to understand what the creature was saying. My guess was that it had been hibernating for the winter, that our entrance into the labyrinth had awoken it early, and that now it was experiencing the pangs of hunger.

It was searching for its first meal in months. And I didn't want either Maribel or me to be a part of its feast.

Painstakingly, I listened to the creature until I began to understand the various sounds it made. The language was so ancient that I couldn't keep from wondering if this was one of those extinct dragon-like animals fabled to have lived long ago. I'd only read about them in the scrolls among Sister Margaret's collection.

Footsteps and torchlight alerted me to the presence of more soldiers coming our way. As before, two were working together.

I pushed myself up from the stone floor, my shoulder and leg stiff and sore.

Hearing my movement, Maribel began to scuffle, and I guessed she was rising to her feet too. "Stay where you are, Maribel," I whispered, unsheathing my dagger and sword, preparing to surprise the approaching soldiers the same way I had the previous two.

Too late, I realized the creature was nearing our cavern from the other side. Was it drawn here because it smelled the blood of the fallen soldiers?

Mentally, I lashed myself for not dragging the bodies away. Now, we were trapped between a starving, bloodthirsty beast and two more elite guards. I'd have to take down the guards first and then we'd need to flee far from the cavern, praying the bodies of the slain soldiers would be enough for the creature's feast.

The coming torchlight began to give shape to the cavern, which meant the soldiers would be upon us in a moment. A growl from the other direction informed me the beast was picking up its pace and would also soon reach the room.

"What was that?" Maribel whispered, staring at the dark entrance, having heard the creature now too. Her expression was taut with terror.

"Make haste and stand close to me," I replied as I backed away from the door.

Needing no further urging, she scrambled over.

I raised my dagger as the footsteps increased their pace into a run, the men likely having heard our whispers or the beast or both.

Maribel stood behind me and clutched my cloak with trembling fingers.

The soldiers thrust their torches into the cave first, blinding me as they moved in. At the same time, a mighty roar resounded from the other side of the tunnel, and a beast filled the doorway behind them.

Chapter
13

Maribel

I screamed.

The creature was like nothing I'd ever seen before. It crawled on four stout legs, each foot containing extended claws that curled under, similar to Sheba's talons. It had the long body of a lizard but was much larger, the size of a warhorse. Its scales appeared to blaze—a mixture of crimson and ebony down its spiked spine, which tapered to a whip-like tail.

When the beast roared again, I cowered behind Edmund. It swung its enormous snout back and forth as though sniffing the air. A frill fringed with sharp barbs formed a fan around its head, making it appear bigger and even more terrifying.

Near us, the two soldiers cloaked in black retreated slowly, their swords drawn but suspended in midair, their fear and shock mirroring my own. The creature, however, wasn't the least intimidated by any of us. It continued into the cave and hissed, releasing a long, forked tongue like that of a snake and revealing dozens of jagged teeth.

Its glassy eyes roved over us, and I wondered how much it could see. Then, with a flick, its tail lashed out and struck against the knight nearest to it. The tail, full of spikes, raked across the soldier's legs, ripping open his breeches and flesh in one strike. The man screamed in agony and slumped to his knees.

At the same instant, the other elite guard threw his dagger, aiming for the creature's heart. The knife glanced off the hard layers of scales and clattered to the floor. The beast roared and lunged toward the second soldier, who already had his sword out and was crouched into battle position, ready to fight.

Edmund released a yell and tossed his knife. I thought he was fighting with the soldiers against the beast, but his knife plunged into the back of King Ethelwulf's elite guard, dropping him to the ground in a motionless heap.

Even as the other injured soldier rose up and swung his sword, the creature wrenched its tail around again, slicing him so that he crumpled to the floor, this time lifeless.

The beast snarled and raised its tail as though to flail Edmund.

Edmund didn't move but instead snarled back. For several endless, frightening seconds Edmund seemed to be arguing with the creature until finally it lowered its tail. It growled at both of us, revealing dagger-like teeth again.

If it hoped to intimidate us, the tactic worked. I pressed against the wall, my heart thudding with a desperate urge to escape.

"Wait, Maribel," Edmund said in a calm tone.

I froze. Would my movement cause the creature to strike at me with its tail or chase me? Where was Sheba when I needed her to dive in and carry me away?

"The creature has a festering sore near its eye—a sliver of some kind. It will allow you to remove the shard and dress its wound." Edmund spoke as if he'd carried on a friendly conversation with the beast rather than roaring and snarling at it for the past few minutes.

"Remove a sliver?" My focus shifted to the reptile's fierce face, its forked tongue protruding, its fangs visible even with its jaws closed. Near the left eye, I caught sight of a bubble of oozing flesh. "I cannot do it, Edmund. Please do not ask it of me."

"We need to show a measure of goodwill to the creature," he continued in a level voice.

I shook. I wasn't sure I was capable of walking the dozen paces to the beast, even if I'd wanted to.

"Do you trust me?" he asked.

"You know I do."

"Then you must help it with your healing touch. You'll likely save us both if you do so."

If I had the power to save us, then I couldn't show any more fear. Pushing down my terror, I swallowed hard before opening my medical bag and retrieving the pain-reducing poultice I'd concocted for Edmund's wounds.

I took three steps toward the injured beast before it hissed at me, nearly hitting me with its tongue. I stopped, remained motionless, and allowed it to sniff the air around me.

Edmund growled low and long, drawing the

attention of the creature. They went back and forth for several more minutes before falling silent. Edmund motioned me forward. "Go ahead. He will allow it."

"He does not appear happy about me in the least." I had the feeling without Edmund's presence, the creature would have sliced and killed me with his tail and added me to the pile of bodies he planned to eat for dinner.

"He'll suffer—possibly even die—if you do not tend him."

"Would that be so horrible?"

"The labyrinth needs its protector."

I didn't understand Edmund's reasoning, but I'd do it for him because he wanted me to. That alone was reason enough. I took several more halting steps until I stood in front of the creature. The stench of its breath and body, like that of decaying flesh, nearly made me gag. But I breathed through my mouth and tried not to think about how close its teeth were and how it could easily snap off my head in one bite.

I refrained from looking anywhere except the spot near its eye. Brown oozed from the wound and dripped steadily to the cave floor. I didn't know the anatomy of this animal, but I suspected the sliver had festered for a long time and become putrid.

Gripping what appeared to be a piece of an iron blade, I tugged at it. The creature growled again, baring its teeth and hissing. But I tried to ignore the danger just inches away and instead focused on what I needed to do. With a final quick yank, the shard came out.

The creature roared and backed away. It shook its head and started to maneuver in an effort to turn itself around. Before it could slip beyond my grasp, I dug my fingers into the ointment and slathered it across the wound in spite of the rusty blood that trickled over my fingers.

The soothing properties of the ointment must have eased the creature's discomfort just a little, for it ceased its thrashing. Seizing the advantage, I pressed a rag against the site to staunch the flow, and again the beast stood still for me, almost better than some of my human patients.

It sniffed the air around me and moved so close to my head I dared not stir, not even to breathe. Finally, with a soft snort, it took a step back. I tried to maintain my grip upon the beast, but it retreated out of reach.

The creature raised its snout and seemed to assess both Edmund and me, as though trying to decide who we were and what we were doing there. Then it released a guttural growl, one that was certainly not friendly and made the hairs on my arms stand on end.

Edmund responded with a low growl, while encircling my arm and slowly towing me until I was standing behind him.

The creature turned away from us and sniffed the body of one of the fallen soldiers, its tongue flickering in and out. It then moved toward the two Edmund had killed earlier. With the beast's attention elsewhere, Edmund gathered his weapons and our belongings.

"We need to go," he whispered, picking up one of the torches still flaming where it lay on the ground by the entrance. With his other hand, he grasped mine and tugged me out of the cavern.

We fled into the winding tunnel, the leather soles of our boots slapping hard against the stone as we ran. When we reached a branch, we stopped so Edmund could consult the map, but then we ran again. And again. The running and stopping seemed endless. I didn't know if we were trying to put as much distance between ourselves and the creature as possible, or if Edmund had other reasons for the speed with which we traveled. Whatever the case, I didn't question him. I was too winded and tired to do anything but stumble along with him.

Finally, Edmund halted and leaned against the tunnel wall. His face was pale and his breathing as labored as mine. "We've reached the edge of the map. We must take one tunnel inward and pray that it loops back around here."

I studied the area of the map he indicated with his finger. We'd crossed exactly half of the bottom part of the maze. Although we were still in the outer region of the labyrinth, we'd arrived at a tunnel that led into a piece of the map we didn't have.

I drew in a deep breath, trying to bring air into my lungs. "If anyone can do it, Edmund, you can."

His expression was grave as he studied our map intently, peered into both tunnels, smelled the air, and then started down one of them. He explored more cautiously now, his pace slower, the torch held high. He halted more frequently to study every detail of our surroundings—the dust, mold, trickle of water on some of the walls, even the direction the fire flickered on the torch.

I sensed danger all around, guessing the engraved block letters on the various branches of tunnels we passed signified additional clues that would lead further into the maze. A part of me longed to explore deeper and locate the treasure so that I'd have something valuable to bring to Queen Adelaide Constance.

But every time I mentioned investigating one of the other passageways, Edmund insisted on sticking to the path he hoped would wind around and lead us back to the outer rim. As we passed by caverns stacked with additional bones, I tried not to think about ending up in one of those piles and kept as close to Edmund as possible.

Although Edmund didn't complain about his pain, his limp grew more pronounced, until finally he stumbled and almost fell.

I caught his arm. "Let me clean and tend your wounds again."

He shook his head. "No, I can't rest until we cross back into the section of our map." The waning torchlight illuminated the paleness of his face and the dark circles under his eyes.

"You are exhausted."

Without giving me a chance to protest further, he started forward again, this time faster. "We're almost there. I can feel it."

I appreciated his optimism and his belief that we would reach the destination, but I feared he was taxing himself and wouldn't endure much longer. When he halted a short while later, his shoulders slumped, and he sank to the floor.

"We're back in the outer rim," he said wearily but with the hint of a relieved smile.

I dropped next to him and began to pull out medicinal supplies. As he studied the map, I cleaned his wounds and reapplied ointment. He traced the remainder of our route, which on paper didn't appear far. But in reality, with all the winding and back-tracking, we still had a lengthy trek.

He didn't sit long before pushing himself to his feet, disregarding my instructions to rest. From the worry in his eyes as he glanced at the way we'd come, I guessed he was concerned about the creature chasing after us. The thought of facing the beast again was enough to push me forward.

As before, we made our way carefully along as Edmund consulted the map at every turn. At last, when the tunnel forked into three branches, Edmund halted. "We're here."

"God be praised." I sagged against the wall, and tears stung my eyes. I lifted up gratitude for both God's help as well as Edmund's ability to guide us in the right direction in a labyrinth that had been designed to confuse, trap, and lead people astray.

Edmund eyed the tunnels. "Let's pray that beyond one of these passageways there really is another opening."

I whispered a silent prayer, not wanting to imagine what we'd do if we couldn't escape through an eastern entrance. I couldn't bear the thought of having to traverse the passageways again, especially with that creature searching for us.

Edmund tested the three tunnels as he had when we'd entered the labyrinth and then decided to veer to the right. After lighting another torch for me, he motioned for me to stay where I was.

"Wait here for me," he warned.

"If you will be safe, surely I shall be too."

"No, Maribel. I want you to wait this time."

I sighed and watched his back until he disappeared

around a bend. He was only trying to protect me. But we needed to remain together.

"Shall I come now?" I called after him.

The echo of a crack was followed by the rumble of what sounded like an avalanche of falling rocks.

"Edmund?"

The rushing of stone turned into a crumbling that tapered away to silence.

"Edmund?" I called again, then waited for several heartbeats. "Answer me, Edmund!"

When no response came, I lurched forward, my heart thudding against my chest. As a plume of dust billowed around me, panic hastened my steps. I turned the bend and stopped at the sight that met me. Edmund lay sprawled on the path. Behind him, an enormous pile of stones blocked the tunnel. The dust still wafted around the heap, and small rocks continued to cascade down.

I rushed to Edmund and fell to my knees. From the backside, I could see no damage. Gently, I rolled him over and ran my hands down his torso, legs, and arms, assessing for any broken bones. Other than scratches on his hands and face, I didn't think he'd sustained any injuries. I skimmed my fingers over his head, his hair feathery-soft beneath my touch. At an egg-sized lump on his temple, I realized he'd probably been hit in the head with a falling rock.

At the pressure of my hand against the swelling, he released a low moan but didn't open his eyes. I only had to probe it a moment to know he'd be fine. He'd been knocked unconscious but hadn't sustained any serious wounds and would rouse soon enough.

I glanced at the avalanche that could have buried

him alive—likely had been intended to trap and kill anyone who attempted to pass.

Relief swelled in my throat. The emotion was so strong it pushed out a sob before I could contain it. Giving way to the rush, I threw my arms over him, buried my face into his chest, and allowed more sobs to escape. My body shook with the realization of how close I'd come to losing him. He'd almost died, and the thought of life without him made the tears flow even faster.

"Oh, Edmund," I whispered against him. "I cannot live without you."

As soon as the words were out, I knew from the core of my being they were true. Edmund was woven into the fabric of my life, so tightly and so thoroughly I couldn't imagine going on without him.

He was not only my best friend, he was my everything—the closest to family and safety and anything good I'd ever had.

Beneath me, he stirred. I started to push up, but his arms slipped around me before I could move away. As though sensing how close he'd come to death, his grip was tight, pressing me to himself in an almost desperate hold.

I clung to him in return. For a long minute, we lay that way, our chests rising and falling together, our relief mingling with each breath. When I finally released him, his arms loosened, but only a little, enough that I lifted my head and met his gaze.

"I thought I lost you," I whispered. Raising a hand to his face, I cupped his cheek and bent down to place a kiss upon his forehead.

At that moment, he arched upward so his mouth

collided with mine.

I was unprepared for the connection. The heat and the pressure of his mouth stole my breath with a gasp. When his lips moved to secure mine more firmly, my heart ceased its beating, and I nearly swooned at his touch.

At the same instant, our lips melded, one of his hands slid to the base of my neck, turning my head just slightly so that our mouths fused again in another dip of warmth.

I'd never experienced anything so pleasurable before, and my heart swelled with a cascade of feelings I couldn't name. All I could think about was Edmund, how much I liked being in his arms, and how I never wanted the kiss to end.

But with a moan, he broke away. "I'm sorry, Maribel," he said between gasps. "I beg your forgiveness—"

I cut him off by bending down and brushing my lips over his again. The moment I did, he captured my mouth in another kiss, one full of the same passion, as if it could somehow save us.

Once more Edmund ended the kiss, this time abruptly. He sat up, scrambled away from me, and quickly stood, grabbing the wall to keep from toppling over.

"Careful. You injured your head." I was surprised by how breathless I sounded. I pushed to my feet and realized I was wobbly too. My legs were weak and my body strangely weightless.

He leaned his forehead against the wall and closed his eyes. His profile was anguished, his lips pressed together, his brows knit. I wasn't sure what was happening between us, what those kisses meant, but I did know Edmund was more important to me than anything else. I didn't want him to hurt, didn't want him to suffer in any way.

Tentatively, I touched his back. His muscles rippled beneath my hand, and I was suddenly aware of the powerful build of his body in a way I hadn't been before. I was surprised and even slightly disappointed when he pulled away.

"Does your head hurt?" I asked, lifting the flap on my medical bag. "My Saint-John's wort tonic will help ease the discomfort."

He didn't respond for a moment and seemed to be waging an internal war.

I pulled out the tiny vial and uncorked it. "Here. Take a few drops."

"No, Maribel," he said in a strangled voice. "My head is fine. But my conscience isn't. I shouldn't have kissed you."

At the mention of our passion, I twisted at the vial with a strange sense of embarrassment. Our kisses had seemed a natural outlet for the emotions of the moment—relief, gratefulness, and even deep concern for one another. But had we been wrong to engage in the kisses?

Edmund apparently believed so. Had I been incorrect to assume he had feelings for me? That his kiss had been the signal of his affection? "Do you not care about me, then?"

His eyes met mine, tortured and yet filled with warmth that soothed my worries. "I care about you more than you know." His voice was low and raw, and his words sent tingles through my body, making me long to draw close to him again. "I fear, however, that kissing you will only coerce you into feelings you're not ready to freely give in return."

Coerce me? "I do freely give you my feelings," I said, not exactly sure what I was giving him except I knew I couldn't live without him. That was clear.

"Then you're ready to forsake your plans to become a nun?"

"Of course not," I said. "Why would I . . ." Stumbling to a pause, I stared at him, starting to make sense of his reasoning. As a postulant on the verge of becoming a nun, I'd soon pledge myself to Christ as His bride, and in doing so, vow to remain celibate and refrain from the pleasures of the flesh. I'd need to live in purity of thought and body. Engaging with Edmund in any physical pleasure—including kissing—was inappropriate, perhaps even scandalous.

Even though I wasn't yet a nun and hadn't taken my vows, he was right. I couldn't offer him my affection, not when it wasn't mine to freely give.

He was studying my face, gauging my understanding of our situation. "I know how long you've waited and how eagerly you've anticipated becoming a nun. And I would not turn you from that. If you give it up, you must choose to do so of your own will and desire."

Was he telling me if I became a nun I'd lose him? That it wasn't possible for me to hold onto both my aspirations and him? While somewhere in the back of my mind, I'd known eventually things would have to change between us, I'd resisted the prospect and had clung to the hope he'd always be there at the convent with me, always available, always nearby.

However, such an attitude was selfish on my part. Someday, he'd want to settle down, get married, and have a family. Perhaps Colette had been correct in her assessment of me, maybe even prophetic. *I shall love you like Maribel never can. I promise to make you happy.*

Another woman, like Colette, could give Edmund the love he wanted and deserved. Another woman could spend her life making him happy. But God had called me to spend my life in service to Him. I'd always believed so. And I couldn't let the passion of a few stolen kisses change the course of my plans and dreams.

As though reading my thoughts, Edmund's eyes filled with sadness. Before I could say anything, he nodded. "I respect your choice and shall do my best to honor it henceforth. I'm only sorry I didn't do so today."

"You are an honorable man." I took his hand in mine, but he immediately pulled away.

"If I am to honor you," he said, his voice almost a growl, "then it is best we refrain from any sort of physical contact."

At the implication of his words, heat rose into my cheeks. Did my touch affect him? "I am sorry. I did not know . . ."

He sighed. "Let us speak of it no more, Maribel."

For a moment, I contemplated all that had happened between us, struggling to make sense of our relationship and where it would go from here. From the severity of Edmund's expression, I guessed he was doing the same.

Although I knew I should feel more remorse for our kisses and the intimacy we'd shared, I couldn't conjure up the proper guilt. It niggled at me, but the memory of the pleasure and sweetness of the time in his arms was something I'd never forget.

I finally smiled up at my friend, the friend who was definitely no longer a boy and most certainly was every inch a man. "I want you to know that though the moment can never be repeated, I do not regret sharing a kiss with you this once."

As the words left my lips, I felt my cheeks flush at my brazenness. Yet certainly Edmund was used to my directness by now. He'd expect nothing less.

He gave me the ghost of a smile in return. "I'm glad you don't regret it."

Hearing him repeat my words, I sensed how insignificant, even insulting, they sounded. "What I meant to say is that I enjoyed kissing you immensely."

My gaze was drawn to his lips, and I couldn't keep myself from admiring their firmness. How had I never noticed before how handsome his mouth was? Yes, I'd always acknowledged the fact Edmund was a fair and noble-looking man. But I'd never paid close attention to his features, perhaps had simply taken them for granted.

He drew in a deep breath. "Maribel."

I tore my attention from his lips and met his gaze. "Yes?"

"You are not making this easy on me."

"What easy?"

"My pledge not to kiss you again." His focus shifted to my lips, and sparks leaped to life in his eyes. In an instant, those sparks flew between us. A flame lit low in my belly. And I had the urge to close the distance and wrap my arms around him.

Perhaps this wouldn't be easy for me either. Perhaps we'd made a mistake in awakening these feelings between us. Perhaps we should have left them dormant. I didn't even truly understand the feelings. Whatever they were, whatever was happening, I needed to ignore it and put it behind me.

I could do that, couldn't I? I looked away from him to the massive pile of rocks blocking the tunnel. With a deep breath, I straightened my shoulders. I had to, for both our sakes.

Chapter 14

EDMUND

BY THE TIME WE CLEARED THE RUBBLE FROM THE PATH, CLIMBED the steep slope toward the surface, and chipped away at the seal, I wasn't sure I'd have any strength to lift the heavy stone that lay over the eastern opening of the labyrinth. Maribel had insisted on treating my wounds again, reapplying the healing ointment. Even so, they pained me more than I wanted her to know.

It also pained me to work so near to her. In the tight space, we were shoulder to shoulder. Her labored breathing brushed my cheek, and her presence filled my senses.

With both of us heaving against the stone, we finally shifted it enough that I could use a lever to pry it the rest of the way, just as I'd done when we'd entered the labyrinth. As we climbed out the narrow crack, cold darkness met us. Our torchlight revealed we were in a low cave that was more of a cleft in the rocks than a true cavern. We could kneel, but our heads brushed against the crusty ceiling.

We extinguished our light quickly so we wouldn't draw attention from any of Theobald's guards who might be in the vicinity, and I vetoed a fire in spite of the frigidness though I doubted our enemy would see the glimmer. From the distance we'd traveled underground to the east, my guess was that we were over a league from the western entrance where hopefully Theobald was still waiting for his guards to reappear from the labyrinth.

As it was well into the night, we curled up in the far corner of the cleft, away from the wind, and fell into an exhausted slumber.

I'd planned to sleep lightly and stay alert to danger, but when I next opened my eyes, the early gray of dawn greeted me. I held myself motionless and attempted to discern what—if anything—had awoken me.

I shifted but found my arms wound snuggly around Maribel and realized she was curled into my torso. With her back against the rock and her front shielded by my body, I hoped she'd kept warmer than I had.

Even as I regained wakefulness, I was keenly aware of her nearness. And my mind began to relive our kisses from yesterday—not one, but two. I'd floated near the brink of heaven with each of them, especially when she'd initiated the contact.

After so many months—even years—of loving her and wishing for her to return the affection, part of me was ecstatic she finally felt something for me besides friendship and brotherly consideration. It was most definitely something more. There was no other way to explain what had happened or the heat that kept flaring between us.

While I was relieved she finally knew the truth about how I felt, at the same time a knot in my stomach twisted hard with the realization our feelings didn't matter. Nothing could ever come of them. Not when she cherished the prospect of taking her vows and becoming a nun.

I could admit that, in the heat of the moment, I'd considered making her forget about her plans. She was eager and inquisitive enough that with more kissing and tender wooing, I might have been able to win her heart and make her forsake her goals. In the short term, I'd gain the woman I loved. But at what expense? Eventually, she might regret her decision, wonder what she'd given up, and perhaps even resent me.

Though it had been hard to tear myself from her, I'd done the right thing. I loved her too much to cause her misery. No matter what the future held, I'd never stop loving her. And I'd never leave her. Perhaps I'd take the role of her personal guard now that Wade was gone. I'd live close to her, protect her, and die for her if need be, whether that was in Norland, Mercia, or the ends of the earth.

She stirred within my embrace. Wrapped together in my cloak, her face was burrowed against my chest. Although she'd plaited her hair in the dark last night to bring a semblance of order to it, the silky strands had come loose again and tantalized my chin and cheek.

My stomach growled, reminding me I hadn't eaten properly in days. At the same moment, several pebbles dropped from the ledge above.

The drowsiness of my short night fell away, and I tuned in to the human footfalls and boot scuffs coming from overhead, likely surrounding our hiding place.

I tensed and inwardly berated myself for not sleeping more wakefully as Wade had attempted to train me to do.

Even if my shoulder throbbed and my leg still ached, I had no excuse for putting us in danger, especially not after working so diligently to make our way through the labyrinth.

How had we been discovered? Had someone spotted our torch when we'd come up out of the maze? I glanced to my side to the stone I'd already slid back in place over the labyrinth. I'd wanted to make sure that if any of Ethelwulf's soldiers found the eastern entrance, we'd hear them attempting to open it and could make a getaway before they discovered us.

I hadn't counted on them finding us so soon from the outside. But perhaps Theobald had hawks scouting the hills.

Could I remove the stone from the labyrinth entrance quietly enough that we could retreat into the depths? I pictured the dark, confusing tunnels, the deadly traps, and the ravenous dragon-like creature we'd escaped only by God's grace. Even after Maribel had removed the sliver and had tended the wound, all the creature had wanted to do was eat. While it had temporarily allowed us to flee unharmed, hunger would drive it to seek us out if we returned to its hunting grounds.

Slowly, I reached for my sword. Which was worse? To face Theobald and his soldiers? Or to chance meeting the dragon again?

Maribel released a contented sigh that would have constricted my chest if not for the danger of our predicament. She tilted back her head just enough to see my face. As she peered at me sleepily from beneath long lashes, her eyes dropped straight to my mouth and filled with hazy desire.

I enjoyed kissing you immensely. Her words from last

night rang in my head along with the awareness that she was thinking of our kisses just as I had moments ago. I could count on Maribel to say exactly what she thought. She wasn't capable of being coy or playacting. She lived out her feelings without holding back.

A puff of her breath, white in the cold air, mingled with mine. I was cognizant our circumstances were less than ideal, that if we'd been alone without our enemy camped on our doorstep, I would have had a difficult time unwinding myself from her and probably would have let our lips touch again.

In the future, I'd have to be careful to establish and keep proper boundaries between us. But for now, I had more serious problems to think about.

At another scrape of footfalls, my fingers tightened around my hilt and my pulse quickened. We didn't have time to climb down into the labyrinth and hide. I was left with no choice but to fight our intruders.

I started to rise and push Maribel farther against the rock out of harm's way. To my surprise, she drew me nearer, winding her arms around my neck. "Edmund." Her whisper contained pleasure, as though she could think of no place she'd rather be than with me. Before I realized what she intended, she bent in and pressed her mouth against mine. At the same instant, a shadow fell over the opening of our hiding place.

I pushed away from Maribel, scrambled to my knees, and withdrew my sword. But I was too late. A dagger was at my throat before I could turn. It bit into my skin, piercing the first layer and causing blood to trickle down my neck.

"Stop!" Maribel cried, kneeling with her dagger extended. Her eyes were as wild as her hair. She was fully awake now, her expression panicked. When she took in the knife at my throat and the blood, her panic transformed into determination.

"Release him," she said firmly to my captor. "It is I you seek."

More voices came from behind us. And more shadows crowded the ledge's opening. I considered whether I could reach my dagger and plunge it into the man's gut before he killed me. As if sensing my next move, he wrenched my arm behind my back with one hand and disarmed me with the other. The pain of the movement tore through the wound in my shoulder, and I gritted my teeth against a wave of nausea.

"You do not need him," Maribel said, this time with slightly more worry in her voice. "I am the Princess Maribel, and if you let him go, I shall willingly hand myself over to you."

The pressure of the knife against my throat eased, but my captor's grip was as unyielding as though he'd wound chains around me. Although I couldn't see anything but his arm, it was enough to know he was a giant of a man and I wouldn't be able to overpower him.

"Your Highness," the man said with a measure of respect that surprised me.

"Bring them out here, Firmin," came a command from outside—a command that sounded distinctly feminine.

The strong guard yanked me backward. And this time I couldn't keep a cry of pain from slipping from my lips.

"He is severely injured," Maribel called out. "Please allow him his freedom."

But the soldier had no intention of freeing me. Instead, he dragged me from our cavern onto a level plateau that ended abruptly with the jagged edge of a steep cliff and a ravine far below.

My mind scrambled to find the place on the map of Mercia I'd memorized. I rapidly scanned the area for landmarks, for any sign of something familiar. But the barren, rocky terrain spread out before us to the horizon—mountainous crags, jagged rocks, and snowy peaks. In a month or two, the first buds of spring would bring some color back to the bleak gray. The few hardy plants that survived the high elevation and harsh climate would grow again. But for now, it was a desolate wasteland with few identifying markers.

Several other knights congregated on the plateau and stepped back as Maribel crawled from our hiding place. As she stood and straightened, she held her dagger out, her expression solemn and filled with resolve. In her other hand, she had the royal ruby, proving her to be one of the lost princesses.

My heart thudded with the need to protect her. I had to make her see that the best way she could save herself was to cooperate with our captors and cease worrying about what became of me. If she lashed out at them in my defense, I feared what they might do to her.

Before I could issue my warning, the guards all around dropped to one knee and bowed their heads before Maribel. Only then did I notice that although they were attired in black cloaks that were the style of Ethelwulf's elite guard, these men weren't wearing the king's coat of arms. Instead of golden lions leaping against a black background, their badges contained golden lions standing against a ruby-colored backdrop.

It was Mercia's emblem, one that hadn't been allowed since Ethelwulf had taken the throne away from King Francis and Queen Dierdal. Were these rebels?

Maribel opened her mouth to speak, but at the sight of the men kneeling around her, she only stared, her eyes widening and the hand holding the dagger faltering.

"Maribel?" came a voice from above us.

Maribel pivoted at the same time I peered up.

There, on the upper ledge of the hiding place we'd just vacated, stood a woman who exuded strength and power in her bearing. She held a sword in one hand and a dagger in the other, and she, too, wore a black cloak over chain mail, breeches, and long leather boots. With her hood up, her face was shadowed, but it was easy enough to tell she was young and noble.

Behind her towered a broad-shouldered man with strong features and an iron build. He was armed and wore chain mail as well, but from the proud way he held himself, I could tell he was no ordinary soldier, that he was someone important.

Surrounding them were additional knights. Farther up the mountain, I glimpsed more soldiers and horses. If they were rebels, then perhaps we had a chance of surviving.

The young noblewoman sheathed her weapons and began to hoist herself from the ledge. Two of the guards nearby rushed to her aid. She ignored their outstretched offers of help and hopped down as nimbly as a cougar. The broad-shouldered man followed behind her.

When the noblewoman crossed to Maribel, I stiffened. My need to stand next to Maribel and protect her swelled with such force I struggled to free myself. At my movement, my captor jerked my injured shoulder, and I nearly collapsed to my knees.

Upon reaching Maribel, she touched the ruby. Then she lifted her hood, letting it fall away. And I knew. The likeness was so evident and natural there was no doubt who this woman was.

"Maribel," the young woman said. "I am your sister, Adelaide."

The fight and frustration evaporated from Maribel's face, leaving wonder in its place. At the same moment, overwhelming relief swept through me, and I almost sagged against my captor. Maribel was safe. Ethelwulf wouldn't get her.

"It may come as a shock to learn you have a sister," Adelaide continued, "but rest assured, you are one of the lost princesses of Mercia."

"No. It is no shock," Maribel replied, staring at her sister with fascination. "Sister Katherine arrived at the convent less than a week ago and brought me the news of my true family—that I have two sisters."

Adelaide exchanged a glance with the young nobleman.

He cocked his head to the west. "Then 'tis she who has brought Theobald's troops into the area."

"'Tis she who has finally brought our search for Maribel to an end," Adelaide countered.

"We are fortunate Theobald did not find Maribel first."

"We are not so fortunate yet." Adelaide returned her gaze to Maribel. "For he will not rest until he has her within his grasp."

Maribel's attention was no longer upon our fate. She was too enamored with her sister to think of anything else. I could see it in her eyes—that childish look of excitement she got when setting out on an adventure.

"Sister." Maribel tested the word and then reached out a hand to touch the queen's cheek. "I am delighted to make your acquaintance. You are very beautiful."

Adelaide hesitated, looking as though she wanted to

touch Maribel too. But she held herself back.

"I never dreamed I had sisters." Maribel moved her hand to the queen's arm and examined her from her head down to her boots. "I always thought my entire family died, that I was the only one who survived."

I was fascinated by the similarities between the two women. Their hair was spun of an identical golden hue, their eyes of the same bright blue. Their features were delicate and elegant. And both were stunningly beautiful.

From the admiration radiating from the faces of the other men, I realized I wasn't the only one fascinated by the resemblance of the two women.

"I held you when you were but a newborn," Adelaide said softly. "And now look at you. You are a grown woman."

"I am grateful God has spared us and kept us safe all these many years."

"So many lost years," Adelaide said wistfully, finally lifting a hand and grazing Maribel's cheek.

"I have had a good life," Maribel replied. "The convent has been a wonderful home, and everyone there has been family."

The queen studied Maribel and fingered her hair.

When the broad-shouldered man next to her cleared his throat, Adelaide dropped her hand. "You will tell me everything about your life. I am eager to hear it all. But presently, we must be on our way. Captain Theobald has scouts swarming the Highlands and will learn soon enough we have found you. We would do well to put as much distance between our forces and his before that discovery."

Her words set the soldiers around us into motion—all except the guard at my back, who still held me with an iron grip.

"Your Majesty," he called. "What would you like me to do with this one? When I found him, he was molesting the princess."

For the first time since we'd been discovered, the queen seemed to notice me. "Molesting?" Her voice sharpened as her eyes narrowed.

"He was taking advantage of your sister, Your Majesty." The knight yanked at my arm, sending pain shooting through my shoulder. The move left me no choice but to drop to my knees or pass out.

"No!" Maribel cried out. "Edmund is my best friend. He would never compromise me."

"Firmin is my most trusted guard," the queen replied. "Are you accusing him of lying?"

Silence descended. With my back bent, I tried hard to focus on the unfolding situation. But the guard knew how to cause me pain and was taking full advantage of incapacitating me. I could hardly lift my head, much less speak through the burning sensations running up and down my arm and back.

"Edmund is a good man," Maribel said, "and he has been helping me escape from King Ethelwulf's soldiers."

"So Firmin is lying?" Adelaide persisted.

What could Maribel say? That she had initiated a kiss with me this morning? She'd been half asleep and probably hadn't realized what she was doing. If she confessed, she would bring shame to herself in front of everyone, especially in front of her sister.

I couldn't let her do that.

I lifted my head as much as Firmin's hold would allow. "The guard isn't lying, Your Majesty. It's my fault. I took advantage of Maribel. I should have kept better control of myself."

The queen scrutinized me before returning her attention to Maribel who shook her head. "No, Edmund is trying to protect me—"

"Do what you wish with me, Your Majesty," I called out, "but I would have no blemish rest upon Maribel."

Was I imagining things, or did Firmin loosen his hold on me?

"We'd just escaped from the labyrinth." Maribel's voice was threaded with panic. "There was a horrible creature there, and we were tired and hungry and cold."

While I appreciated her effort to spare me any discipline, I was more determined to protect her. "I have no excuse, Your Majesty."

"Labyrinth?" The queen interrupted us both. "Here?"

"Yes," Maribel responded. "And if not for Edmund, we would be hopelessly lost in it."

"What kind of labyrinth?" Adelaide asked, but the broad-shouldered man next to her gestured, drawing her attention.

"We shall have plenty of time for conversation once we are far from the Highlands," he said. "For now, we must be on our way."

Adelaide nodded. Then she crossed to me with determined steps. When she stood directly in front of me, Firmin repositioned his hold, giving me no choice but to look up at the queen.

"Who are you?" she asked.

"Sister Katherine tasked me with accompanying Maribel to Norland and seeing her safely into your hands, Your Majesty."

"Yet you have sullied her reputation and in so doing have cast a stain upon our fledgling cause. Furthermore, you have likely harmed Maribel's chances of making a good match."

Even though we'd done nothing more than kiss, I understood how compromising our predicament appeared. We'd been sleeping together very closely with our arms around each other.

"Have no fear," Maribel said. "I am in no need of a match. I am a postulant and will soon take my vows to become a nun."

The queen ignored Maribel and kept her focus upon me. "Tell me your name and where your family is from."

"I am Edmund Charles Chambers. My family was from East Mercia of Chapelhill. They are all dead. Murdered in the purge during the early days of Ethelwulf's reign."

"And you alone escaped?"

I nodded but said nothing else. I wasn't willing to revisit the past, not even for the queen.

Her brow quirked, and she studied me more carefully. "Chambers of Chapelhill?"

"Yes, Your Majesty."

"How old were you when your family perished?"

"I was but a lad of four."

Adelaide looked again at the broad-shouldered man who'd been pushing us to go, and silent communication passed between the two. "Then you are Lord Chambers of Chapelhill." Her words were a statement and not a question.

Since I was the only living son of my father, I supposed his title had passed to me. Nevertheless, I'd been raised by a simple soldier turned blacksmith, and the idea of being considered a lord was almost laughable.

"To what lengths will you go to protect Maribel's future and her reputation?"

"I would die for her if need be." The words were out

before I realized just how passionate my tone was.

Again, I couldn't be sure, but Firmin's hold seemed to ease even more.

"Then you will marry her." The queen's declaration contained a finality that echoed against the stones around us. She didn't wait for my assent. Instead, she spun and strode away.

Chapter 15

Maribel

I stared after Adelaide. She wanted Edmund to marry me? She couldn't be serious.

"Edmund and I cannot get married," I said.

"You must." Adelaide climbed up the embankment without breaking her stride.

Scrambling after her, I bunched my long gray habit to keep it from impeding me, but still, I lacked the physical prowess Adelaide clearly had. "You have apparently misunderstood me. I have made plans to become a nun and will do so when I turn eighteen."

"I understood you," she replied, leaping from one rock to the next. "But you are royalty and as such must resign yourself to a new life and the roles that come with being a princess."

"Surely a princess can also be a nun, can she not?" At least I hoped so.

"As the firstborn twin, if something happens to me, you would become the heir."

I'd never considered such a possibility. "I should

like to give that role to my twin sister, if I may."

"You might not have that option."

I heard what Adelaide was leaving unspoken, that we had no way of knowing if Emmeline was still alive. And if she was, we'd likely need to fight against King Ethelwulf to claim her. "Nevertheless, I have never intended to marry. And I plead with you to reconsider what you have requested of me."

Adelaide stopped so abruptly I almost toppled backward. With her gloved hand on the hilt of her sword and the wind billowing her dark cape, she looked every bit a warrior and queen. "I can forbid my soldiers to speak about your indiscretion with Lord Chambers, but the word will leak out eventually."

Lord Chambers? For a moment, I was confused about who Lord Chambers was until I remembered that was what Adelaide had called Edmund when he'd shared his identity. "I shall bear the burden of a ruined reputation myself." I lowered my voice, aware we were drawing the curious looks of Adelaide's men. "Moreover, since I have no need of a match, the soiled reputation will not interfere with my future."

"It will interfere with our cause." Adelaide spoke with a gravity that made me realize just how little I knew about the *cause*. "We have many supporters for the rebellion both within Mercia and Norland. They long to rid the isle of the evil practices, lewdness, and corruption King Ethelwulf's reign has brought. I chance losing their support if I tolerate improprieties among my courtiers, especially from a sister."

"I claim an abiding friendship with Edmund and nothing more."

"You have been traveling with him unchaperoned

and sleeping with him."

The heat of mortification speared my cheeks. "Only for warmth."

Adelaide lifted a brow, her eyes telling me she'd seen the truth of the situation between Edmund and me, and I wouldn't be able to hide anything from her.

"In addition to being titled, wealthy, and landed, it is clear Lord Chambers loves you and will marry you," Adelaide continued more gently.

Edmund loved me? Of course Colette had said as much, but how could Adelaide conclude something so soon after meeting us?

"If he is willing to suffer death on your behalf," Adelaide said, as if hearing my question, "then he will find it no hardship to marry you."

I glanced down the hill. The ox-like guard who'd discovered us together had released Edmund. In the gray morning, he was pale from his injuries, but he held his head with dignity, his lean face containing strength and appeal that would likely turn the heads of many women.

When he sensed my attention upon him, he looked up. His bright green eyes were filled with his concern. For me.

Adelaide followed my gaze. "'Tis evident you also care about him."

"I do care," I admitted, picturing the labyrinth when I'd thought he'd died. I couldn't claim we were only brother and sister or only friends. My relationship with him had changed. My feelings for him had blossomed from some part of me I hadn't known existed.

Nevertheless, it was a part of me I needed to shut

off and lock away, a part of me that would cause us trouble if I didn't utilize self-control.

Adelaide's keen eyes swept over the silent terrain. "The truth is King Ethelwulf seeks you for the purpose of marrying you to his son and uniting the houses of Warwick and Mercia. If you wed Lord Chambers with all haste, we shall eliminate King Ethelwulf's motivation to kidnap you. In doing so, we shall also eliminate his attempt to subdue the rebellion."

The night of the attack, Colette had spoken of the king's marriage plans for me. But at the time, I hadn't understood what that meant. Now I shuddered at the reality of his plans.

"With so much at stake," Adelaide continued, "I hope you can resign yourself to my decision. Perhaps someday you will even thank me for bringing you together with the person you love."

She turned, then, and resumed her climb, leaving me to stare after her. I wanted to deny her, to call out my objections, to tell her I'd never thank her for preventing me from realizing the goal I'd worked toward my entire life. After all, she'd only just met me. How could she presume to know more about my feelings for Edmund than I did? And how could she think that I could so easily give up my plans to become a nun?

But this was neither the time nor the place to raise further objections. Besides, she was the queen, and as such, I must treat her with the respect she was due as my sovereign, even if she was my sister.

On the slope, a bitter, winter wind slapped my cheeks and stung my ears. I resolved to speak with her later. Surely she'd accept my plans if only I could explain to her how important they were, how long I'd dreamed of becoming a nun. Perhaps if she witnessed me using my physician's skills, she'd understand.

The stones bit into my hands and occasionally my knees as I climbed to the level area where a band of soldiers waited with the horses. When I reached steady ground, Adelaide was already in conversation with her scouts, who were monitoring Captain Theobald's position in the west.

We were soon on our way through the craggy outcroppings that led farther into the higher mountain passes. The climb in elevation was gradual but slow due to the rocky terrain. In order to steer away from King Ethelwulf's soldiers, who were still distracted with the labyrinth, we kept to the east but always veering north to Norland.

Adelaide relinquished her horse for Edmund and me and rode with the broad-shouldered man, who I learned was her husband, Christopher, the Earl of Langley. As the path was narrow and we traveled single file, I didn't have the opportunity to get to know her.

Instead, I plied Edmund with my questions.

"She lived at Kentworth Castle with the Langleys while growing up," Edmund whispered in answer. "The former Earl of Langley appeared so loyal and dedicated to King Ethelwulf that no one had reason to question Adelaide's identity. It was the perfect hiding place for her all those years."

I tried not to lean back into Edmund—for fear of putting strain on his injury and also to prove to my sister that although I might care for Edmund, I could control my feelings and actions around him. She need not worry I would bring any further blemish to her efforts to reclaim the throne.

"So, Christopher was one of the earl's sons?" I wasn't sure how Edmund was privy to the information surrounding my sister. But I suspected Wade had divulged more to Edmund after his trips than I'd realized.

"The oldest of the brothers died in childhood, leaving Christopher the heir."

I watched my sister's profile from a short distance behind. Her poise, her beauty, and yet her fierceness. There was so much about her I didn't know, that I longed to learn. "I wonder why she chose to marry Christopher?"

"He rebelled and ran away to Norland many years ago. Once there, he proved himself a valuable asset to King Draybane of Norland, becoming like a son to the king. Their marriage solidifies an alliance between Norland and Mercia."

"Then she did not marry him for love?" With Adelaide's talk of love regarding Edmund and myself, I had expected it was important to her—that it would play no small role in her own match.

Edmund's gloved hand rested on my waist. His fingers pressed slightly, making me all too conscious of his nearness, of the heat of his touch through the layers of my garments.

He shifted as though he, too, was aware of our closeness. But the movement only reinforced the fact that there was no place to go, that his thighs securely hugged mine within the tight confines of the saddle. He lifted his hand from my waist and rested it on his leg as if that could somehow make the difference, but I was only made all the more aware of his long fingers.

"From what I have heard and now seen," Edmund whispered, "theirs is indeed a match of love, as well as one of alliance."

I studied the couple and noted the trusting way Adelaide reclined against Christopher to converse and how he bent in and spoke into her ear intimately. "Yes," I whispered over my shoulder to Edmund. "They do seem to love each other."

Edmund didn't respond, making me conscious again of his nearness. I could almost feel the beating of his heart against my back.

"What shall we do once we are in Norland?" I asked, bringing up the question that thus far during our ride we'd avoided. "Adelaide surely will not force us to get married against our wishes."

"Then it is still against your wish, Maribel?" Edmund's voice rumbled low near my ear.

I knew he was referring to our talk down in the labyrinth after we'd kissed, when he'd asked if I was ready to forsake my plans to become a nun.

My chest constricted. I didn't want to hurt him, didn't want to make our situation difficult, and most certainly didn't want to cause strife with my sister so soon after meeting her. But I'd never imagined anything beyond the convent walls. How could I start now? What would that kind of life be like?

Everything I'd labored over for years was at the convent in the apothecary—all my herbs cataloged so carefully, all my experiments recorded in detail, all the medicines I'd developed. I couldn't give everything up and waste the countless hours I'd spent trying to become a master healer.

Of course, I loved the simplicity of a cloistered life, the community of sisters, and the devotion to God. I wanted to serve Him wholeheartedly. But if I was completely honest with myself, I knew my desire to become a nun had more to do with retaining my right to act as a physician than with my desire for a holy, secluded life.

I only had to think back to all the times I'd longed to explore, see more of the world, and have adventures beyond the convent walls. Would I have those longings if I was destined to be a nun?

What if I considered Adelaide's plans? What if I married Edmund and started a new life elsewhere? For a heartbeat, I imagined myself by his side as his wife, never having to leave him. But in the next heartbeat, I pushed away the fantasy. Even if I moved my herbs and medicines to a new home, how could I continue to practice as a physician? People accepted nuns who were skilled in medicine. But outside of midwifery, women weren't allowed to be physicians or surgeons. In fact, those who dabbled in medicine were often considered witches.

I sighed. "If God has gifted me with a healer's touch, how can I not use the gift?"

Edmund took hold of my hand and squeezed it. The measure was one of friendship and was laced with understanding and support. "Have no fear, Maribel," he said quietly. "We're not beholden to the queen."

At his sensitivity, tears stung my eyes. I was struck again, as I had been since before our journey started, by what a good man Edmund had become.

"You did not have to take the blame for our predicament," I said softly. "I was the one who kissed you."

"I shouldn't have placed us in such a position." His declaration from earlier came back to me: *I would die for her if need be.*

Some part deep inside had known this to be true. Edmund had always been willing to sacrifice for me. The question was how much was I willing to sacrifice for him? The answer sobered me. I'd too often, in my enthusiasm for things, pushed forward with little thought to how my choices affected him. Including the kiss.

"I should have been more careful, Edmund." Even if I hadn't been fully awake, I shouldn't have reached for him, should have considered how difficult our closeness was for him when he'd vowed not to touch me again.

"We'll get through this together," he said quietly.

We traveled for some time in silence, his hand enfolding mine with his reassurance. Ahead, Adelaide and Christopher rode hard, obviously skilled equestrians. Edmund and I were less so, having had few opportunities to ride over the years. Thankfully, his brief moments of communication with the horse kept us from lagging too much and slowing the guards that followed us.

The gray sky overhead blended with the rocks rising up around us. Since everything looked the same, I couldn't tell where we'd been or where we yet needed to go. Who would guess that somewhere far beneath these hills lay a dark, winding labyrinth with all its dangers? In fact, we could very well be riding directly above the tunnels we'd recently traversed, quite possibly above an ancient treasure.

With so many obstacles deterring past kings from

finding the treasure's location, no wonder it had become nothing more than an old tale. Even now that Edmund and I had discovered the labyrinth and how to access it, there was no guarantee of a treasure inside, and the dangers inside were innumerable.

Nevertheless, I needed to share everything I'd learned with Adelaide as soon as I could. For certainly Captain Theobald would inform King Ethelwulf about the labyrinth too. If the king was smart, he'd likely suspect the labyrinth held the elusive treasure, and he'd send more men to explore.

Of course, the king wouldn't have the map to help him navigate the maze. And he wouldn't have the three keys necessary for unlocking the treasure—if indeed Edmund's presupposition about the keys was true.

With Adelaide's key and now mine, we only lacked one. If we located our other sister—my twin, Emmeline—before King Ethelwulf found her, then we'd most definitely have the advantage.

By midday, I was saddle sore and hungry. Edmund's stomach rumbled, too, and from the stiff way he held his arm and shoulder, I guessed his injury was troubling him. Thus, I was relieved when Adelaide halted in a secluded rocky area to rest our horses. From our position overlooking the surrounding highlands, we'd be able to see King Ethelwulf's men approaching if they were on our trail.

The absence of sunshine and the stinging of wind had numbed my fingers and toes. As Edmund lifted me to the ground, I could hardly stand for the scarcity of feeling in my limbs. He caught me and slipped his arm around my middle.

One of the guards nearby pointed up and several bowmen, including Christopher, readied bows and arrows.

Edmund glanced skyward. "No! Don't shoot her."

Christopher already had his bowstring pulled taut and his arrow nocked. His gaze darted to Edmund before narrowing once again on the bird. "We cannot let it escape and return to the captain with our location."

"She won't." Edmund released me and started toward Christopher. "She's mine. I've trained her from a hatchling. And she's only come to deliver game and make sure Maribel and I are unharmed."

With that, Edmund trilled a quiet call. Sheba whistled back as she continued to hover above us.

"At ease!" Christopher shouted to the other bowmen even as he released the tension in his own string and lowered the bow.

Edmund whistled again, and this time Sheba flapped downward until she landed upon a boulder. She dropped a hare from her talons before turning her dark eyes upon me.

With a soft, almost silent, warble, Edmund retrieved the gift and offered it to me. My stomach lurched with the need for the roasted meat, and I nodded at the bird gratefully.

When Sheba lifted and took flight, everyone stared at Edmund.

"You're a Fera Agmen," Christopher said once Sheba was gone.

Edmund hesitated in his response before bowing slightly, apparently deciding to trust this group with his rare skill.

"Then the gray wolf is a friend as well?" Christopher inclined his head to the path behind us.

"Yes."

I strained to see Barnabas, searching the trail as well as the surrounding rocks, but I didn't glimpse him anywhere.

"You should have told me earlier," Christopher admonished. "I had a mind to shoot him and roast him as the queen loathes wolves."

"Please, do not harm him. We have other meat." I quickly dumped the other prey Sheba had provided for us before our descent into the labyrinth. The few small animals wouldn't be enough to feed all Adelaide's men but would provide something.

"We cannot start a fire." Adelaide stepped forward, eyeing Sheba's gifts. "If Theobald does not see our smoke, one of his scouting hawks surely will."

I tried not to let my disappointment surface and instead reminded myself that even if I went hungry a little while longer, at least Edmund and I were safe and alive.

"Maribel has not eaten a full meal in several days," Edmund said. "She must have something soon."

Adelaide didn't reply and instead returned to her horse. She dug in her saddlebag, retrieved a bundle, and approached me. "You will have my ration."

"Let her have mine." Christopher reached for his saddlebag.

"No," Adelaide said. "You need more sustenance than I do. She will have mine."

The giant of a guard who rode close to Adelaide frowned and began to unlatch the leather strapping on his bag. Adelaide stopped him with a touch to his arm and a shake of her head. "No, Firmin. If Captain Theobald attacks, you and all your men will need your strength."

"So will you, Your Majesty."

For the first time, I noticed the strain on their faces and realized an army of this size and this caliber of men would be difficult to feed, especially in the winter. They were apparently so low on food supplies they'd divided the remaining amounts into rations.

As if coming to the same conclusion, Edmund toed the game. "I'll ask Sheba and Barnabas to hunt for us today. And then tonight, everyone will be able to feast on fresh meat."

Adelaide dipped her head in gratitude.

"Can your eagle tell you if Theobald's guards draw nigh?" Christopher asked.

"She'll let me know if danger approaches."

"Very well," Christopher said. "Then we shall eat and rest for a few moments without worry."

My frozen limbs could hold me no longer, and I sank to the closest rock and pulled Edmund down next to me. I unrolled the small bundle to find several slices of dried venison, a few dates, and a piece of hard rye bread.

"You must have some, Edmund." I placed the food into his lap and opened my medicinal bag.

"I'll be fine until this evening when we make camp."

I rummaged through my supplies and found the healing ointment. "Eat while I tend your wounds."

He started to protest again, so I promptly shoved venison into his mouth. At the surprise flickering in his eyes, I smiled and busied myself with pulling back his cloak and shirt to expose the spot on his shoulder. It was red and raw and in need of rest from the strain he continued to exert, but I couldn't detect any bile or putridness. I started to speak, but before I could give him my prognosis, he, too, wedged some venison into my mouth.

It was my turn to be surprised. At the mirth in his eyes, I realized he was just as determined as I was. He wouldn't let me go hungry any more than I planned to let him.

I bit down on the tough meat, relishing the smoked saltiness. As I chewed, I applied the ointment, gently rubbing it into his flesh. When I finished, I adjusted his shirt and cloak and then reached for the drawstring at his waist so I might add ointment to the wound on his thigh.

Before I could loosen the string, Edmund caught my hand. "Not now, Maribel," he whispered in a strained voice. A faint reddish hue colored his cheeks, and he darted a glance sideways in the direction of the knights.

I shifted my gaze. The men were staring at us as they ate their rations. Had they never seen a physician at work? Well, they would now.

Again, I slipped my fingers underneath Edmund's shirt and tugged at the drawstring of his breeches. He caught my hand more firmly within his, the red stain in his cheek creeping higher. "If you pull down my breeches," he growled low, "your sister will have us married within the hour."

"I am only tending your injuries," I replied even as I withdrew. I didn't like having to refrain from doctoring, but these men wouldn't understand why a young, unmarried woman had the license to touch a man to restore him to health. Perhaps they already considered my ministrations of his shoulder wound inappropriate.

And so it would be with everyone. Even if I was more skilled than most male physicians and surgeons, it wouldn't matter. My doctoring would be frowned upon because I was a woman. Not only would people be unwilling to trust me, but they'd also assume I was inferior. They wouldn't want me treating them and likely wouldn't give me permission to tend to their families either.

Yet, as a nun devoted to a celibate life, people would readily put their confidence in me. They wouldn't question my motives or reputation. All the more reason to continue with my plans to take my vows.

"Lord Chambers, you have sustained a terrible wound," Adelaide said from behind me, making me jump at her nearness. I hadn't realized she'd crossed to us.

"Maribel has worked hard to keep it from festering," he replied, rising in my defense.

I gave him a grateful smile. "The wounds upon his legs need doctoring as well."

"My guard Darien knows a little about medicine." Adelaide met my gaze directly. "He will take over Lord Chambers' care."

"I have been trained for years in the art of healing. If I may, I should like to tend Edmund just as I have been doing."

"Until you are wed, you must refrain from such displays."

Although not unkind, her tone brooked no room for argument, and I could do nothing but bow my head in deference. I understood how my ministrations appeared to everyone else, especially as Edmund and I had traveled together alone for days and then been discovered in an indecent situation.

But surely, I'd be able to convince Adelaide to allow me to doctor Edmund in private, away from the eyes of the men. She seemed to be a rational and intelligent woman. She was attired as a man in breeches and chain mail. She wielded her weapons as a man. And she rode her steed like a man. Surely, of everyone, she would permit me to act as a physician even though it was man's work.

"How were you injured?" Adelaide asked Edmund. "During your flight from Captain Theobald?"

"Yes, Your Majesty. If I hadn't reacted when I did, the arrow would have pierced my heart."

"The two wounds on his leg are from when we visited St. Cuthbert's," I added. "We were attacked by spiders."

"What were you doing at St. Cuthbert's?"

I looked at Edmund. Should we tell Adelaide everything we'd discovered?

Edmund nodded, as if reading my thoughts. "She'll need to know eventually."

Christopher joined Adelaide as I relayed the events of the past week—Sister Katherine's delivery of the key, our discovery of the clue inside, the trip to St. Cuthbert's, finding a piece of the map, and then our adventure in the labyrinth.

"My key also led us to a piece of the map. I have the parchment in my possession at all times." Adelaide patted her side and the bulge of a leather pouch. "We decided it was a map but didn't know its origins."

"Edmund is skilled with maps. During his training as an elite guard, he had to memorize every inch of Mercia's terrain." I was boasting, but I couldn't help it. I was proud of Edmund for his brilliance.

"You're trained as an elite guard?" Christopher studied Edmund more carefully.

"My guardian did his best to train me," Edmund said. "But I was a helpless cause."

"Edmund is very skilled at many things," I boasted again. "He was the one who figured out the piece of the map was for the labyrinth."

"I have never heard of a labyrinth within Mercia's bounds," Adelaide replied.

"Only the oldest of legends mention it," Edmund explained. "But now we have discovered for ourselves that it does indeed exist."

Adelaide's sharp eyes took on an excited glimmer. I sensed we were kindred spirits in our love of adventure.

"By connecting your map to mine," I said, "we may possibly be able to reconstruct the rest."

"Then we will not need Emmeline's piece?" Christopher asked.

Edmund shook his head. "We might be able to make do without the third section, but we'll need her key. If the treasure is indeed hidden in the labyrinth, it will likely require all three keys to unlock."

"Perhaps we should go directly to find Emmeline and retrieve the last key," I suggested. "Especially since her key might be the only thing left standing between us and the hidden treasure."

Adelaide and Christopher shared a look.

"I am anxious to meet her as well," I added. She was, after all, my twin, and I was curious to see what she was like.

"I have several scouts searching for her," Adelaide said.

"Since we are still in Mercia, we may as well join the search."

"As much as I would like to find our sister, I have pushed my men to the limit of our supplies. If we had not spotted your light last night and located you this morn, we would have started the journey home."

I nodded in understanding. Edmund and I had quickly devoured the few food items Adelaide had given us. I could only imagine how hungry the men were on such low rations.

"Moreover," Adelaide said, "I must be forthright with you. There is another obstacle to the treasure besides Emmeline's missing key." She paused as though making certain she had both my and Edmund's attention.

"I'm sure there are many obstacles left to overcome," Edmund said, "many we won't know about until we come face-to-face with them."

"I no longer have my key." At Adelaide's admission, silence fell over us, except for the soft chatter of the soldiers at rest nearby and the whistle of the winter breeze.

I looked from Adelaide's stricken expression to Christopher's. "Then we shall find it. If we go back to the last place you had it and search, I am sure we can locate—"

"King Ethelwulf has it."

Her statement silenced us again.

"The explanation is much involved," she said finally, "one I shall divulge in due time. For now, however, we must be on our way to Norland."

I wanted to question her further, but at Edmund's touch to my arm and at the warning in his expression to let her go, I held back. As Adelaide and Christopher strode away, I told myself we would somehow recover the key from King Ethelwulf. That we could possibly still unlock the treasure without it. Or that Sister Katherine had been wrong and Adelaide didn't need the treasure to regain the throne.

But all my hopeful thinking didn't take away the premonition that claiming the treasure and throne would be harder—much harder—than any of us had imagined.

Chapter
16

EDMUND

AT DARK WHEN WE STOPPED TO MAKE CAMP, THE SOLDIERS WERE in high spirits over the game Sheba dropped at my feet as well as the buck Barnabas delivered. Maribel added to the feast with a savory soup made from edible roots.

I hoped with our contribution we'd gain the goodwill of the men and that they'd forget about our indiscretions. However, the moment Maribel joined Adelaide in her tent for the night, Christopher sat down by the fire next to me and spoke of it straightaway.

"How long have you loved Maribel?" His dark eyes were trained on the dancing flames, but like me, the rigidness of his posture told me he was alert to every sound and movement in his periphery. Even though the night was black and starless, the firelight illuminated the crags that formed a buffer from the wind.

I noticed he hadn't asked whether I loved her, only how long. Were my feelings that evident? Whatever the case, I decided honesty with this powerful nobleman was best. He seemed like the kind of man who'd be able to decipher the truth whether I admitted it or not. "I cannot remember a time when I haven't loved her."

"Were you not chaperoned at the convent?"

At his insinuation of further impropriety with Maribel, my gut tightened at the same time as my fist. I had to bite back the need to swivel and punch him. "I would not have you dishonor Maribel's good name."

"You have already dishonored her with your actions." His voice was hard and unrelenting.

Thankfully, the soldiers were talking around a second fire a short distance away and were oblivious to our tense conversation.

If I had any hope of freeing Maribel from marrying me against her will, I needed to explain the true nature of our relationship. "Maribel was not aware of my love for her until this week. Before then, she saw me only as a brother and friend."

"What changed?"

"Facing death makes a man say and do things he might not otherwise." My mind replayed the moment at the end of the labyrinth when the ground began to crumble beneath my feet, how I'd leaped in the air and thrown myself away from the gaping hole to keep the stones from burying me. "Overcome with the relief of cheating death, I kissed her. I couldn't hide my feelings any longer."

"And you discovered she felt the same for you?"

I shook my head. "She may care about me, may even feel something for me. But it cannot compare with my devotion to her."

"She loves you too. Everyone can see it."

My heart gave an extra beat at his observation. Even if he was right, however, it couldn't stop me from trying to clear her name and give her the freedom to continue her work as a physician. "Maribel is a naturally loving person. But her love for me isn't strong enough for marriage." I met Christopher's gaze, hoping he'd see the truth of my words.

"With time, her love will grow stronger."

"With time, she will grow to despise me if I trap her into a union." Although I'd marry Maribel in the blink of an eye, I'd never force her. Nor would I allow the queen to force her.

"You should have thought of that when you slept with her."

"Nothing happened between us. We were both cold and exhausted. I did what I could to protect her and keep her warm."

"And that involved kissing her again?" Christopher was direct and truthful. Under normal circumstances, I would have appreciated his frankness. But not at this moment, not when so much was at stake.

"I was half asleep and didn't realize what I was doing." I lied, of course. Perhaps Maribel had still been half asleep, but I'd been fully awake and had known exactly what was happening. If we hadn't been in imminent danger, I wasn't sure I could have resisted her for long. Even though I'd vowed not to kiss her again. "It was a mistake."

"Now you must rectify that mistake."

Dried brush in the fire crackled, shooting sparks into the air and reflecting the unsettled emotions sparking inside me. I chose my next words carefully. "You must know I desire nothing more than to marry Maribel. But she wishes to become a nun so she can continue using her abilities as a physician. She's spent years perfecting her medicines and learning her skills. God has gifted her, and she doesn't want that to be for naught."

"She can marry you and still help heal others."

"Very few would accept a woman physician. She'd likely be shunned. However, if she becomes a nun, people will more readily look to her for healing."

Christopher stared into the fire as though contemplating my words. Finally, his shoulders relaxed, and he made himself more comfortable against a boulder. "I would like to disagree with you, but I am afraid people are established in their ways. She would face many prejudices and obstacles as a woman practicing medicine."

"Precisely."

"I regret she will have to give up her aspirations."

"Would you have the woman you love give up her aspirations for you?"

Christopher glanced to the tent where the women had retired. The hard lines around his eyes softened. "Never."

I felt no need to respond, for my answer echoed his. Instead, I laid my head back and studied the darkness overhead, the thin layer of clouds and the faint light of the stars that lay beyond. The quietness of the night was eerie. Except for the voices of the soldiers around the fire, I heard none of the usual sounds from owls or bats or even wolves. This high, mountainous part of the Highlands seemed devoid of all life.

"I empathize with your dilemma," Christopher said. "But you must also comprehend the precarious nature of the rebellion. Adelaide needs the support from as many people as possible and can ill afford to alienate anyone with rumors of impropriety within her family."

"I do understand," I offered. A great deal more was at stake than just Maribel's dream of being a physician. As one of the lost princesses, she was now part of a larger plan, one that went beyond her personal goals to those of an entire nation. Mercia had languished far too long and required healing on a much bigger scope than she'd be able to provide as a physician.

"We all must make sacrifices." Christopher's voice was tinged with the sadness of one who'd already suffered. "And I am sorry for Maribel's sake that she will have to sacrifice her ambition. But you must convince her that her goal now lies not in healing just a few but in seeing all of Mercia whole and healthy."

His words echoed my thoughts. They resounded with both wisdom and truth, and I realized he was a man I could respect. He was clearly an honorable and wise advisor to the queen.

"If for no other reason, you must persuade Maribel for her own safety."

"Her safety?"

"Ethelwulf sought Adelaide so he could wed her to his son, Prince Ethelrex. By such a union, he hoped to end the rebellion."

My heart thudded faster. Colette had spoken of the king's intentions, but I'd put them from my mind, too busy with trying to survive to give her words credence. Apparently, I needed to be more vigilant than I'd realized. "Since the queen is now wedded to you, then you believe Ethelwulf will attempt to capture Maribel for the prince?"

"I have no doubt of it."

I blew out a tight breath. I couldn't let Maribel fall prey to his plans. "I understand the gravity of the situation. However, Maribel can persuade others but is not easily persuaded herself."

"Then she resembles her sister," Christopher said wryly.

I bent forward and tossed several more handfuls of brush onto the fire, knowing we needed to turn in for the night but not quite ready for our conversation to be over.

"They are both strong and beautiful women," Christopher added. "And they will not be tamed. Nor should they be. Even so, there are ways to soften their wills."

"Soften? How?"

Christopher grinned. "You will learn."

I thought to the kisses in the labyrinth, to the way Maribel had melted in my arms. "I don't want to manipulate her."

Christopher's grin widened. "I could never manipulate Adelaide, nor would I dare try."

"Then what would you suggest?"

"A little affection can oft go a long way."

A little affection? I could show my affection, couldn't I?

The nuns had indulged Maribel's whims, as had I. She'd grown up sheltered, among a community who loved her and would never harm her. As a result, Maribel loved and trusted freely. And I didn't want to do anything that might jeopardize her faith in me—especially coerce her into marrying me for her safety as well as the greater good of Mercia.

Yet, as much as I wanted to support her becoming a nun, I knew Christopher was right. Not only was her destiny intertwined with the queen's and Mercia's, but her safety was at stake. I couldn't allow Ethelwulf to force her to wed his son.

We had to get married. Soon. And when that moment happened, I wanted her to love me. She'd never be able to love me with the same fervor as I loved her. That would be impossible. But as Christopher advised, I needed to do more to claim her affection.

All these years, I'd remained silent and patient in my feelings for her. Was it time to finally pursue her with more ardor, to be more vocal and demonstrative? If she saw how much I loved her, perhaps she'd love me in return and be able to willingly give up her goal of becoming a nun. It wouldn't be easy and she'd miss her work. But would my love for her be enough?

I'd have to try to win her. It was the only thing left to do.

At first light, we departed. Once again I rode with Maribel, squeezed behind her in the saddle. She was drowsy and leaned her head against my shoulder as though she would sleep longer.

For a minute, I held myself away from her, just as I had yesterday. But after a few moments of trying to maintain my distance, my new resolve from the previous night's conversation with Christopher needled me, reminding me I must make an effort to show her my attraction and woo her at the same time.

I wiggled my gloved fingers on my thigh, trying to gain the courage to reach for her hand and hold it in mine.

We rode behind Christopher and Adelaide again today, and though the shadows of the early morning shrouded the couple, I noticed the way Christopher had wrapped his arm around Adelaide's waist. He bent forward and murmured in her ear. She responded by leaning back into him as if she'd taken pleasure in his contact.

Did I dare follow Christopher's lead? Of course, he was married and had every right to hold his wife. But still, if I had any hope of winning Maribel, I needed to do more.

I stretched my fingers, and then before I could talk myself out of anything, I slipped my arm around her middle. The move seemed to jolt her awake. She started and stiffened.

Embarrassed heat climbed into my neck, and I was grateful for the shadows that hid my flush. I was tempted to withdraw, but I swallowed my timidity and leaned forward until my lips brushed her ear.

She sucked in a sharp breath, which told me she was fully awake now and aware of my nearness. She didn't move, as though waiting for me to do more.

But what? What should I do next? Perhaps say something?

My mind began to spin. What could I say to Maribel to show her my ardor? I hesitated, but then realized I was breathing in her ear, which was mortifying. I swallowed hard. "Have I ever told you how beautiful you are?"

Once the words were out, I wanted to slap my head. Couldn't I come up with something more original? More poetic? More chivalrous? Perhaps tonight at the campfire, I would ask Christopher for advice on how to woo a woman. I obviously had no skill at it.

To my surprise, Maribel's hand slipped over mine where it rested on her waist. Her fingers splayed against mine. I wished we weren't wearing gloves, that I could feel the smoothness of her skin. Nevertheless, warmth spread through my chest at the realization she hadn't pushed me away, that she'd even accepted my attention.

"You told me my hair was pretty the other day," she said, almost shyly. "But no, you have never mentioned that you think I am beautiful."

The heat in my neck rose higher. I wanted to find a way to lighten the mood, to shift the conversation to something playful, as I usually did when the topic turned too serious. But I was already wading into unfamiliar territory, and I couldn't back out now.

I bent in again to her ear. "You are, without question, the most beautiful woman I know."

She laughed lightly, a pleasant sound. "Edmund, you only know two women—Colette and me."

My mind flashed with a dozen witty responses, but I threw them all away. Instead, I pressed closer. "You are the only woman I need to know."

The seriousness of my tone must have surprised her as much as it did me because I could feel the quick catch of her breath again.

I didn't want to frighten her with an abundance of zeal all at once, so I sat up straight. I tried to think of something else to say, but my thoughts jumbled together so much that I almost missed Sheba's distant call.

The hint of warning penetrated my haze. I listened more carefully, and this time her communication was clear. Men were pursuing and closing in around us.

"Lord Langley," I shouted, urging my steed forward.

Christopher glanced at me over his shoulder.

"We need to prepare for battle. Ethelwulf's soldiers are nearly upon us from the southwest."

At my terse warning, Christopher reared his horse around and began issuing orders. His men immediately scattered to do his bidding. I scanned the surrounding area to find a safe place for the women. Up ahead sat a grouping of boulders. The formation of the rocks would provide a wall of sorts to shield them from arrows and any other dangers.

Even as I spurred the horse toward the safe spot, Sheba's squawk resounded closer. Christopher glanced up to the sky, apparently now hearing her. She flew high, circling above us.

"How much time do we have?" Christopher called as he scanned the rocky terrain, likely deciding where to position himself now that his knights were scrambling into places.

"A few minutes. Maybe a little longer." Sheba usually gave me more advance warning. My guess was that yesterday's hunting had worn her out, and she hadn't noticed the enemy's approach as early as she might have otherwise.

Christopher nodded curtly. "I shall remain hidden and take out as many as I can with my bow and arrow. You stay with Maribel and protect her."

"What about the queen?"

A glance around showed that Adelaide, with several other knights, was already riding back down the path we'd traversed.

"Firmin will defend her with his life." Christopher motioned toward the giant soldier galloping behind her.

"I'll protect her along with Maribel among those boulders yonder."

"If the battle becomes too dangerous, I shall bring her to you." With that, Christopher urged his horse toward higher ground.

Thankfully, Maribel didn't protest as we dismounted and took cover among the rocks. And I was grateful she was of the mind to hide away, unlike her sister who had plunged headlong into coming danger.

"Stay low and near the horse," I cautioned Maribel.

"And if anything happens to me, you must get back on and ride away as fast as you can."

I'd considered asking Sheba to carry Maribel, and perhaps I still would. Even if the eagle was weary, she could lift Maribel out of harm's way faster than the horse could.

"What about you?" Maribel crouched behind a boulder that was double her size.

I already had my sword in one hand and dagger in the other. Although my wounded shoulder ached, it was healing well thanks to Maribel's careful attention. I hoped I would find the strength I needed for the battle. "I'll be fine, Maribel. I may not have learned everything Wade tried to teach me, but I can fight well enough."

As I spoke, a cry of alarm rose into the air, the sign the enemy was upon us.

Chapter
17

Maribel

The battle echoed all around me. The clash of metal against metal, the pounding of hooves, the shouts of commanders, and the groans of the wounded and dying.

Terrified, I huddled in the spot where Edmund had insisted I wait. Although I couldn't see him, I knew he crouched nearby. He'd already engaged in combat with a soldier who'd ridden past. While I hadn't been able to see the fight from my hiding place, I'd heard every gravelly footstep, every clank of swords, and every grunt, even the one that told me Edmund had wounded his opponent.

When Edmund had checked on me a moment later, I'd wanted to throw my arms around him and demand he stay hidden with me. But the grim set of his lips and the crimson dripping from his sword had frozen me in my spot. The idea of men taking the lives of other men went against everything I'd ever learned and been trained to do as a healer.

Mostly, I was worried something would happen to Edmund, that he'd be hurt again.

Have I ever told you how beautiful you are? His words from earlier reverberated through my body. *You are the only woman I need to know.*

I wasn't sure what had prompted his boldness, but his declaration had done something to my insides I couldn't explain, almost as if they'd expanded within my chest, making the space there larger and in need of more of him.

Shutting my eyes and fingering my rosary, I lifted a prayer for him, for Adelaide, for all the rebels. I'd already come close to losing Edmund on several other occasions over the past week. I didn't want anything to happen today.

At a crunching step behind me, my eyes flew open. Before I could turn, a gloved hand slid over my mouth as the scent of leather and horseflesh assaulted my nostrils. The strong hand bruised and nearly suffocated me with the pressure as I was dragged backward.

It took several seconds for my mind to register what was happening, that the enemy had discovered my hiding place and had crept in from behind. Once the realization hit me, I started to kick and twist and cry out, even though the sound was muffled.

A sharp prick against my spine stopped me. "Don't fight me, Your Highness," came a low voice. "You'll fare much better if you cooperate."

As my captor began to force me back once more, I ceased my struggle, the painful tip of a knife urging me to submit and move faster.

Sheba cried out and circled overhead. Had she seen my predicament? I willed her to swoop down and carry me away.

"Shoot that eagle," my captor issued the command, "before it causes us any more trouble."

"No!" I screamed, but the hand cupped across my mouth stifled the sound.

"Ah," my captor sneered. "The eagle is your pet?"

"Maribel!" Edmund shouted, racing around the boulder.

The prick in my back moved to my throat right beneath my chin. "Don't come any farther," my captor said. "Or I'll take pleasure in carving the princess up."

Edmund halted. He was only a dozen paces away, and yet it felt like a league. In an instant he took in the situation, his eyes flickering to me, my captor, and then behind me. The lines in his face hardened, and his shoulders stiffened. He gave a sharp whistle just as the twang of an arrow punctured the air.

I couldn't lift my head, but at the angry oath from the bowman, I guessed he'd missed Sheba.

"Let the princess go, Theobald," Edmund demanded in an unyielding tone, one I'd never heard him use before.

Theobald? The captain who'd murdered Edmund's family?

The captain's grip remained unrelenting. "So Princess Constance decided to have a Fera Agmen guard her sister."

Apparently, King Ethelwulf's people still called Adelaide by the name our parents had given her. And they apparently also refused to acknowledge her title as queen.

"Your skills might have given you a warning of our advance," the captain continued with his condescending tone, "but it won't prevent us from taking what we came to get." He jerked me back painfully, and the rocks that scraped against my legs caused me to cry out.

At my muffled sound of pain, Edmund aimed his knife at the captain.

The man gave a low chuckle as though amused by Edmund's display of valor. Then, as he jerked me again, he spoke to the two knights accompanying him. "Kill him."

"No!" I screamed against my captor's hand, thrashing now, heedless of the knife at my throat. I needed to free myself and come to Edmund's aid.

But Captain Theobald yanked my arm behind my back, twisting it tightly. I screamed in agony, unable to see or think or breathe for several long moments. He hadn't dislocated the bone, but it hung in the balance. And I had the feeling he'd done so intentionally. He was clearly the expert on how to instill fear and pain.

"You've given me quite the chase, Princess Maribel," he said close to my ear. "If the king wasn't anxiously awaiting your appearance at court so that you could marry the prince, I'd make you pay for all the men you've cost me."

As he dragged me along with him, the pain became so excruciating I wavered on the brink of unconsciousness.

EDMUND

As much as it enraged me to allow Theobald to drag Maribel away, I had no choice at the moment. If I acted too soon, he'd call for reinforcements, and then I'd be even more outnumbered.

His two men lumbered my way, knives and swords drawn, although the smirks on their faces told me they didn't consider me a threat. Like the rest of the king's elite guards, they were handpicked from among the largest, strongest, and most physically fit men in the land. At a young age, they'd entered special training for pages and squires. Upon knighthood, like Wade, they'd committed to serving the king with their lives, ready to die in the line of duty if need be.

I was neither large nor muscular the way they were, the way Wade had been. But I was still adept with my weapons. And quick.

Even so, I needed the element of surprise if I had any hope of rescuing Maribel.

I tried to reassure myself Theobald wouldn't harm her the way he had my family. As Christopher had pointed out, Maribel was an important commodity in the fight over Mercia's throne. If King Ethelwulf married his son to one of King Francis's daughters, one of the lost princesses, he'd solidify his family's hold on the throne and undermine Adelaide's claim.

Even though I told myself Theobald wouldn't dare harm Maribel, at least severely, his sneering face continued to flash in my mind—the same madman who had shown delight in slitting open my father's abdomen and torturing him was the same one pressing a knife against Maribel's unblemished throat.

I adjusted my grip on my knife and took aim at the weak spot in the right guard's armor. My fingers twitched to toss the weapon, but I forced myself to wait.

"You better call upon your eagle to help you," one of the soldiers said as he crept closer.

I'd considered it, but the bowman who had shot at Sheba before was likely still among the boulders and would take aim at her again the moment she appeared.

In the distance, Theobald rounded a tall wall of boulders. The instant he disappeared from sight, I sprang into action. First, I flung the knife. It rolled through the air end over end with a speed and precision the guards didn't see coming. Before they could show their surprise, the knife sliced into the right guard's throat, and he fell lifeless, his eyes still open but unseeing.

The second guard hesitated, his gaze following his dead companion's path to the ground. It was the instant of advantage I needed. I charged forward with my sword aimed at the other weak spot in a knight's armor, the slight opening in the armpit. When the guard raised his arm in self-defense, I jabbed low and hard, piercing sideways so the blade wedged between his ribs and into his heart.

He, too, dropped without uttering a sound. I prayed the lack of noise from the fight wouldn't alert Theobald. I'd count on his arrogance and his belief that his strong and competent guards would obliterate me before I could protest.

I wasted no time in retrieving my weapons. As I rose,

my gaze snagged upon the pointed ears and long snout poking out from a nearby clumping of stone. "Barnabas."

The wolf perked up and yipped at me, chastising me for not responding to him when he'd called. I'd been too consumed with Maribel to pay attention to anything else.

At the thought of Theobald and any more of his men lurking nearby, I growled at Barnabas. "Go away. It's too dangerous for you here."

He growled back in a low, menacing tone that was laced with his frustration with me.

I didn't have time to fight with Barnabas right now. "Go on," I commanded as I sprinted the way the captain had disappeared with Maribel, needing to catch Theobald before he reached the rest of his army.

When I rounded the bend, Theobald was only ten paces away, dragging Maribel by her arm, which hung at an odd angle—one that would allow him to manipulate her painfully but not cause any permanent damage.

Ahead was the bowman, climbing away with his back facing me. Evidently, the archer believed his companions would be able to kill me easily as well. I took aim with my dagger and released it. The knife impaled him and brought him down in an instant.

At the sight of his companion on the ground, Theobald spun. His eyes rounded with surprise as he took me in, unscathed and with my sword drawn. For just a heartbeat, he couldn't mask his shock over my defeat of his elite soldiers. But then, his expression transformed into anger, even rage, at the realization I'd outwitted him.

He pinched Maribel's arm tighter, causing her to moan in her half-conscious state.

Though I wanted to charge forward and skewer him on the end of my sword, I schooled myself into impassivity. If he learned I loved Maribel—that I cared for her even a fraction of what I did—he'd have absolute power over me. He'd use her to bend me to his will. And then I'd never be able to free her.

"Who are you?" he asked, studying my face closely, likely looking for any weakness.

I pretended to examine his face just as carefully, although I didn't need to. His ugly scar and pointed black beard, the tightly woven warrior braids across his scalp, the dark bottomless eyes—I'd lived with the image of him embedded into my worst nightmares these many years.

"I am Edmund Charles Chambers of Chapelhill." I waited for recognition to spark. But there was nothing, which only fueled the bitterness I held for this man. He'd slaughtered my family and didn't even remember it. My noble father, my kindhearted mother, and my four older siblings had been nameless faces to him, mere pawns in a political game. They'd meant nothing except for the twisted pleasure he'd derived in hurting them.

"You have been the Princess Maribel's guard all these years?" He slipped his hand toward his belt, no doubt to reach for his dagger.

In two strides I had my sword pointed against his heart. With his hold on Maribel, he was crippled, although I couldn't underestimate this man. I'd be wise to kill him now before he could act.

But a part of me wanted him to know exactly why I was killing him. I dropped my sword to his hand and sliced through his glove, drawing blood. "Don't move again or you'll lose your hand."

Maribel moaned once more. Even though I burned with the need to free her, I continued my ruse of impassivity.

"I can see you've had exceptional training," Theobald said casually. He was using the tactic of stalling. It was one Wade had taught me as well.

"I suppose I have you to thank for my training." The bitterness that had festered in my heart oozed into my voice.

His fingers twitched, and I pushed the tip of my sword deeper into his hand. The strain of the muscles in his neck was the only indication of the pain I was causing him.

"Yes," I continued, "if not for you murdering my family, I wouldn't have been an orphan, wouldn't have been rescued by one of King Francis's elite guards, and wouldn't have been trained at the Highland Convent as both a warrior and Fera Agmen."

If my words startled him, he didn't give any hint. Like me, he was probably skilled at hiding his true emotions. "Chambers of Chapelhill . . ." He spoke the name slowly as if trying to place it.

Then his lips curved into a cold, heartless smile, one that made his eyes darker and more dangerous. "I know why that name sounds familiar. Because I just recently executed your grandfather for turning against King Ethelwulf and giving aid to the rebellious Princess Constance."

My grandfather? Although he'd been away visiting his smelters in Middleton when we'd been arrested, my father had learned through other prisoners that Grandfather had been killed upon his arrival home to Chapelhill.

Why, then, was Theobald speaking of Grandfather as though he'd survived? Was it possible he'd been alive all these years and I hadn't known it? And now Theobald had murdered him too?

Rage swelled deep inside my chest. From Theobald's widening smile, I guessed my expression was no longer emotionless, that my surprise and anger were written there, and that I'd given him the reaction he'd wanted.

I couldn't restrain the bitterness I'd harbored for this man. With a roar that contained my hatred, I swung my sword toward his throat. I wanted him to pay for all the hurt he'd caused my family and me.

Before the blade could make contact, Theobald kicked my feet from beneath me, knocking me sideways and throwing me to the ground.

Even as my shoulder and arm landed, a sickening realization pooled in my gut. Theobald had known mentioning my grandfather's death would tempt me as nothing else would. I'd let down my guard. I'd allowed my feelings—namely my need for revenge—to cloud my judgment. And now, I'd most likely lost Maribel in the process.

Though the impact of the hard earth jarred my wounds and took away my breath, I rolled and sprang up. Before I could straighten, Theobald shoved me down and pressed his knife against my throat. A piercing pain was followed by the warm trickle of blood over my collarbone.

I grasped for my sword, but I'd lost it during my fall, and it lay too far away.

Even as I strained, Theobald's blade sank deeper, burning hot. His grin inched higher, and his eyes probed mine as though to see into my soul. "It's always a pleasure to take care of unfinished business. I'm not sure how you escaped the punishment your family deserved, but you'll escape no longer."

He released his knife from my throat and lifted it in readiness to plunge it into my heart. It was my only chance. As he brought the knife down, I threw him off balance and rolled sideways so that the weapon clanked onto the rocky ground where I'd lain seconds earlier.

I scrambled toward my sword. But before I could reach it, Theobald screamed out. I spun to see that Maribel had plunged a dagger into his back. Somehow during my struggle with Theobald, she must have regained consciousness enough to crawl to the bowman, pull out his dagger, and now had used it to help save me.

She took a quick step away from Theobald, her face filling with horror, her eyes wide upon the weapon protruding from him.

Theobald's pain seemed to turn him into a rabid animal. He bellowed, then swung out and slapped Maribel's face with the back of his hand. She cried out and fell to her knees, blood spurting from her nose.

I used the moment of his distraction to pick up my sword and leap toward him. As I raised my weapon against him, he pivoted and met it with his own. Even with a dagger in his back, I only needed one parry to realize his sword-fighting skills surpassed mine. Although I could defend myself well enough, I sensed I wouldn't win this battle unless I wore him down. With his blood loss and injury, it was my only hope.

I heard Barnabas growl before I saw him. I didn't have time to tell him to stay away. He attacked Theobald from behind. At the moment the wolf sank his fangs into Theobald's thigh where he lacked chainmail, I realized my animal friend was offering up his life for mine, for he would surely sustain mortal wounds unless I disarmed Theobald.

With a shout of protest, I lunged toward Theobald just as he pivoted to strike Barnabas. The momentum of my hit forced Theobald's sword out of his hand. It clattered to the ground and skittered away from him.

I sliced my sword into Theobald's fighting arm and then gorged his other, incapacitating him. All the while, Barnabas dug his fangs in deeper.

As I withdrew my sword and prepared to strike another blow, Theobald buckled to the ground and tried to crawl away. But he was weakening from his injuries and couldn't get far before Barnabas growled and tore into Theobald's thigh in a different spot, causing the captain to cry out again.

"I'll have the wolf rip you apart in little pieces!" I yelled. "It will be a slow, agonizing death, just the kind you deserve after the way you tortured my father."

"No, Edmund!" Maribel stared at Barnabas and Theobald, her face pale, almost sick.

"He deserves it," I said bitterly. I growled low in my throat and told Barnabas to feast upon Theobald's flesh.

The wolf growled in response and began to tug at Theobald's leg, wrenching it back and forth as though to cleave it from his body.

"Edmund, please!" Maribel turned her eyes upon me with the full weight of her revulsion. "You are a better man than this, than him."

I watched as Theobald writhed with agony, his blood pooling on the rocks beneath him. I was justified in seeing him die this way, wasn't I? He'd brutally killed my family. And he'd admitted to murdering my grandfather. Surely, he was better off dead so he could no longer inflict his terror upon innocent people.

Barnabas again tore viciously at Theobald, this time lower in the leg. The captain arched up in agony, his breath and moans gurgling in his throat.

Maribel's blue eyes pleaded with me. Tears streaked her cheeks, along with the blood that trickled from her nose. "I understand why you want to hurt him. But giving in to revenge will not release the bitterness. Revenge only feeds the hate until it grows like mold, turning your heart black."

I didn't care about my heart turning black. All I wanted was for Theobald to die a torturous death. But Maribel's tears moved me. I didn't want to disappoint her, didn't want her to look at me with revulsion any longer, didn't want to lose her trust and faith—not when I needed to win her love.

My muscles tightened with resistance, but I somehow managed to order Barnabas to pull back. He ceased his slow torture and glanced up at me, his sharp teeth still deep into Theobald's calf. Blood covered his snout and fangs. His eyes were wild, and he growled a protest. He'd already gotten the taste of blood and didn't want to let go of his prey.

His instinct mirrored mine, but I issued another command, this one sharper than the last.

The wolf reluctantly released Theobald, who now lay motionless on the ground. If he wasn't unconscious yet, he was close to it and would soon die, whether Barnabas killed him or not. The captain had already lost a great deal of blood, his injuries were severe, and he was alone and separated from his men.

Barnabas raised his head toward me. I praised him for saving my life, for helping to protect Maribel, and then I gave him the freedom to return to his family.

The wolf hesitated. I appreciated his loyalty and friendship. But he'd done more than enough for me over the past week. It was time for me to discharge him from any further obligation so he could live at peace. If he continued with me into Norland, I feared what might happen to him.

With a final good-bye, Barnabas trotted off and disappeared among the boulders as if he'd never been there.

Chapter 18

Maribel

Edmund scooped me up like a rag doll. I didn't protest since my legs felt as if they were made of flax. Though I'd readjusted my arm and shoulder, the area still burned as did my nose, which thankfully wasn't broken. I was also weak with relief—relief that Edmund and I were safe and relief that he'd stopped Barnabas from torturing Captain Theobald to death.

Perhaps the captain did indeed deserve to die for his crimes. However, torturing him wasn't the answer. If Edmund had continued, his actions would have caused a stain upon his conscience that would have haunted him forever.

When we returned to the sight of the skirmish, Christopher and Adelaide met us, their faces creased with worry. Edmund explained what had happened, and Firmin and several of his strongest guards rushed off to retrieve Captain Theobald, but upon finding him dead, they left his body for the vultures.

After wiping the blood from my face, I set to work

cleaning and stitching Edmund's neck. When I finished, I moved on to doctor the other soldiers who'd sustained wounds. With Adelaide's medical man, Darien, injured, no one complained or resisted my ministrations.

From what I gathered, Sheba's warning of the impending assault had allowed our rebel group to take an offensive position. They'd been able to attack King Ethelwulf's men first. The unexpected frontal assault had pushed the king's men back until finally the few soldiers who hadn't been struck down managed to escape.

"He is not one of ours," Adelaide called to me as I knelt in front of a wounded soldier who had propped himself against a rock. His ankle was twisted at an odd angle, and blood had pooled underneath. One of his arms also appeared to be broken, and he had a large gash on his forehead.

The soldier eyed me warily. Beneath the grime of travel and battle, his features were boyish, and I guessed he was my age or younger.

"Leave him," Adelaide said from where she and the others had begun to ready their horses. "His own will come back for him eventually."

"Then I shall staunch the blood flow to ensure his survival." I was already rifling through my medical bag for the supplies I would need.

I glanced to the battle area where a handful of enemy soldiers moaned in pain. Then I returned my attention to the young man in front of me. "Have no fear," I said gently. "I only want to help you."

I worked quietly for a few moments, feeling the boy's eyes upon me. When he stiffened, I glanced over my shoulder to see Adelaide standing behind me, her knife drawn. "You are disregarding my orders, Maribel."

"I cannot ignore these men."

"They are the enemy."

"Holy Scripture and our Lord Himself implores us to love our enemies and bless those who persecute us."

Adelaide was quiet for a moment, hopefully contemplating the Lord's command. Then she sighed. "We need to be on our way."

"We can spare a few more minutes, can we not?"

Again, she was silent. I could sense her men watching our interaction, waiting to see what the queen would decide. "Very well, Maribel," she said. "I shall spare you half an hour longer. King Ethelwulf may still have additional men in the area, and we cannot let down our guard."

I wanted to protest that I needed more time than that, but before I could, she knelt beside me. "It is not long, but with my aid, you will be able to accomplish more."

Her intense gaze met mine. There I saw a mixture of both compassion and kindness. "Instruct me on what to do, and I shall be your assistant."

My heart swelled with gratefulness. And for the first time since meeting my sister, I knew I'd love her. Heretofore, I'd seen her as a strong leader and a fierce warrior. Now I saw her as a wise and caring queen to whom I would gladly pledge my life.

Side by side, we worked to bring comfort to the wounded enemy soldiers. I quickly cleaned and stitched gashes, set bones in place, and bandaged lacerations. I cast Edmund a thankful smile when he followed us, giving sips of water to those too wounded and weak to fend for themselves.

When Christopher called for us to go, I rose and left the injured men behind even though it pained me to do so. Some would not last long without further medical attention. But I couldn't delay our entire company, especially since Adelaide had already compromised for me. I'd done all I could and must be content with that.

For a long while, Edmund and I rode silently. In some ways, I was in shock over all I'd seen, never having witnessed so much violence and bloodshed. A part of me was saddened by the destructiveness of men toward each other, the ease with which they could harm and slay one another, along with the bitterness and hatred that could fester.

Edmund's face, taut with hatred, haunted me. I'd only ever seen him calm and in control of his emotions. So, having witnessed the killing glimmer in his eyes, the bitterness in his voice, and the coldness with which he'd stood by and watched Barnabas maul the captain was so unexpected I wasn't sure I knew my friend anymore.

I shifted in order to glimpse his profile. The muscles in his jaw and chin were taut and his lips pursed into a tight line. His expression contained a hardness that hadn't been there before, as if he, too, had been changed by what he'd experienced today.

As if sensing my attention upon him, he dropped his gaze to my face. I was afraid of what I'd see in his eyes and was happy the green radiated with warmth. When he managed a smile, albeit a small one, my happiness expanded.

I smiled in return. "You are not too peeved with me?"

His expression finally gentled. "I'm proud of you. You not only showed great courage in the face of danger, but you also gave love and compassion to the king's men, who have offered you nothing but threats."

"'It is more blessed to give than to receive,'" I said, quoting one of the many Scripture verses Sister Agnes had taught us.

He reached for my hand, and I gladly welcomed his hold, although I couldn't stop from thinking about the way he'd wound his arm around my waist earlier in the day and the way he'd spoken in my ear, when his intimate tone and breath had caused my insides to tremble.

Our pace was less brutal than yesterday's, but we still rode with urgency. The cold winter wind had given way to a warmer breeze, and with the brightness of the sun overhead, it was easy to believe spring was drawing nigh, although in the Highlands, the weather could change without notice.

I reclined against him, closed my eyes, and let the rays of rare sunshine warm my face.

Edmund's fingers laced through mine. "I almost lost you," he whispered against my temple.

When the captain had dragged me off, I'd thought my fate sealed, that I would have to marry King Ethelwulf's son. "Thank you for coming after me," I whispered. "You saved me from having to get married."

Edmund tensed. "Maribel," he said, hesitantly. "I spoke with Christopher last night."

"I like him. He is kind and sweet to Adelaide."

"He's also shrewd and knowledgeable."

"Together they make an impressive ruling team."

"Then you're willing to follow their leadership and support their cause?"

"Of course." Adelaide had more than proven herself to me. After all the risks she'd taken riding into Mercia to rescue me, how could I not follow and support her?

Edmund took a deep breath. "Even if that means you must get married?"

"There is no need," I replied. "Once I become a nun, I can support Adelaide, perhaps even more so."

"Maribel," Edmund said, his voice wistful, almost sad. "After speaking with Christopher and understanding what is at stake, I believe your destiny is intertwined with your sisters. You must work with them, as Sister Katherine indicated, to restore Mercia."

"I shall do so gladly."

"Then will you gladly do what you can to keep Adelaide's reputation and the cause unblemished from any taint of misconduct?"

As I realized what he was asking of me, a twine seemed to wrap around my middle and form a tight knot. "I thought you understood how I felt. And I thought you would support me."

"I do understand." He bent in so that his breath tickled the loose strands of my hair at my neck. "But Mercia is suffering. The people are languishing. Perhaps God is calling you to a greater healing purpose as a princess than you can accomplish as a nun."

I let Edmund's words settle inside me. I sifted and sorted them. And he pressed no further. As sensitive as always, he knew I needed time to think and pray.

By the end of the long day, when we neared the outer edge of the Highlands, I'd laid to rest my plans and dreams of becoming a nun and physician. Edmund—and Christopher—were right. I might not be able to practice the medicine I loved to the extent I'd always wanted to. But I had to acknowledge I'd been born for something greater—healing a nation that was dying under a dark grip and saving a people trapped and afflicted and scarred with festering wounds.

When we stopped to make camp for the night, I spent the last of the daylight hours doctoring those who'd been injured in the battle. I was nearly out of my healing lotion by the time I approached Edmund where he helped to roast the prey Sheba had caught, along with a buck one of the expert bowmen had shot.

The food rations Edmund and I had split earlier in the day hadn't been nearly enough to satisfy the rumble of hunger in my belly. And now the smoky waft of roasting meat beckoned me.

"Your turn," I said, lifting my small crock. With Darien yet weak from his injuries, surely Adelaide couldn't object to my tending to Edmund's wounds—at least not tonight.

"I am faring well enough." In the twilight, his lean but wiry frame stood out against the backdrop of the dark hills. His windswept hair and unshaven face lent him a ruggedness that was different, though not unpleasant.

"I shall not take no for an answer." I couldn't stop from admiring the deftness of his movements and the way his body was built. He was a good-looking man in every way, and my stomach fluttered with a strange desire for him.

At the waywardness of my thoughts and longings, a flush infused my cheeks. Attempting to put on the physician role that would make me impartial to my patients, I tugged him away from the roasting spit he'd put together and made him sit. He didn't resist as I cleaned the wound on his neck and then tended his shoulder. I worked in silence, not quite sure how to bring up the issue from earlier and yet knowing he was too kind to push me to talk before I was ready.

As he stood to return to the fire pit, I stopped him with a touch to his arm. "Edmund," I said softly, the darkness of the oncoming evening giving us some privacy. "I am prepared to accept a new future."

He hesitated. "Are you certain?"

I nodded. "I shall miss the life I thought I would have. But if this is what God desires, then He will help me find contentment."

Edmund searched my face. When his shoulders slumped a moment later, I guessed he hadn't found what he'd been looking for. I wanted to apologize, but I had no idea for what.

"Am I making the right choice, Edmund?" I asked, as uncertainty rushed in.

"I wish we had the freedom to make whatever decisions we wanted," he replied. "But sometimes life chooses a course for us, and then we must make the best of what we're given."

"Do you not desire to marry me, then?" I'd assumed he was willing, had perhaps even wanted it. Had I read more into his words and actions than he'd intended? Was it possible he was marrying me out of obligation too?

"I'd hoped you'd learn to love me first," he

whispered, almost as if he was embarrassed to say the words. "But since that doesn't appear likely, I'll pray that perhaps someday you will."

"I do love you." I reached for his hand and clasped it.

He pried his away. "Of course you love me, Maribel, as a friend and my sister. And perhaps you even harbor some affection for me. But you do not love me the way I've always loved you."

Colette's words came back to haunt me. *She will never love you the way you love her. She is too caught up in her own life to think about anyone else.* Colette hadn't believed I'd be able to make Edmund happy. Was she right?

"I shall try, Edmund." I took hold of his arm, clinging to him. "I shall do all I can to make you happy."

He didn't pull away again, but I could sense a distance between us that hadn't been there before, that perhaps his disappointment had taken up residence in that space.

"Please," I said. "I could not bear to earn your censure or to have things change between us."

He sighed and then brushed his free hand across my cheek. "None of this is your fault. Have no fear. We'll get along as we always have. I promise."

I smiled up at him, hopeful. "Good. If I must marry, I can think of no one else I would want to spend my life with than you."

I meant my words to reassure him, but again, as before, his shoulders deflated. And this time when he moved to return to the fire, I didn't stop him.

A short while later, as I huddled in my bedroll next

to Adelaide in our tent, she grasped my hand. "I was proud of you today, Maribel. You showed love to our enemy and urged me to do the same. And I thank you for the reminder."

The darkness of the night prevented me from seeing her face, but I could feel her warmth beside me. I relished this time we had before falling asleep, these few minutes of conversation. She'd shared about her life growing up with the Langleys and everything that had transpired last summer after Sister Katherine had visited her with the news regarding her royalty. Likewise, I'd told her all about my childhood with the sisters at the convent.

"I have resigned myself to giving up my pursuit of becoming a nun," I whispered. "And I shall willingly marry Edmund."

She didn't reply. I'd come to understand from our conversations as well as from watching her that she valued wisdom above all else. She'd confided in me how she'd prayed the ancient words of King Solomon, that God would bless her with the gift of wisdom more than wealth, health, and valor.

From everything I'd witnessed, I knew God had indeed answered her prayers. Adelaide acted shrewdly and decisively and justly, with more wisdom than even the wisest of the nuns I'd known.

After a long pause, she finally replied. "If your healing abilities are truly a gift from God, let us pray He will open a way for you to use your gift no matter where you are or who you are with."

My fingers slipped to my rosary. I would pray, for it was all I had left.

Chapter 19

EDMUND

WE CROSSED INTO NORLAND BY MIDDAY. ALTHOUGH THE TERRAIN remained rugged and rocky, our gradual descent from the higher elevations was marked by warmer air and an easier trail. Eventually, we passed through the timberline that was thick with evergreens and a few deciduous trees.

The knights were lighter in spirit for prevailing in their mission to find Maribel and for defeating Ethelwulf's forces yesterday. There was also plenty of talk about the feasting that would occur once we reached Brechness, Norland's capital city.

I empathized with the plight of the soldiers, for my stomach ached with the need for sustenance. However, my heart ached much more.

You saved me from having to get married. Maribel's declaration reverberated in my head. It was a constant reminder that even if she'd given up her plans for becoming a nun and resigned herself to marrying me, she didn't *want* to be married—not to me, not to anyone.

Yes, she loved me and would do her best to be

content with our marriage. She wasn't the type of woman to be spiteful or bitter, and she would try to find the positive in whatever circumstances came her way. But her love and her desire would never be equal to mine, no matter how much I might try to win her affection and her heart.

I had to resign myself to the reality that had been there all along. Although part of me ached for more, I could do nothing less than go on loving her, even though she might never reciprocate the same way. I'd continue to accept her for who she was, and I'd have to be satisfied with what she was able to give me, even if it would never be enough.

"Upon our arrival in Brechness, you will be married with all haste," the queen said in answer to Maribel's question about our upcoming nuptials as we rode next to the royal couple. "No later than the day after we arrive."

"So soon?" Maribel's question contained a note of distress that pricked my already sore heart.

"Yes. Then, once we have time to make the arrangements, we shall host a feast and dance for all the people to meet you."

"Are there many who have escaped from Mercia and now live in Norland?" Maribel asked.

"Those who openly support the rebellion have had to flee Ethelwulf's wrath," Christopher said from where he sat behind Adelaide. "But we know of many who remain in Mercia who will join with us when the time comes to march against Ethelwulf."

My grandfather had remained when he should have left. Anger burned like acid in my gut every time I remembered Theobald's confession of recently killing him.

"When shall we march against King Ethelwulf?" Maribel shifted against me in the tight confines of the saddle. The movement only made me want to wrap my arms around her, but I fought the longing.

"Our army is growing larger and stronger," the queen said. "But until we have the treasure, we have decided not to proceed."

"What difference will the treasure make?" I asked. The scent of pine and damp earth filled my nostrils and brought back dormant memories of riding through the forestland with my father and grandfather.

"We do not know exactly," Adelaide responded. "But according to the ancient prophecy, a young ruler filled with wisdom will use the ancient treasure to rid the land of evil and usher in a time of peace like never before seen or ever seen again."

"So you believe you must have the treasure in hand before you can rid Mercia of evil?" I pressed.

The queen nodded. "Sister Katherine also indicated the three of us sisters must work together if we hope to defeat King Ethelwulf."

"Perhaps if your scouts follow Sister Katherine, she will lead us to Emmeline."

"Unfortunately, we have lost her trail. She is skilled at evasion and masking her scent. As such, she likely will not allow us to find her again until the time is right."

On the northern breeze, I caught the distant but urgent communication of a horse. I sat up straighter and strained to listen.

"What is it?" Maribel asked, twisting to watch my face.

I peered ahead, but couldn't see the creature yet. Now that we were moving into the open country, the ground had leveled, and we'd left the rocks and snow behind.

Even most of the evergreens were behind us, too, as we entered the fertile farming plains that Norland was known for. This time of year, the ground was fallow and hard. But in a few weeks, the peasants would be out plowing in preparation for the spring planting.

The horse was still too far away to understand completely. Nevertheless, I sensed its urgency once more. "I believe a messenger is riding to us from the northeast."

"Then someone is coming from Brechness." Christopher narrowed his eyes upon the fields to the north. "Can you estimate the distance away?"

I listened again and shook my head. "Perhaps a quarter of an hour, maybe less."

I was right. Within a few minutes, a rider appeared on the treeless horizon, racing at full speed.

"A courier bearing King Draybane's standard," Christopher said. "Something must have happened for the king to send a messenger."

The queen and Christopher kicked their steed into a gallop and left us behind.

The level fields were dotted with clusters of trees that signaled creeks flowing out of the foothills. Everywhere we looked, the signs of life and color contrasted with what we'd known in the Highlands, and Maribel had been excitedly exclaiming over everything all day.

I thought back to her question the day we'd gone out to find valerian and had found Sister Katherine instead— the day that had changed everything. Maribel had asked me if I'd ever considered life beyond the Highlands. I'd told her I never wanted to be anywhere except with her.

It was still true. But a new discontentment had begun to settle inside me since our conversation of the previous evening. I wanted her to feel the same way I did. Even though I knew it wasn't fair of me to expect it from her, even though I'd stated my intentions—to her and to myself—to be satisfied with friendship, I still couldn't stop from wishing she never wanted to be anywhere except with me.

In little time, we caught up to the queen and Christopher, who had dismounted and were talking with the messenger. From the exhaustion lining his young face and the foam lathering his steed's mouth, he'd obviously ridden unceasingly to reach us. And from the creased foreheads and grave expressions of the royal couple, I guessed the news had not been good.

"'Tis the pale pestilence," the queen said. "The disease is sweeping through Norland and has already infiltrated the army."

I recoiled at the same moment as Maribel. We may have been sheltered, but like everyone else, we knew about the pestilence, how devastating it could be, and how quickly it could spread. The word itself was enough to instill fear in any heart.

Whenever there had been outbreaks of the pestilence, the news Wade had brought back to the convent had always been devastating and haunting—whole villages dying, entire city streets perishing, graveyards piled high with bodies waiting for burial.

Christopher met my gaze. "We must find a safe place for Adelaide and Maribel."

I nodded my agreement. Their well-being was of the utmost importance. We hadn't escaped Ethelwulf's clutches only to die in Norland from disease.

"We shall deliver Maribel to safety," Adelaide said, "but I shall proceed to Brechness straightaway and do what I can to be of assistance."

Christopher scowled. "You cannot risk it. You will be no good to the people and your army dead."

"The people and my army will not need me as queen if they all perish. After travailing to recruit and train our army, I cannot abide standing by and doing nothing."

The largest group of the queen's rebel army lived in barracks in Brechness alongside King Draybane's army. I could feel her desperation and fear at the possibility of the pestilence spreading among the men. The disease was no respecter of age, class, or profession. It could reap the seasoned warrior as easily as an infant.

If the pestilence infiltrated her knights, how would she be able to attack Ethelwulf? Her army, though growing, was not nearly as large or strong as Ethelwulf's. Even if King Draybane lent his men to her cause, she wouldn't outnumber Ethelwulf's seasoned army. Already, she was at a disadvantage and couldn't afford to lose a single man.

"King Draybane and the court have left Brechness by ship," the messenger said, "and are traveling south to Loughlin. He bids you meet him there and take refuge until the worst of the pestilence has passed."

"Yes," Christopher responded quickly. "Ride ahead to Loughlin. Inform the king we shall join him within a day."

The queen nodded to the knights who had reined a short distance back and now awaited the news. "Lord Chambers will accompany Princess Maribel, along with the rest of the men. But Lord Langley and I shall ride on to Brechness."

Christopher's expression was granite. "I shall speak with the queen in private." He grasped the queen's arm and led her a dozen paces away, not nearly far enough to conceal their animated and heated conversation.

As I helped Maribel down from our steed, she gripped

my hand with determination. "I must go to Brechness in my sister's stead."

"No, Maribel," I said. "You heard the queen—"

"You know as well as I do if anyone can lend aid, it is I."

"No one can stop the pestilence."

"I may not be able to stop it, but I may be able to ease the suffering of the dying."

"And risk catching it yourself?" I shook my head. "It's too dangerous."

Maribel observed the queen and Christopher argue a moment longer before clutching my hand harder and peering up at me with her beautiful, bottomless blue eyes. "If I go, then we might be able to persuade Adelaide not to."

The earnestness and sincerity of Maribel's statement reached inside and gripped my heart just as firmly as she held my hand.

"What if this is why I was born? What if this is why God allowed Sister Agnes to save me? So I could, in turn, save Adelaide?"

If Maribel wanted to make this sacrifice for her sister, how could I argue with her? Past experience had taught me not to. I didn't want her going to Brechness and submerging herself into a city riddled with the pestilence. But I wasn't forceful and outspoken like Christopher, whose frustration radiated from every tense muscle in his body.

I had no doubt he'd physically restrain the queen if he needed to. I, on the other hand, couldn't say no to Maribel, not even now when I wanted to.

Christopher jammed his fingers in his hair and shook his head.

"She will go unless I step in for her," Maribel whispered.

"He won't let her," I whispered back.

"Then at least her mind will be at ease to know I am in the city doing all I can for the sick and dying."

I nodded, and my chest swelled with love for this woman before me. This was one of the many reasons I treasured Maribel. Because she wanted to help others. She truly cared about the hurting and the hopeless. That's why I couldn't say no. I couldn't squelch her beautiful inner spirit.

"Your Majesty," I called. "My lord."

The couple glanced at me, their anger and frustration with each other evident in the way they stood apart, arms crossed, and shoulders stiff with defiance.

"Maribel and I shall go to Brechness in your stead," I said. The two began to protest, but I continued regardless. "Maribel is a skilled physician and may be able to provide comfort to the dying. She'll go and represent you among the people, spreading your goodwill and concern."

"I give you my word that I shall work day and night to bring relief," Maribel added. "I have developed many herbal remedies over the years that can reduce pain and perhaps even slow the spread of the disease."

This time neither spoke. Instead, they studied Maribel and me until I began to squirm under their scrutiny.

"I would not put the princess at risk any more than I would the queen," Christopher started.

"But it is a wise plan," Adelaide interrupted never taking her eyes from Maribel. "You will use your gift of healing to comfort the dying and bring order to the chaos. On behalf of King Draybane, we bestow upon you access to the royal apothecary along with any other supplies you may need."

Maribel bowed her head in subservience, but I could see the excited glimmer in her eyes. Even with the danger we would face, Maribel relished another adventure and the opportunity to help those in need.

As always, I'd be right by her side protecting her and shielding her and keeping her out of harm's way as best I could. I'd been her guardian since we'd been little. Perhaps that's all I'd ever be. And perhaps I'd have to be satisfied with that.

Chapter 20

Maribel

I knelt next to a dying soldier and swung an aromatic pomander above his head. I'd had dozens of waxy balls crafted and strewn through the barracks. Made with musk, ambergris, and civet, along with rosewater and aloes, the fragrance was meant to fend off disease. But so far it had failed to stop the spread of the pale pestilence, as had my other remedies.

I'd hardly slept since Edmund and I had arrived in Brechness two days ago. As one of King Draybane's primary residences and Norland's greatest seaport, the city was set upon rocky cliffs overlooking the East Sea. The high position provided a natural defense against King Ethelwulf, who had terrorized and attacked Norland oft throughout the years in his quest to gain all of the Great Isle.

The granite cliffs might have saved Brechness from King Ethelwulf, but they couldn't protect the city from the ravages of the pestilence. By the time we'd arrived, those who could flee from the city had, leaving behind the weak and infected, along with the poor and those who had no place else to go.

I lowered the pomander and rested a hand against the soldier's forehead. He shook with the chills even as his face perspired from fever. His arms and legs contained the telltale signs of death—pale, onion-sized lumps that were painful to the touch. His breathing was labored, and he coughed intermittently, beginning to spew blood. I feared there was nothing more that could save this soldier. He'd been ill when I'd arrived and would likely die soon. His body would be added to those already piled up outside the barracks awaiting transport to the cemetery.

I released a frustrated sigh past the mask of rosemary and flower petals that covered my nose and mouth. Then I moved to the soldier on the next pallet. The dining hall had been transformed into a makeshift infirmary and was now lined from wall to wall with infected men.

"You didn't expect to see me here this morning, did you, princess?" came the soft-spoken voice of Captain Colton, who'd greeted us when we'd first arrived at Brechness. He was a kind, middle-aged man who hadn't left the sides of his dying men over the past two days.

At the sight of him lying motionless on the floor, his weather-crusted face flushed with fever, I gave a cry of protest. "Not you, Captain Colton. You cannot get sick. We all need you too much."

He offered me a small smile, one that was tight with the pain he was attempting to hold back.

I turned to Edmund, who knelt next to me. He'd been with me every moment, following my instructions as he aided me in tending the patients. The dark circles under his eyes attested to his lack of sleep. Nevertheless, his expression contained a determination that matched mine, as well as compassion.

"What do you think?" I whispered. "Shall I try the new tonic on Captain Colton?"

I'd given the royal apothecaries detailed ingredients for several of the remedies I'd developed at the convent. Fortunately, the palace was stocked with every herb I'd ever heard about and even some I'd never known existed. The apothecaries had located all the dried herbs necessary to make my concoctions, including blessed thistle, butterbur, and cloves.

Yesterday, I'd administered the tonics and ointments among the soldiers at the barracks and then later at the cathedral where many of the sick and dying had been brought, hoping for a miracle.

But as far as I'd been able to tell, none of the remedies had made a difference. Dozens of people had died overnight anyway, and now their lifeless corpses awaited pickup from the grave diggers who came through town with their carts to collect and bury the dead. Smoke from the torches of burning juniper on every street corner could hardly mask the stench of death and decay.

In desperation, I'd spent all of last night working on my healing tonic, the one I'd been trying to perfect ever since it had failed to revive Sister Agnes. I'd combined many herbs including sage, rosemary, rue, camphor, garlic, clove, lemon, cinnamon bark, eucalyptus, and several very rare Eastern herbs.

As I'd worked, I'd been haunted by the possibility my tonic had actually accelerated Sister Agnes's death.

The wrong dosage of just one of the ingredients or the negative interaction of a compound with another could have a deadly effect.

Of course, I'd told myself Sister Agnes had been dying, that I couldn't sit back and simply watch her waste away without trying something. Even if my medicine had still been largely in its experimental phase, I'd needed to find a way to offer a remedy. Had I been wrong to test the medicine upon her?

Since that time, I'd made some adjustments in the tonic, but what if it still wasn't ready? What if it hurt rather than healed the sick?

Edmund's expression behind his rosemary-and-flower-petal mask was grave. I had no doubt he sensed my inner turmoil and understood it. "You've worked hard all these years to find the right ingredients in the right amounts." The mask muffled his voice. "These sick men will surely die without the medicine. They may still die with it. But you won't know until you try."

"What if it aids their dying or causes them more pain?"

"You've been careful, Maribel. Besides, if it does either of those things, it would be minuscule compared with their current pain and suffering."

Edmund's rationale calmed the nervous flutter in my chest. He held my gaze for a moment, the green of his eyes both soothing and encouraging. Then he handed me the bottle. His expression told me he believed in me and supported my decision.

I took the vial and nodded my thanks, hoping he could see how much I valued him. Returning my attention to Captain Colton, I uncorked the bottle. "Captain, you are a brave man. Would you be willing to take a dose of my latest creation? I cannot guarantee it will help you, but I would certainly like to try."

I hadn't been able to ask Sister Agnes for her permission, and I regretted that as well. She'd already been delirious by the time I'd decided to give her the tonic.

The captain's lips trembled before he replied. "I'd be honored to try, Your Highness." His eyes pinched closed, and the muscles in his face contracted with a fresh wave of pain. His chest began to rise and fall rapidly with the effort of breathing.

I poured a scant amount of the medicine into a tin cup. Edmund lifted the captain's head from his pallet, and I emptied every drop from the cup into his mouth before Edmund lowered him.

"Whatever happens, Your Highness," the captain rasped in a stilted voice, "you have brought comfort and peace and kindness in the midst of our turmoil and sorrows. That is truly enough. And we thank you for it."

It wasn't enough for me. I wanted to do so much more. I wanted to ease the suffering of the people. I wanted to represent Adelaide well and bring her honor. And I wanted to help save her army and, in doing so, salvage the rebellion.

For long minutes, I remained by the captain's side waiting for any sign the medicine might be working, praying it would at least bring him some relief from his pain. When he released a loud wheeze, my head jerked up, and I realized I'd fallen asleep in my exhaustion. I rubbed my bleary eyes and then gasped at the sight of the captain's nearly blue face.

"He's not breathing!" I called to Edmund. Without

waiting for Edmund's help or response, I shook the captain.

He didn't move, didn't breathe, didn't blink.

I felt for the pulse of life in his neck and his wrist but found none. I opened his mouth and checked for obstructions to his breathing but there was nothing. I pressed my ear against his chest and heard only silence in place of a beating heart.

He was dead.

I cried out in dismay. Had my tonic killed him?

The brown vial in my hands seemed to burn my flesh. Suddenly I hated it, hated myself, and hated medicine. Why had I ever thought I'd be good at being a physician? Why had I assumed I could bring healing to anyone? Why had I believed God had gifted me?

I hadn't been able to make a difference when it really mattered. I'd failed to develop a medicine that could truly help. In fact, I seemed to bring more trouble than good everywhere I went. After all, Edmund had been injured numerous times because of me. I'd even brought trouble to the sisters at the convent.

Would they all have been better off without me? With another cry, I raised the bottle, wanting to dash it to pieces against the wall.

Edmund's hold restrained me. "It's not your fault, Maribel. The pestilence took him, not the medicine."

"No, it was the medicine." Tears clouded my vision and brought an ache to my throat. I tried to throw the bottle again, but Edmund wrenched it from my hand.

Before I knew what he was doing, he uncorked it, pushed away his mask, lifted the vial to his lips, and took a long sip.

I screamed in panic and grabbed at the container. "No, Edmund! You must not have any!"

But I was too late. He swallowed hard and then tugged up his shirtsleeve revealing two pale, swollen lumps.

My heart ceased beating. "You have the pestilence." He nodded.

Only then did I notice the perspiration on his forehead, the tremor in his hands, and the pain in his eyes. He'd withheld the symptoms from me for hours. He'd stayed next to me faithfully tending the sick even though he'd been suffering himself.

My tears slipped over and a sob rushed out before I could stop it. I threw myself at him and clung to him. "No, no, no."

He slid his arms around me in return and hugged me as if saying good-bye.

The tears flowed faster. "Edmund, you cannot leave me. Please."

His hold sagged, and he swayed. I could sense he was losing consciousness, perhaps even losing his life the same way Captain Colton had.

He rested his head against mine. "I have loved you with all my heart, Maribel." His words were a breathless whisper. "And I always will."

Then his body slackened, and his dead weight pressed upon me.

Chapter 21

Maribel

Edmund was dead and I hadn't been able to say good-bye and tell him everything pouring into my heart—a cascade of overwhelming emotions, mainly that I loved him in return. Not merely as a friend and companion. Not merely as my brother. Not merely as a man. No, I loved him with my entire being, with everything that was within me.

Perhaps my love had always existed. Or perhaps it had been slowly growing. Whatever the case, I knew now that my selfishness had prevented me from acknowledging it. I'd been too consumed with my future ambitions. I'd been too caught up in what I'd wanted and hadn't considered his feelings or needs.

Now it was too late. I could only hold him as silent sobs wrenched my chest.

Suddenly I felt something. The faintest twitch in one of the muscles in his arm.

I sat up. Was he still alive?

When he released a soft moan, I gulped down my

sobs. "I need help with Lord Chambers!" I called to the servants who were present at the barracks and distributing bread and water to the patients well enough to eat. "He yet lives, and we need to transport him to the palace immediately."

An hour later, Edmund was still alive in his chamber. I hovered above him, wiping his forehead with a cool cloth. Across from me, a manservant bathed Edmund's arms and chest with cool water. Edmund's temperature was slowly dropping as the fever left his body. The pale lumps on his arms and legs also seemed to be diminishing in size, but I was afraid in my desperate need to see him well again, I was only imagining the change.

As I swayed in my exhaustion, a servant behind me offered me a chair, which I gratefully accepted.

"Allow me to bathe his forehead, Your Highness," the manservant said kindly. "Then you may rest."

I couldn't resist as he took the cloth from me. He dipped it into the basin of cool water on the bedside table and then gently wiped Edmund's face. My own hands free, I reached for one of Edmund's, bent down, and kissed it. As I did so, I laid my head on the feather mattress. The softness beckoned to me in my exhaustion and worry. I closed my eyes, only intending to rest for a few minutes. But I was asleep before I could take another breath.

"Maribel," a voice croaked my name.

I opened my eyes in a haze, trying to gain my

bearings. A strong, musky odor filled my nostrils. Was I in the apothecary room?

"You must go now," the voice said.

Go where? I blinked and tried to focus, but shadows surrounded me.

"Maribel." The voice became more insistent. Edmund's voice.

I jerked upright to find myself sitting in a chair at the edge of his bed. My gaze scrambled to find his. At the sight of his eyes wide open and peering back at me, I cried out with relief and delight and threw myself upon him.

"Oh, Edmund." I pressed my cheek to his and relished the scruffiness of his unshaven stubble against my skin. "I thought I'd lost you."

He coughed weakly.

I pulled back and quickly assessed the spots on his arm. From what I could tell, the nodules were smaller and the swelling was gone.

"The medicine worked," he whispered.

Had it? My pulse hummed with a new thrill. Was Edmund truly safe? At the very least, he was alive and his fever was gone.

How long had I slept? I glanced at the window to gauge the passing of time, but the thick tapestries were pulled to keep the pomander aroma within the chamber. The manservant from earlier was absent, but another servant stood near the door, watching and waiting for my instructions.

Edmund's gaze drifted to the servant before focusing on me again. "You need to distribute the medicine among the army and the people."

"I cannot leave you." I grasped his hand and

brought it to my lips. Touching a gentle kiss there, I allowed myself to love this man as I'd never done before. "You are more important to me than anything, even more than my desire to be a physician."

His beautiful green eyes captured mine in an intense connection.

"I want to be with you, Edmund," I whispered, knowing I was being bold. But after almost losing him again, I couldn't bear to leave him for even a minute. "We have much to speak about."

He squeezed my fingers, albeit weakly, before his lips curved into a smile—a smile which lit his eyes and brought life back to his features. "We'll have plenty of time to talk later. For now, you must have the apothecaries make more of your medicine and dispense it with all haste."

His admonition stirred my compassion for the people. I'd always thought I was pursuing my medical skills to help people and serve God. But over the past days, God had been showing me that I'd been more concerned about my own fulfillment and advancing myself. Could I move forward and do the work not for what I might gain but for what I might give?

"Go," Edmund said softly. "You'll be able to save many more if you hurry."

I nodded and stood, holding his hand a moment longer. I was tempted to ask him if he'd truly meant what he'd said earlier when he thought he was dying, when he'd told me he loved me with all his heart and always would.

But then I realized it didn't matter. Just as I'd been selfish about my desire to become an important physician, I'd been selfish in my relationship with

Edmund. I'd only focused on myself and what I wanted or needed from him. I hadn't thought about what he needed or what might make him happy. I had to learn to love unconditionally, without having to get something from him in return.

"God gave you the healing gift, Maribel," Edmund whispered. "When He gives you the opportunity to use it, you cannot say no to Him."

"You are right." Maybe I wouldn't use my gift the way I'd planned, but I could always be on the lookout for the work God would give me to do.

Apparently, satisfied with my answer, Edmund's lashes fell. From the even rise and fall of his chest, I could see he was slumbering again, this time peacefully.

I whispered a prayer of thanksgiving, bent and kissed his forehead, then left his chamber, knowing exactly where I must go and what I must do.

Chapter 22

EDMUND

BY THE THIRD DAY OF LYING ABED, I WAS BEYOND FRUSTRATED with my inability to get up and help Maribel. Every time she came to my chambers to check on me, her beautiful face was lined with weariness. Even though she argued that she was getting enough sleep, my inquiries of the servants revealed that she rarely rested—only when exhaustion claimed her and only for short periods of time.

I learned she had the royal apothecaries busy night and day following her formula and making the healing remedy the servants now called the Cure. Every hour, the servants reported to me the stories of family members, relatives, and friends who'd been saved from death because of Maribel's medicine. They wept openly, with both joy and relief, and hailed Maribel as a healing angel.

There were still many who had succumbed to the illness, such as Captain Colton, who didn't receive the dose of the medicine soon enough to heal. And most of the sick, like myself, were still weak and bedridden. But we were alive. The spread of the pestilence had all but ceased. And it was because of Maribel's intervention.

"You must find Princess Maribel," I instructed the king's steward, "and you must bring her back to the palace so she can rest. Don't let her give you any excuses this time."

The steward bowed, but not before I caught sight of his face, red from exasperation. "I have tried on every occasion you have ordered it, Lord Chambers. But the princess always insists on going to one more place or visiting one more person."

I sighed my own frustration at Maribel. The man spoke the truth. No doubt she'd refuse once again to come home.

With only the slightest groan, I pushed up and perched on the edge of the bed. Fighting a wave of dizziness, I forced myself to stand.

"My lord." The steward rushed to my side. "You should not be out of bed yet. The princess has forbidden it."

I grabbed the bed frame to keep from buckling. Not only were my limbs like custard, but my head pounded like a church bell. Nausea churned in my gut, and I wanted nothing more than to fall back onto my mattress.

"Please have a horse readied for me." I swallowed the rising bile and took several deep breaths, pushing away the dizziness and pain. I was strong. Wade had taught me to persevere through adversity, and I would do so now.

"There is no need to trouble yourself, my lord." The steward held my arm and steadied me. "I shall gladly go once more to fetch the princess."

I shook my head, my determination taking root. "No. It is past time for me to be on my feet. I'll be fine after I walk around for a few minutes."

Within the hour, I was dressed and atop my horse. A small retinue of palace guards accompanied me. Although I was still dizzy, I'd regained enough strength in my arms and legs to move around on my own, even if slower than my usual pace.

As we rode out of the palace gates and through the city, I breathed in deeply, savoring the salty sea air that brimmed with mist from the waves crashing against the granite cliffs. The stench of death and smoking juniper was gone. Instead, a cool north wind drifted from the sea, carrying the scent of fish and brine. The breeze had a bite meant to remind us winter wasn't yet over, even though the sun shone brilliantly.

The harbor below was silent, with only a few ships awaiting unloading. Most vessels feared weighing anchor so close to a city that still bore the ravages of the pestilence. It would be some time before normal trade and travel resumed.

The streets were quiet as well, with only a few vendors selling wares and shopkeepers with windows open for business. Our horses' hooves echoed against the flagstone and against the many shops and homes made from stone. With the sun glistening on the thatched roofs, I was struck by what a beautiful city Brechness was with so many buildings made of granite quarried in nearby mines.

The cathedral spire rose in the air above the rest of the town. Apparently, Maribel had taken up residence in the holy place since that's where so many of the sick and dying had congregated. As we neared the cathedral, the streets became much busier. By the time we arrived at the entrance to the place of worship, we had to wedge our way carefully inside, stepping over men, women, and children sprawled out on pallets.

Fortunately, many priests and nuns mingled among the sick, feeding and tending to their needs. Whereas the stench of death and despair had lingered in the air only a few days ago, this morning hope and life seemed to stream through the stained-glass windows and hover over the masses.

Near the altar, I spotted Maribel kneeling next to an old woman lying on a pallet. The two guards who accompanied her stood a short distance away, giving her the space she needed to work, but maintaining a boundary just in case Ethelwulf decided to chase Maribel into Norland. I didn't expect the king would let news of the pestilence stop him from trying to capture her. Likely, he'd only cease pursuing her if she were wed to another. Then she'd no longer be useful to his schemes.

Although we hadn't discussed marriage since we'd received news of the pestilence, I couldn't put it off. With the threat of scandal still hanging in the air and the danger from Ethelwulf, I needed to convince Maribel to go through with the wedding soon.

You are more important to me than anything, even more than my desire to be a physician.

I let her words from several days ago roll around my mind, savoring them as I had many times since the impassioned declaration. I didn't quite know what to make of her admission. Perhaps it had been borne from desperation and fatigue. Even so, I cherished the words, along with the look in her eyes when she'd spoken them, almost as if she'd seen me for the first time as a man.

I'd hoped to see that same look again on the brief visits she'd made to my chambers to check on me, but I hadn't. I wasn't disappointed—at least that's what I told myself. With Maribel, I'd learned to keep my expectations from rising too high.

She stood, pressed a hand to her forehead, then pivoted to scan the people around her as though assessing whom to tend next. At the sight of me in the middle of the nave, she froze.

I stopped and tried to gauge her reaction to seeing me there. I had the feeling she'd scold me severely for getting out of bed. But would she leave the cathedral with me willingly, or would I need to pick her up and forcibly carry her out? I'd told myself during the ride over that today I wouldn't let her sway me from bringing her back to the palace to rest. If she told me no, I'd find a way to soften her will, just as Christopher had suggested.

Stiffening my spine for the task, I continued toward her, preparing for both her resistance to leaving and the need to make her do so lest she fall ill herself.

Her eyes followed my movement, never swerving from me. Something in her blue depths welcomed me. And as I neared her, my stomach flipped at the realization that the *something* was desire. She desired me—not just for my companionship and help, but because she'd missed me and wanted to be with me. Was it possible her love for me as her brother and friend had finally deepened into something more passionate?

As I came to a halt in front of her, she peered up at me expectantly. Even though her face was smudged with dust and grime, she'd never been more beautiful. And for several heartbeats, she rendered me speechless.

"You should be abed," she said quietly.

"So should you," I managed to reply.

"There is too much work yet to be done." She swayed slightly from her fatigue.

That was all the incentive I needed. Although still reeling from my own brush with death, I scooped her up, sweeping her off her feet and cradling her against my chest. "You need a respite from your doctoring, Maribel."

"I cannot leave all these people. They are still so sick." But even as she protested, she relaxed against me, allowing me to hold her.

I started back the way I'd come, stepping carefully around the pallets filling the floor. "They will get along for a little while without you. But I cannot be without you a moment longer."

At my tender words, I felt her melt in my arms. And I inwardly smiled, realizing Christopher had been right. Rather than persuade Maribel, I'd simply needed to soften her resolve.

"I have missed you," she whispered as I carried her toward the door.

"And I have missed you," I whispered in return, heedless of the dozens of people watching us from all corners of the cathedral.

She smiled, and at that moment I was clay in her hands. She could have asked me for the world and I would have done anything to give it to her.

"I love you, Edmund."

Her words stopped me. It wasn't the first time she'd made the declaration. But the way she spoke the words— in a low, almost desperate tone—told me this was real and she wanted to be with me in the same way I wanted to be with her.

She lifted a hand to my cheek and caressed it. "I want to marry you and spend my life loving you. I can think of nothing I desire more."

My heartbeat pulsed hard at the words I'd never

thought she'd say. I almost couldn't believe I'd heard her correctly. What had made her change?

"The night you almost died of the pestilence," she answered my unasked question. "I learned a great deal about myself regarding my selfishness."

In the growing quiet of the nave, I wondered how much of our conversation carried to those around us. I started again toward the door, wanting to protect her from further gossip and scandal.

"Stop, Edmund." She squirmed in my arms.

I kept moving forward. "We'll talk more in private."

"I want to get married before we leave the cathedral."

This time her words made me stumble so that I nearly dropped her. I halted and studied her face. Was she jesting with me?

"We should do it now." Maribel's eyes sparked with sudden excitement. "While we are here and while we have a priest present to marry us."

I'd been admonishing myself to work harder to convince her to go through with the wedding soon. I'd never imagined she'd be the one to bring it up. And I'd certainly never imagined she'd want to get married this day, at this moment.

Part of me cautioned against doing anything hasty, that Maribel deserved to have a lovely wedding in a pretty gown with her sister present. But the other part of me wanted nothing more than to marry this woman I'd loved my whole life and finally make her mine.

"It would put my mind at ease to have you wed," I said, trying to keep the waver of my own excitement from my voice. "Then we'd no longer have to worry about Ethelwulf working to steal you away to marry his son."

Maribel watched my expression as though attempting

to read it. "You will marry me foremost for love, will you not? You spoke of your love once when you thought you were dying, but have not spoken of it again."

I could always count on Maribel getting right to the point and saying exactly what she meant. Even in a room full of people. Since she had no inclination to wait until we were alone to have our overdue conversation, I had to put aside my reservations and speak what was on my heart.

Slowly, I lowered Maribel to her feet so that she stood once more. Then I knelt before her and reached for her hand. "Maribel, I meant what I said on my deathbed. I have loved you with my whole heart for as long as I can remember and I always will. Would you make me the happiest man in all the Great Isle—in all the world—by marrying me and becoming my wife?"

Soft gasps came from all around, along with murmurs of delight from among the people. Perhaps this public proposal of marriage would bring even more goodwill toward Maribel.

She smiled down at me, and tears glistened in her eyes. "I accept your offer, Edmund. I only pray one day I will be worthy of the honorable, kind, and noble man that you are."

Chapter 23

Maribel

I was tired beyond anything I'd ever experienced. But I was also happier than I'd ever been.

King Draybane's steward had hastily procured a clean gown for the wedding. One of the nuns had helped me wash and change while Edmund spoke with the priest to enlist his services.

Now I stood at the front of the sanctuary, before the altar next to Edmund. And I was getting married.

Word had spread quickly regarding Edmund's proposal and our hasty wedding plans. Behind us, the nave was crowded not only with patients who seemed eager to witness our nuptials, but also many of the populace who remained in Brechness.

I ran a hand over the tight bodice of my gown, marveling at the tiny stitches of embroidery that decorated the waist. The bright red laced with roses was exquisite and likely belonged to Adelaide. I'd never worn anything but the traditional nun's habit, so the close-fitting confines and heavy layers of the garment felt strange.

Yet every time uncertainty swelled and threatened to undo me, I glanced into Edmund's eyes. Although he'd attempted to mask his appreciation of how I looked, he was unable to disguise his fascination and enjoyment of the changes in my appearance.

"Are we ready to begin?" the priest asked. As one of the kindly older men who'd lent his aid day and night for the past week, I could see the fatigue in his face. Nevertheless, he'd agreed to make us man and wife in the sight of God and men.

Edmund reached for my hands. Devoid of gloves, our fingers slid together smoothly, sending tingles over my skin. His face was pale and drawn from his recent illness, but I was struck as never before at what a distinguished, handsome man he was.

"Dearly beloved," the priest said, "we are gathered together here in the sight of God to join together this man and this woman in holy matrimony; which is an honorable estate, instituted of God in Paradise, and into which holy estate these two persons present come now to be joined. Therefore if any man can show just cause why they may not lawfully be joined together, by God's Law, or the Laws of the Realm, let him now speak, or else forever hold his peace."

"I object," came a voice from the far side of the cathedral.

Startled, I spun, as did most everyone. Amidst gasps and murmurs, those who were standing lowered themselves to their knees.

There in the open double doorway stood Adelaide, the sunlight streaming in upon her. She wore a stunning royal blue gown. Her golden hair was piled on top of her head, and a crown was centered among the glorious waves. She was breathtaking and regal, with an air of power and confidence that filled me with awe.

Behind her stood Christopher, attired in regal court garments. Without his chain mail, I hardly recognized him.

The queen glided forward into the cathedral, and the people cleared a path for her. As she strode forward, her face was unreadable. When she stopped several feet away from the altar, Edmund tugged on my arm and began to kneel. I followed his example in bowing to the queen. Since meeting her, I'd thought of her as a warrior and leader. But today, seeing her in all her glory, I realized she had the aura of a royalty and would make a magnificent queen.

"Your Majesty." I bowed my head before her.

For a long moment, I remained subservient. When I finally dared to lift my head, she held out her hand to me, revealing a signet ring with the royal emblem that had once belonged to the house of Mercia—two golden lions standing rampant with a ruby at the center.

I kissed it, and then she assisted me back to my feet. When Edmund had taken his place next to me, I met the queen's gaze. I was surprised to see pride and joy shining in her blue eyes that were so much like my own. Since she'd voiced her objection just moments ago, I'd expected to see censure.

"I am heartily glad to see you, sister." I dipped my head again.

"As I you," she replied with a smile.

I couldn't help but return the smile, the gladness of our reunion filling me. We'd had so little time together to make up for the years apart. I hadn't been sure if we would survive the pestilence to see each other again, and I lifted a grateful prayer God had seen fit to spare us both.

"I did not think you would object to our wedding," I said. "I thought it would please you."

"I only objected because I did not want you to begin without my presence by your side." She moved to stand next to me, and Christopher did likewise with Edmund.

At her show of support, my heart swelled with a gladness it couldn't contain.

"After all," Adelaide continued, "I could not miss the wedding of my most esteemed royal court physician, could I?"

My pulse stuttered. "Royal court physician?"

Adelaide lifted her chin and let her gaze fall upon the masses of people on the floor, along the walls, and crammed into the back. "Her Royal Highness, the Princess Maribel, has worked a miracle among the displaced of Mercia as well as the good citizens of Norland. Because of the gift bestowed upon her by Almighty God, she has brought healing to this city and all of Norland. In honor of her service and her skills, I hereby announce from this day henceforth, she is to be esteemed, respected, and sought after as the greatest physician in all the land."

Loud cheers and clapping echoed throughout the cathedral, and I couldn't keep the tears from filling my eyes. My dearest dream had come true. The people were ready to accept me as a woman physician. Not only did they accept me, but they lauded me.

Edmund's hand slid into mine once again. And

when our eyes met, I knew God had blessed me indeed with more than I could ask or imagine. He'd given me this incredible man to spend my life with, and He had opened the way for me to continue to use my gift of healing.

Only when I'd let go of my selfish ambitions and been willing to embrace His greater plans, had I found true contentment. In the end, He'd provided an even better way for me to use my healing skills than I could have done as a nun. He'd increased my scope, and now I would be able to help so many more people.

Adelaide's proud gaze came to rest on me. She didn't have to say anything for me to know what she was thinking—that God had indeed answered our prayer in a way we'd never been able to envision on our own.

"I have been speculating during the return voyage from Loughlin," she said softly. "Perhaps there is more to King Solomon's hidden treasure than mere riches. What if the real treasure lies within us? With the gifts God imparts to us? What if those combined gifts are the keys to ridding the land of evil and restoring peace?"

I nodded eagerly at Adelaide's astute observation. "Wisdom and healing are indeed great treasures. Already God has used these gifts to bring about much good." Adelaide's wisdom had gained her an alliance with Norland as well as acceptance among the rebels of Mercia. And now my medicine and healing touch had saved our army, along with countless people who supported our cause.

What about Emmeline? Wherever she was and whatever she was doing, had God given her a gift as well? Were our gifts the treasure? Or was there more we still needed to seek down in the labyrinth?

Although I wanted to voice my questions, Christopher cleared his throat loudly and gained Adelaide's attention. He inclined his head to the crowded nave, raising his brows meaningfully.

She nodded in reply and then turned to face Edmund. "We have brought someone back with us from Loughlin. Someone who was loathe to miss your wedding."

"Your Majesty?" Edmund asked politely.

Adelaide beckoned at a man from the crowd. "Your grandfather."

Chapter
24

EDMUND

MY GRANDFATHER? I SCANNED THE FACES BEFORE ME. SURELY THE queen was mistaken. "Captain Theobald killed my grandfather for aiding the rebellion."

"No." The queen focused on a figure approaching from the back. "The captain planned to arrest your grandfather for assisting in my escape from Mercia. Fortunately, friends became privy to the plans and warned us. Thus, we were able to intervene and save him in time. He has been residing in Brechness until he left at the outbreak of the pale pestilence."

My heart twisted with the news and with the realization that I'd almost murdered Theobald, not just for what he'd done to my family but also because of my grandfather—especially because of my grandfather.

Theobald had taunted me, lied to me, and tried to use my need for revenge to turn me into a bitter and angry man. It had almost worked. What if I'd killed him that day thinking I was taking revenge for my grandfather's death? How would I have been able to stand here today and hold my head high? How would I have been able to look my grandfather in his eyes without thinking about what I'd done?

Was it time to finally stop trying to forget about all that had happened and instead forgive? Was that where true freedom was found?

Once again, the crowd parted as a stoop-shouldered, white-haired man shuffled toward the altar. The man I remembered had been tall, having brown hair with only a smattering of white at his sideburns. That man had walked with purpose and certainty. Was this old man really my grandfather?

It had been over seventeen years since I'd been dragged away from my childhood home in Chapelhill. Seventeen years since I'd last seen my grandfather. Seventeen years since he'd hugged me good-bye in a hard embrace. So much had changed during that time.

As he drew nearer, he halted and sucked in a wheezing breath, as if seeing me was too much for him. Christopher was at his side in an instant, lending him a supportive arm, holding him up, gently encouraging him the final distance to the altar.

I was grateful for Christopher's quick aid, for I couldn't make my legs or arms work, nor could I manage to think of anything to say.

Maribel slipped her hand through the crook of my arm. In an instant, her strength and steadiness seeped into me and reminded me we would face the future together, side by side, as husband and wife.

"Grandfather?" I said tentatively.

"Edmund." His voice wobbled, and he studied my face, his eyes welling with unshed tears. "You look like your father."

I nodded. "If I am ever half the man my father was, then I will be blessed indeed."

At my words, tears spilled over onto Grandfather's lined cheeks. "I believe you were saved by God's mighty hand to rise up and do greater things than your father ever did."

When our gazes connected, I saw there the man I'd always known, the wise and loving grandfather. The stresses of the years might have aged him and changed his outward appearance, but inwardly he was still the honorable nobleman I remembered.

"I have searched for you all these many years," Grandfather said. "I prayed every day that if you were alive God would help me find you."

I couldn't begin to imagine the heartache and worry he'd experienced at my disappearance. "I'm sorry, Grandfather. I believed you were murdered like everyone else—"

"Do not be sorry, my child," he said. "If God had answered my prayer the way I wanted and allowed me to find you, King Ethelwulf would have killed you by now. Instead, God put you someplace safe, where you could be trained and prepared for taking care of the princess and for contributing to the fight that is yet to come."

In my heart, I sensed Grandfather was right—that I'd been in the best place possible. If not for being at Highland Convent, I would have missed knowing and loving Maribel. Even so, my heart ached at all the years I'd missed being with my last remaining relative.

Maribel's fingers closed around my arm in a gentle squeeze. The look in her eyes told me she understood exactly how I felt, that she regretted the many years she'd been separated from her sisters. But her touch also reminded me we had the present to spend with our loved ones and hopefully many more years in the future. We couldn't focus on the regrets of what was lost. Instead, we needed to cherish what we had left.

Grandfather held out a shaking hand. I grasped it and bent to place a kiss upon his knotted knuckles. Instead of allowing me the kiss, he pulled me forward with surprising strength and wrapped both arms around me in an embrace as hard as the ones he'd always given me as a boy.

I hugged him back, letting the years slip away, letting my love for him swell until my throat ached.

When he finally released me, his cheeks were wet and his eyes bright. "Now, shall we have a wedding?"

I wasn't sure what the appropriate course of action was in our situation. I'd just been reunited with my grandfather, and I wanted to spend time with him. And yet, I also didn't want to put off marrying Maribel another day.

As if sensing my inner turmoil, my grandfather smiled and took a step back. "I can think of no greater joy than to watch my grandson get married. I never believed I would see you alive again. And now, here I am, standing with you and witnessing your wedding. If I die tomorrow, I will be a satisfied man."

"Let us not talk of death," I urged.

"You need not fear, Edmund," Maribel said. "I shall not allow your grandfather to become even the slightest bit ill. If I have my way, he will live for many, many years."

At Maribel's sweet expression, her earnest eyes, and the love there just for me, I was overwhelmed with gratefulness. I'd lost so much long ago, but I'd gained even more through the adversity I'd endured.

Christopher led Grandfather to the spot next to me, ceding his place of honor. Grandfather seemed to stand taller, and pride shone from his eyes.

As Christopher positioned himself on the opposite side of Grandfather, the queen smiled. "Shall we begin the wedding?"

"I say yes," Maribel replied, her eyes dancing once more with excitement. She was radiant in her gown. The rich ruby color brought out the blue of her eyes and made her hair shine more golden. Once again, as when I'd first glimpsed her, my mouth went dry with just how beautiful she looked.

If I'd wanted to kiss her all those years she'd worn her drab, colorless habit, I thrummed with the need now that she was alive and vibrant the way she was meant to be. My gaze dropped to her smiling lips, to the delicate curves, to the memory of the forbidden kisses we'd shared in the labyrinth.

Starting today, I'd get to kiss her as much as I pleased and for as long as I wanted. The thought burned through me so that I couldn't keep myself from reaching for her waist and drawing her near.

"If Your Majesty will permit it," I said to the queen, "I would like to adjust the order of the service just slightly."

"How so?" Adelaide answered.

"If I may," I said, dipping toward Maribel, "I'd like to kiss my bride first rather than last."

Without waiting for permission, I bent in and touched my lips to Maribel's. The tender clinging pressure was my promise that from this day forward, I would love and cherish her foremost, till death parted us.

At the gentle return pressure of her lips, I knew she was promising me the same.

Chapter
25

KING ETHELWULF

"YOU ALLOWED PRINCESS CONSTANCE AND PRINCESS MARIBEL TO escape." I spat at the two soldiers lying on the dungeon floor.

"We tried, Your Majesty," croaked one of the men through cracked, dried lips. He attempted to sit up, but he was too injured and weak to make it higher than his elbows. "But somehow they learned of our ambush and were prepared when we attacked."

Inwardly, I seethed at the stupidity and failure of my elite guard. I'd already questioned other surviving soldiers and discovered most of what had happened before I'd sentenced them to be hanged, drawn, and quartered. Yet, an insatiable need for more information drove me to the dungeons again.

Several servants holding torches stood by with burning incense pots to cover the stench of decay and the rancidness of bodily waste. Even so, I had to breathe through my mouth in order not to gag.

"And what exactly happened to Captain Theobald?" I demanded.

"He was injured and killed, Your Majesty," said the other guard, whose wounded arm had putrefied. "We found his body ravaged by wild animals."

I shook my head at the captain's ineptness. He was fortunate he'd died. After failing me one too many times, I would have hanged, drawn, and quartered him too. I didn't care that the man had served me well in my early campaigns to regain Mercia. He'd failed me now when it mattered most.

At the very least, I could give him credit for following Princess Maribel to the labyrinth. The discovery had been monumental. I hadn't known the extensive network of tunnels in the Highlands existed. After speaking with my trusted advisors, we'd concurred that Solomon's hidden treasure was likely there. But the caverns and patterns of the labyrinth were so extensive, and the traps so deadly, none of the soldiers who'd gone down had come back alive.

Instead of losing more men, I'd decided to have my scholars attempt to discover a map or more information regarding the labyrinth. While they'd uncovered mentions of labyrinths and mazes in fables in other countries, they'd found nothing substantive about a real one here in Mercia, mainly speculations that had been passed on among the elite guard regiments.

I'd almost begun to believe someone had purposefully destroyed every manuscript containing evidence or clues regarding the labyrinth, perhaps with the hope of erasing the memory of it from history.

Nevertheless, I'd tasked the scholars to keep searching, sending them out to confiscate each history book they could find. Even if they succeeded in compiling more information, my closest advisors had reminded me we only had one key, and we'd likely need the other two in order to unlock any hidden treasure we might find.

That made the loss of Princess Maribel all the more frustrating. I'd been counting on getting her key to add to my collection. And now apparently Princess Maribel was in Norland within the safety of Brechness. I'd even heard rumors over the past day that she'd single-handedly stopped the spread of the pestilence and saved the army. I'd also heard she'd married a young nobleman from Mercia, Lord Chambers.

"Did the princesses tend your wounds?" I asked, although I already knew from questioning the others yesterday that only these two had refused treatment—at least of the men who'd lived until another detachment of knights had arrived.

"No, Your Majesty," said one of the men gruffly. "We didn't let them touch us. We would rather have died than betray you."

The damage was already done, however. Word had spread quickly that the lost princesses had worked together to bind the wounds and provide relief to my soldiers. I had to give Princess Constance credit. She was perceptive, using her sister's compassion to draw on the emotions of the rest of the people. As it turned out, she and Princess Maribel were being lauded as angels for their selfless conduct.

Princess Constance was not only endearing herself to my people, but she was gaining more loyalty every day. I had few noblemen I could truly trust, mostly those who could be bribed. If she kept winning favor, she would face little resistance when she invaded and would likely be able to march all the way into Delsworth.

Unless, of course, I could find the third lost princess first.

"Rex," I bellowed.

Near the stairway, my oldest son shoved away from the wall and stalked out of the shadows. "Yes, Your Majesty."

The light of the flickering torches heightened his massive size, his thick arms and torso. It emphasized his broad shoulders and strong hands which could snap a man's neck in two pieces as easily as a chicken bone. At twenty, he was handsome with fair hair like his mother's. He wore it in tight warrior braids, along with the black chain mail and cloak of my elite guard.

I saw the way the young noblewomen looked at him as if he were a prize to be won. I noticed the way my courtiers flaunted their daughters in the hope of catching his attention. So far, since his arrival in Delsworth, Ethelrex had taken more interest in his warrior training than he had in women. But it was time for that to change.

"I have given you command over my elite guard in place of Theobald."

"Yes, Your Majesty." He bowed, the menagerie of weapons at his belt clinking ominously.

"As commander, you must take up the quest to find the final lost princess."

"Very well, Your Majesty." Although Rex kept his voice from showing his emotion, I sensed his anticipation and knew he would relish the opportunity to prove himself, especially since I hadn't allowed him to participate in any of Theobald's missions over the past months.

I'd done my best to protect Rex these many years from rebels and dissenters who might plot to murder him. I'd even gone so far as to send him back to the safety of the royal residence in Warwick where he'd spent his childhood and youth being educated and trained by the best knights and scholars in all the isle.

However, now with the threat of rebellion growing stronger, I'd decided it was time for him to come to my aid. He was no longer a young boy needing my protection. Rather he'd become a force of contention, someone to be feared, a warrior fiercer than Theobald.

"I shall do whatever you ask, Your Majesty," he said.

I nodded at him curtly. "At least Theobald proved useful in wresting information from the Highland Convent abbess. The third princess is named Emmeline, and she is somewhere in Inglewood Forest."

We'd hoped to follow Sister Katherine once again to the princess, but she'd all but disappeared after leading us to Princess Maribel. Since then, not even my strongest trackers had been able to pick up her scent.

"You must find Princess Emmeline," I said severely, hoping to emphasize the serious nature of the mission. "I do not need to remind you of the gravity of our predicament if you should fail me."

Rex dropped to one knee before me. "I vow I shall not return without her." He reached for my hand and kissed it three times as was the custom when making a vow. In the darkness of the dungeons, my royal onyx ring gleamed even blacker, but he seemed not to notice or crave it.

"When you find her," I said, having faith that my son would do as he pledged, "you must not let any harm come to her."

"Very well," he said. "I shall guard her myself."

I smiled. He would be doing much more than guarding her. "You must take Father Patrick and marry her the moment you have her in your possession."

Though I sensed he would rather put off marriage for a while, he was an obedient son. He bowed his head in acknowledgment of my order. "Shall I leave at first light?"

"There is no need to wait." I strode past him toward the stairs, having had enough of the stale dungeons. "You may leave as soon as you are packed."

"Very well, Your Majesty."

I stopped at the bottom of the steps. "And take Magnus. He is in need of additional discipline."

My younger son had too much free time at court and wasted it with women. I regretted now having neglected to send him to Warwick for the same education and training as Rex.

"I fear he may slow us down." Rex's statement was respectful, but I could sense the irritation he harbored toward his brother.

"I trust you will find a way to keep him in line, just as you do with your soldiers."

Rex inclined his head in acceptance of my answer. He would do as I asked whether he liked it or not. Taking Magnus would make his quest more difficult. But it would also force him to learn how to control his brother—a skill, among many, he would need in the future.

"Oh, and when you find the princess, you must make sure you retrieve her key. It is of vital importance I have the key."

Again Rex bowed.

As I ascended the dungeon steps, I wondered why I had not thought to send Rex sooner. He was determined and trustworthy. If anyone could find the princess and the key, I had faith my son would.

Jody Hedlund is the best-selling author of over twenty historicals for both adults and teens and is the winner of numerous awards including the Christy, Carol, and Christian Book Award. She lives in central Michigan with her husband, five busy teens, and five spoiled cats. Learn more at JodyHedlund.com

Young Adult Fiction from Jody Hedlund
The Lost Princesses

Always: Prequel Novella

On the verge of dying after giving birth to twins, the queen of Mercia pleads with Lady Felicia to save her infant daughters. With the castle overrun by King Ethelwulf's invading army, Lady Felicia vows to do whatever she can to take the newborn princesses and their three-year old sister to safety, even though it means sacrificing everything she holds dear, possibly her own life.

Evermore

Raised by a noble family, Lady Adelaide has always known she's an orphan. Little does she realize she's one of the lost princesses and the true heir to Mercia's throne . . . until a visitor arrives at her family estate, reveals her birthright as queen, and thrusts her into a quest for the throne whether she's ready or not.

Foremost

Raised in an isolated abbey, Lady Maribel desires nothing more than to become a nun and continue practicing her healing arts. She's carefree and happy with her life...until a visitor comes to the abbey and reveals her true identity as one of the lost princesses.

Hereafter

Forced into marriage, Emmeline has one goal—to escape. But Ethelrex takes his marriage vows seriously, including his promise to love and cherish his wife, and has no intention of letting Emmeline get away. As the battle for the throne rages, will the prince be able to win the battle for Emmeline's heart?

The Noble Knights

The Vow

Young Rosemarie finds herself drawn to Thomas, the son of the nearby baron. But just as her feelings begin to grow, a man carrying the Plague interrupts their hunting party. While in forced isolation, Rosemarie begins to contemplate her future—could it include Thomas? Could he be the perfect man to one day rule beside her and oversee her parents' lands?

An Uncertain Choice

Due to her parents' promise at her birth, Lady Rosemarie has been prepared to become a nun on the day she turns eighteen. Then, shortly before her birthday, a friend of her father's enters the kingdom and proclaims her parents' will left a second choice—if Rosemarie can marry before the eve of her eighteenth year, she will be exempt from the ancient vow.

A Daring Sacrifice

In a reverse twist on the Robin Hood story, a young medieval maiden stands up for the rights of the mistreated, stealing from the rich to give to the poor. All the while, she fights against her cruel uncle who has taken over the land that is rightfully hers.

For Love & Honor

Lady Sabine is harboring a skin blemish, one, that if revealed, could cause her to be branded as a witch, put her life in danger, and damage her chances of making a good marriage. After all, what nobleman would want to marry a woman so flawed?

A Loyal Heart

When Lady Olivia's castle is besieged, she and her sister are taken captive and held for ransom by her father's enemy, Lord Pitt. Loyalty to family means everything to Olivia. She'll save her sister at any cost and do whatever her father asks—even if that means obeying his order to steal a sacred relic from her captor.

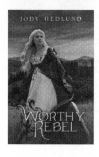

A Worthy Rebel

While fleeing an arranged betrothal to a heartless lord, Lady Isabelle becomes injured and lost. Rescued by a young peasant man, she hides her identity as a noblewoman for fear of reprisal from the peasants who are bitter and angry toward the nobility.

A complete list of my novels can be found at jodyhedlund.com.

Would you like to know when my next book is available? You can sign up for my newsletter, become my friend on Goodreads, like me on Facebook, or follow me on Twitter.

Newsletter: jodyhedlund.com
Goodreads:
goodreads.com/author/show/3358829.Jody_Hedlund
Facebook: facebook.com/AuthorJodyHedlund
Twitter: @JodyHedlund

The more reviews a book has, the more likely other readers are to find it. If you have a minute, please leave a rating or review. I appreciate all reviews, whether positive or negative.

Made in the USA
San Bernardino, CA
24 May 2020